SNOWY NIGHTS AT THE LONELY HEARTS HOTEL

Karen King

SNOWY NIGHTS AT THE LONELY HEARTS HOTEL

Bookouture

Published by Bookouture in 2018

An imprint of StoryFire Ltd.

Carmelite House
50 Victoria Embankment
London EC4Y 0DZ

www.bookouture.com

ISBN: 978-1-78681-553-8
eBook ISBN: 978-1-78681-552-1

As this story is about two sisters it seems only fitting to dedicate it to my sister, Joy. Thanks, sis, for always being there for me. xx

Chapter One

'You're working late again, Saffy. I thought you'd be out on the town tonight celebrating breaking up for the Christmas holidays,' said Freddie, the security guard, as he popped his head around the office door. 'You're finishing tonight, aren't you?'

Saffron Baxter pushed a stray lock of her chin-length caramel bob back behind her ear and looked up from her computer screen. 'Yes – I've got a couple of holiday days to use up still. I'll be off as soon as I've done this spreadsheet. We've got a product meeting first thing on 2nd January and Ajay wants me to send the research data over before the Christmas holidays so he can take a look at it. I'll be ten minutes max,' she promised.

'You'll have to be. I need to lock up and go home,' Freddie told her. 'I'll be back in ten minutes, no later.'

'Almost done.' Saffy turned her attention back to inputting her research data into the spreadsheet. She loved working for buycreative.com, an online company that brought small creative businesses and individuals together to sell their goods online. It had been going for six years now and was very successful. Saffy had been working there for three years, and as part of the digital product marketing team it was her job to work with the individual creatives to help them achieve the maximum sales for their business. It involved a lot of research but the end product, helping a small craft firm or a solo artist to achieve more sales, was worth it. What she really wanted to do though was be a business development manager and find new creatives to add to their list of partners. One of the development managers was leaving next month and Ajay had hinted that he was intending to promote someone from the office, and she was hoping it would be her. Saffy knew that two other product researchers were after the job too, but if she could produce an impressive product development plan then she might be able to convince Ajay that she was the best person for it, so it was worth working late to get it finished. Then she was off to meet Robbie and Meg, two of her oldest friends, for a pre-Christmas drink at Perry's, the new wine bar in town.

True to his word, Freddie returned exactly ten minutes later.

'Finished,' Saffy said cheerily as she switched off her computer. She pushed her chair back and grabbed her black leather holdall from under her desk. 'I won't be a sec.' She nipped over to the women's cloakroom, took a lacy electric blue sleeveless top from the holdall and swapped it with the pin-striped shirt she was wearing. She replaced the thick black tights and ankle boots with sheer tights and black stilettos, thus transforming her black pencil skirt into a passable going-out outfit. She put her work clothes and boots into the holdall, then quickly added a touch of powder to her face, replaced the light pink lipstick with shimmery red, ran a brush through her unruly bob – the bane of her life – added another sweep of Luscious Lash mascara to enhance her dark brown eyes, took her camel trench coat from the hanger and was out again.

Freddie looked amused. 'Well, that's quite a transformation!'

Saffy grinned. 'I don't have time to go home and change so it'll have to do.' She blew him a kiss. 'See you in the New Year. Have a good

Christmas!' Then she hurried out of the office. She was a bit late but Robbie and Meg wouldn't mind.

Buttoning up the neck of her coat, she stepped out of the warm building into the cold night air. People bustled by, laden down with bags from their late-night shopping or gathering in the coffee and wine bars that dotted the street. It was almost cold enough for snow, Saffy thought as she thrust her hands into her pockets, wishing she'd remembered to wear her gloves this morning. She hoped it did snow. Everywhere looked so gorgeous all twinkly and white, really Christmassy.

Colourful fairy lights twinkled overhead, illuminating the street in a multi-coloured glow and a huge decorated tree shimmered and sparkled in the square. Saffy smiled and quickened her step. She loved Christmas; the decorations, the tree, the lights, the carols booming out in the shops, the drinks with friends and most of all the parties. Her diary was full of nights out planned for the following Christmas week, and she wasn't back at work until 2nd January, thanks to being owed two days' holiday. The rest of the office didn't finish until lunchtime on Friday; Ajay had given everyone Christmas Eve off. Life was good. She turned the corner and hurried towards the sparkly lights of Perry's.

Meg was already there, sitting at a table by the window, a glass of white wine in front of her. She stood up and waved as Saffy walked in. Saffy waved back, went to the bar, got herself a glass of rosé – she always found white wine too heavy – and made her way over to Meg.

'Sorry, I had some work to finish,' she said as she sat down. 'No Robbie yet?'

'No worries, I've only been here a few mins, we had a meeting after work.' Meg's short, blonde hair was still immaculately in place, as was her make-up. As manageress of a well-known beauty counter at the high street store she knew all the tricks of the trade. Saffy, Meg and Robbie had attended the same high school and now all worked in Birmingham city centre so often met up after work. They all travelled to work by train, which meant they could chat over a few drinks without having to bother about getting a taxi home.

Meg looked over Saffy's shoulder towards the door. 'Here's Robbie now. He looks a bit excited.'

Saffy turned and saw Robbie heading towards them, fair hair sticking up like a hedgehog, tartan scarf flung over his shoulder, black coat half-buttoned up. 'I've got something to tell you,' he said, as he pulled out a chair and perched on the edge of it. 'But first you've both got to promise not to breathe a word.' He smoothed his hair down with his hands, which he then folded in his lap, obviously bursting with excitement.

Saffy and Meg exchanged amused glances and said together, 'We promise.'

Robbie leaned forward. 'I'm going to propose to Duncan on Christmas morning,' he announced dramatically.

Saffy beamed. Robbie and Duncan had been together four years now and although totally different to each other – Robbie, a publicist, was like an excitable puppy while Duncan, an accountant, was calm and unruffled – they made a perfect pair. 'I'm so pleased. You two are made for each other.' She leaned over and kissed Robbie on the cheek. 'Congratulations.'

'Duncan hasn't accepted yet,' he pointed out.

'He will. He's mad about you.' Meg clapped her hands and squealed in delight. 'Oh this is so gorgeously romantic. We could have a double wedding.' Meg and her partner Stefan had got engaged in the summer. 'What a shame you aren't with someone, Saffy. We could make it a triple wedding.'

Saffy gave a mock shudder. 'Listen, it's fantastic that you guys are getting your happy ever after – Meg's right, of course Duncan will say yes, Robbie – but even if I was dating the sexiest guy on the planet I wouldn't be getting married any time soon. There's too much I want to do with my life.'

'She hasn't got time for romance, she's planning on taking over the company,' Meg whispered, leaning forward conspiratorially.

'Knowing her, she'll succeed, too,' Robbie whispered back. 'I reckon our Saffy can do anything she puts her mind to.'

Saffy grinned at them. 'Never mind changing the subject to me and my career, I want to hear all about your proposal plans. When are you going to do it? Have you thought what you're going to say?'

'And have you bought the ring yet?' Meg added. 'Stefan proposed to me with a Haribo jelly ring because he wanted us to choose the ring together. I've still got the jelly ring,' she added. 'It's in my memory box.' Meg was such a romantic; she kept everything from their dates – cinema tickets, restaurant bills, the lot.

'That's just it, what do I do about the ring?' Robbie asked them. 'It doesn't seem right to propose without one, I want to swoop the ring out of my pocket and put it on Duncan's finger as soon as he says yes, but what if he hates the ring I choose?'

'Are you sure he will want a ring?' Saffy asked. 'Not everyone does.'

'He will, Duncan loves jewellery.' Robbie stood up. 'I need a drink, do you two want a refill?'

❄

It was late when Saffy finally returned home. The drinks with Robbie and Meg had progressed to a visit to a local club but it had been a fun evening. Robbie had finally decided to propose using a lock of his hair for the ring, then he and Duncan could go out and buy a ring together on Boxing Day. Thank goodness she didn't have work tomorrow so could have a lie-in, Saffy thought as she climbed into bed. She was knackered. As soon as her head touched the pillow she could feel herself drifting off to sleep.

She wasn't very happy to be woken by the phone ringing at half past seven the next morning. Why hadn't she turned it down when she went to bed? Saffy groaned, reaching for her handset so she could mute it and groaned again when she saw the image of her sister Hannah's face staring at her from the screen. The last thing she needed right now was another awkward conversation with Hannah asking her to come down for Christmas, complaining that she was a stranger to the twins, and was the only family they had nearby now Mum and their stepdad Jon had moved to France. She was about to ignore the call when she remembered that Hannah, her husband Lee and their three-year-old twins, Miles and Lily, were on holiday in Tenerife – they always took their holiday after the summer rush and just before Christmas. Hannah wouldn't be calling unless it was important.

'Hannah… are the twins okay? Lee?'

'The twins have caught measles and Miles has complications, a fever and ear infection. So we can't fly home tomorrow.' Saffy could hear the tremor in Hannah's voice. 'We can't come home for Christmas.'

Saffy's heart went out to her sister. She knew how important Christmas was to Hannah, she loved the whole atmosphere, the idea of family and friends being together – which was why she nagged Saffy to join them every year, not understanding that as a young singleton Saffy preferred to party. 'I'm so sorry, Hannah. I bet you and Lee are really worried. The twins will be okay, won't they?' she added. 'I mean, measles isn't that dangerous any longer, is it?'

'It can be. Lily doesn't seem too bad at the moment, although she's really miserable, poor thing, but Miles is burning up terribly. The doctor said that they can't fly home until Boxing Day, at the earliest.'

Hannah's voice broke. 'I feel so guilty. It's all my fault. They had a cold when it was time for their injection and I forgot to rebook it. We've been so busy at the B&B this summer.'

'Stop beating yourself up, the days go so fast it's easy to forget stuff,' Saffy said, feeling sorry for her usually totally in control sister, who sounded so distraught. 'Is there anything I can do? Do you want me to contact anyone for you?'

'There is something…' Hannah hesitated. 'But it's a big ask and you'll probably say no. It'll be too much for you.'

Hannah had a habit of expecting the worst of Saffy just because she'd had a few troublesome years in her teens. She didn't seem to accept that Saffy was now grown up and quite capable, thank you very much. Saffy held back a snappy retort, knowing that her sister was stressing about the twins. 'Ask away. If I can do it, I will.'

'I'm gutted that we won't be back for the Christmas party. It's become a tradition now and everyone looks forward to it. They'll be so disappointed if it's cancelled.'

She'd forgotten about the party. Hannah and Lee had started hosting the Christmas party when they first opened their B&B six years ago and Hannah had found out that a young single mum living nearby was spending Christmas alone. She'd immediately invited the mum and her children to spend Christmas Day with them and then had decided to open the invitation to other single parents too. The party had been a huge success, so Hannah and Lee had hosted one every year since. Another reason Saffy hadn't wanted to go down for Christmas. She wasn't as fond of family events as Hannah and didn't fancy spending her Christmas Day surrounded by kids.

'I'm sure people will understand. Do you want me to tell everyone what's happened?'

'It's too short notice for the parents to organise anything else, Saffy. Some of them won't have budgeted for Christmas dinner so it'll be a real struggle for them to provide one.' Hannah paused. 'I was wondering if you would go down and host the party for us?' Her words were coming out in a rush now. 'I can't ask Mum because Jon is still recovering from his bypass so they're having a quiet Christmas at home in France.'

And I want a fun Christmas with my friends. Saffy tried to think of a way to refuse without Hannah getting the hump. If she agreed it would be goodbye to drinks on Christmas Eve, followed by a lazy Christmas morning then a Christmas dinner party at Robbie and Duncan's – hopefully celebrating their engagement – Boxing Day with Meg and Stefan and all the other socialising she had planned. 'Please say you'll do it. It's all organised,' Hannah continued. 'The turkey and veg are ordered. I can get them delivered to the house for you, the cupboards and freezer are full of food, and there's plenty to drink. I sorted it all out before we went away. All you have to do is cook the dinner, serve it out and organise a few games for the afternoon – oh and put the Christmas decorations and tree up.'

Chapter Two

'It's a lot, I wouldn't have any idea what to do—' Saffy started to say but Hannah cut in.

'I might have known you'd be selfish and refuse. We all know you'd rather spend your Christmas out partying but can't you think of someone else for once? If we let these poor single parents down they'll not only have to try and provide a Christmas meal for their children, we'll be robbing them of the chance to let their hair down and enjoy adult company.' Hannah's voice was getting firmer. 'Don't you remember what a struggle Christmas was for Mum? She would have loved to have Christmas dinner cooked for her and to mix with other adults. That's why I do this every year. I remember how Mum struggled to provide for us.'

Here comes the guilt trip, Saffy thought, bracing herself. Hannah, at thirty-four, was five years older than Saffy, so had always had to look out for her and never let her forget it.

'When I think how I had to look after you when we were young, be a substitute mother, take you around everywhere with me while Mum worked… You've no idea what that was like for me. And now, not only can you not be bothered to come and see your nephew and niece, you're too selfish to help me out when I need it. I've always been there for you.' She sniffed. 'All you care about is your work, and your friends. You're just like Dad.'

That stung. 'Look, Hannah, it's a big ask. I've got plans for Christmas Day and Boxing Day, I'll have to let people down too.'

'The people you'll be letting down aren't lonely and short of money.' Hannah changed her tone to one that was cajoling instead of accusing. 'I wouldn't ask you if I wasn't desperate not to ruin Christmas for these single families. I'm worried sick about the twins as it is, I don't need the worry of this too.'

Saffy bit her lip. Hannah was right, she must be going out of her mind with worry. The least she could do was run this party for her. If it was all organised perhaps she could go down Christmas Eve, put the Christmas tree and decorations up, organise the dinner and come back after the party. Then she could still go to Meg and Stefan's on Boxing Day. And Robbie and Duncan always had a party New Year's Eve so it wouldn't be too bad missing their Christmas one.

'Okay, I'll do it. I'm sure I can manage to organise a party for a few hours.'

'Oh thank you, Saffy.' Hannah sounded almost tearful. 'I'll message you all the details, and Logan, one of our neighbours, has our spare key and will help you if you need anything. I'll WhatsApp you his number. Oh and there's a couple more things…'

Saffy braced herself. Hannah was such a perfectionist she probably wanted to tell her exactly how to decorate the house and tree. 'Go on…'

'We always have a real Christmas tree so you'll have to get one. Logan will help you…'

Okay, so maybe she'd have to travel down Sunday night so she had time to locate and buy a Christmas tree.

'That's fine.'

'And Logan is looking after Oscar, but he's a single parent and works from home and I don't want to leave our mad English springer spaniel with him for another week. Poor Oscar must be wondering what's happening too, and would be much happier in his own home, so could you possibly go down as soon as you can? When do you finish work?'

Saffy bit her lip as she considered her reply. She didn't want to tell Hannah that she had already finished work. But Hannah had always been able to suss out when she was lying.

'Saffy…?'

'I've finished, I go back 2nd January,' she confessed, knowing what was coming next.

'Oh, that's brilliant. You can go down today then, can't you? I'll let Logan know. Thank you so much, Saffy. You will wait for us to come home before you go back, won't you? We'd all love to see you.' And she was gone.

Well, bang goes my Christmas, Saffy thought. That was typical Hannah; one moment she'd persuaded Saffy to host a party on Christmas Day, the next she'd talked her into going down to Cornwall for over a week. She'd be lucky if she got home for Robbie and Duncan's New Year's Eve party at this rate!

Her phone pinged. She glanced at the screen and saw that it was a WhatsApp message from Hannah. *Thank you, Saffy. I really am grateful. I forgot to say how many will be coming to the party. There will be ten parents and twenty-five children – ranging from a six-month-old baby to a couple of twelve-year-olds.*

What? Saffy read the message again. Thirty-five mouths to cook for. And to entertain. What would she do with them all? She wasn't as at home with kids as Hannah was. In fact, they scared her! Why had she let Hannah talk her into this?

Another message followed, containing details of where the Christmas tree decorations and trimmings were (and that Hannah always put them up Christmas Eve, like their mum always did), games she usually played with the kids, Logan's telephone number and strict instructions to ask him if she needed any help as he knew how Hannah organised the party. Having persuaded Saffy to organise the Christmas dinner she was now obviously worrying that she wouldn't do it properly. Hannah always seemed to think she could do everything better than Saffy. Well, if she thought this Logan was so good why hadn't she asked him to organise it all?

Saffy sat up in bed, hugging her knees. What had she let herself be talked into? Then she immediately felt bad. Her sister had sounded really distressed on the phone. She was worried sick about the twins and trying not to let everyone down, that's all. Poor Hannah, what a way to spend Christmas. She knew how much her sister would be missing home, especially at this time of year. It was selfish to bother about having to give up her own Christmas plans when Hannah had so much to think about.

Well, she'd better let Robbie and Meg know the change of plan. She called Robbie first.

'That's a bummer, Duncan has a surprise theme this year and you'd have loved it. Still, you can't let your sister down, can you?' Then his voice brightened. 'You'll be back for our New Year's Eve party, won't you?'

'You bet! I'll be back for the weekend.'

'Well good luck, Saf. It's not really your thing is it, organising a huge party for families, but I'm sure it'll be fun. We'll miss you though.'

'You'll have plenty of other guests to keep you busy,' replied Saffy. Robbie and Duncan loved entertaining and she knew there would be at least a dozen other guests there. Shame they weren't free to come down with her; organising the Christmas party would be a doddle for them. 'Seeing as I'm not coming to the party you can tell me the theme now, can't you? Let me know what I'm missing.'

'No can do. Duncan will kill me. You'll have to check out the pics on FB to find out.'

Whatever it was it would be flamboyant. Duncan never did anything by halves. 'Have fun anyway. And good luck with the proposal – I can't wait to see the ring you both choose. I'll have to give you your present on Saturday,' she said.

'You too, hun. And good on you for helping your sister out. Christmas spirit and all that.'

Saffy couldn't help feeling a bit wistful as she ended the call. Robbie and Duncan's parties were always such good fun, she wished she could be there.

Don't be selfish, she told herself as she dialled Meg's number.

Meg sounded disappointed, and a bit envious, when Saffy told her. 'Hey, we'll miss you but that's so kind of you. And it sounds fun, I almost wish I was coming with you. I think Christmas in Cornwall would be lovely.'

Saffy looked over at her white Christmas tree decorated with blue and silver baubles twinkling in the corner of her flat. She'd spent hours decorating it but it looked nowhere near as artistic as the one in the magazine she'd copied. She was good at her job but nothing practical that she did ever turned out how she wanted it, so it was no wonder Hannah was worrying about the party. Hell, Saffy was worrying about the party! If she messed up she'd probably never hear the last of it from Hannah. Her bossy older sister was always so in control, and organised.

And stranded over in another country with two very poorly children, Saffy reminded herself. Well, she wasn't going to let Hannah down. She was going to make a success of this party. All she had to do was treat it like a project. Plan it all out carefully, stick to the agenda then it would all be fine.

❄

Logan Carter read the message from Hannah again. The twins were laid up with the measles and they wouldn't be allowed to fly home for another week, but her younger sister, Saffy, was coming down later to organise the Christmas party and take over looking after Oscar, so everything was still as planned. Could he give Saffy the spare key Hannah had left with him and help out if Saffy needed it?

Hannah had often spoken about Saffy, who had only been down to visit once the entire time Logan had lived in Port Breok. Not that he'd met her; he and Chloe had been away visiting his parents in Scotland that weekend. Apparently Saffy was a career girl who worked hard and partied hard and didn't have time to come down to Cornwall and visit her only sibling and young nephew and niece. She sounded a bit like Jade, his ex. He was surprised that Saffy had given up her Christmas – which would no doubt have involved lots of kid-free partying – at such short notice to come down to Cornwall and organise a Christmas party for a group of single parents. Not as selfish as Jade, then.

Well, it was good of her; everyone would be really disappointed if the party was cancelled, especially Chloe. His little daughter was only six and Christmas was still a big event for her. He and Chloe had been going to the LH Christmas party (named after the initials of Liwus Helyk, Hannah and Lee's B&B) ever since Hannah had seen them move in across the road just before Christmas five years ago and had invited Logan to join them. They'd both really enjoyed themselves and now looked forward to it every year. Hannah and Lee were fantastic hosts, there was always plenty of food and fun games to play. Christmas Day wouldn't be the same without their party and he was glad that it would still take place, even though Hannah and Lee wouldn't be there. Of course, it would seem strange with Hannah's sister in charge, but he was happy to muck in and was sure the other parents would too. He messaged back to say that he hoped the twins would be better soon and he'd be glad to help any way he could and to tell Saffy not to hesitate to contact him if she needed anything.

His phone pinged again as an email came in from the client he was designing a new bungalow for. They had originally planned completion for the summer but had made so many alterations to their original design that they'd driven Logan, and the builders who were waiting to start work on it, mad. At this rate they'd be lucky if the bungalow was completed for next winter! Working from home as an architect wasn't easy, not when you had a six-year-old to look after. It was Chloe's Christmas play at school today, and her carol service tomorrow.

Oscar barked and dropped a ball by his feet, tail wagging expectantly.

Logan stroked the dog's head. 'Sorry, boy, but I've got work to do. No time for playing today.'

As if he understood, the dog lay down, resting his chin forlornly on his front paws.

Logan sighed, sat down at his desk and fired up his laptop. First things first; Chloe broke up from school tomorrow so he needed to get as much work done as he could before then.

❄

Saffy pulled on her coat and grabbed her car keys. Her suitcase was packed, she'd even had time to go shopping and buy gifts for Hannah, Lee and the twins. She'd left the presents she'd received from friends under her Christmas tree; she'd open them when she came home.

As she loaded the car she cast her mind back to the one and only time she'd visited Hannah and Lee, for the twins' christening when Hannah had asked her to be godmother. Their beautiful six-bedroomed pebbledash cottage was named Liwus Helyk, which was Cornish for 'colourful willow', after the gorgeous willow tree in the back garden. And it was only a few minutes' walk from the beach. She remembered staying in a pretty room with an en suite, overlooking the harbour, but couldn't recall much else about it. Hannah and Lee had bought the cottage with the intention of running a bed and breakfast business during the summer and from what she gathered it was very popular. She felt a bit guilty that she hadn't been down again even though Hannah had invited her to stay several times. She had always been too busy doing other things – working, partying, dating. Well, now she was going to be spending more than a week there, most of it on her own. She'd have Oscar, she told herself; they could enjoy some long walks along the beach. And maybe she could take a look around the local craft shops too. She might spot someone suitable for buycreative.com. If she could go back with a couple of potential partners that might impress Ajay enough to give her that promotion.

Chapter Three

'Can I put the decorations on top of it, Daddy, please?' Chloe begged as she watched Logan pipe icing around the edges of the cake.

Logan finished the curl of icing then looked at his precious daughter's eager face. 'Sure you can.' He smiled. 'How about we go and choose some new decorations for it on Saturday?'

Chloe clapped her hands excitedly, her dark bunches bouncing animatedly. The thick dark hair was definitely from Jade, but the smiling blue eyes were a replica of his. And, thankfully, she showed no sign of having Jade's temperament. 'Can I ice a bit of the cake too? I'll be really careful.'

Logan concentrated on filling the piping bag with more icing while he considered this. He'd taken up cake-making and decorating as a way of relaxing and spending time with his daughter, partly spurred by the constant guilt of spending hours working on his laptop while Chloe watched TV or played. Then, a couple of months ago, Hannah had admired the Dory birthday cake that Logan had made for one of the children in the village and asked him to make the Christmas cake for the party. Logan had been a little hesitant, but it was a way of contributing and paying Hannah and Lee back for their hospitality, so he'd agreed. Now he was trying not to fret over it, but his competitive streak was kicking in and suddenly it was ridiculously important that the cake was a success. He pushed down the competitiveness. He'd started this hobby so he could do something with Chloe, he reminded himself, and none of the families coming to the Christmas party would mind if the icing was a bit askew. He handed her the piping bag. 'Go ahead.'

Chloe's face lit up in delight. 'I'll be really careful,' she promised.

Logan guided Chloe's hand as, tongue sticking out between her teeth, she squeezed the icing down through the nozzle and carefully wove a rather wonky swirl of icing around one edge of the big square cake – big enough for about thirty people to have a slice, he was hoping.

'That's brilliant,' he told her.

Chloe grinned triumphantly. 'Can we save a piece for Mummy too?' she asked. 'She will come and see us at Christmas, won't she?' The little girl bit her lip anxiously as she waited for his answer.

Logan fought down the familiar surge of anger whenever Chloe asked to see her mum. It wasn't that he still had feelings for Jade – they had disappeared years ago when he'd realised how self-centred she was – but his ex-partner's casual attitude to their daughter infuriated him. She'd finally walked out on them both just before Christmas, when Chloe was only eight months old, although she had hardly been home before then. And rarely visited Chloe since, just flying over for a couple of days when she could spare the time from her high-powered job in Brussels as MD of an international gift company. He couldn't understand how she could be so cold-hearted towards their little girl.

'You've never understood how important my work is,' Jade had complained when Logan had pointed out that she hadn't seen their baby daughter for two weeks and he was struggling to hold down his job and arrange babysitters. They were still together at the time. 'I never wanted kids, you know that. I love Chloe but this isn't the life I planned.'

Chloe had been an 'accident' and Jade never let him forget it. They had only been together for six months and had got carried away one night after a party. Neither of them had a condom on them so had decided to chance it – something Jade had never forgiven Logan for. She'd carried on working right up until two days before Chloe was born and started again when she was two weeks old, despite Logan begging her to give herself longer to recover and the chance to spend some precious time with Chloe. At first, Chloe was left with a succession of childminders if Logan was at work, then Jade booked her into a day nursery when she was just three months old. One Sunday afternoon, Logan had arrived home from a weekend business trip to find four-month-old Chloe crying alone in her room while her teenage babysitter entertained friends. Furious, he'd picked up and cuddled Chloe, told the babysitter in no uncertain terms that she would never be babysitting for them again and vowed that from now on Chloe would come first. He tackled Jade when she returned home from Brussels later that evening, but she merely replied that she'd had to go away on a last-minute business trip and the babysitter was the daughter of a friend so she'd trusted her. 'Chloe is as much your responsibility as mine,' she retorted. 'Why should I have to give up a career I love? You're not giving up your career, are you?'

That was when Logan made the decision to work from home and take care of Chloe himself. The company he worked for had been very understanding and agreed he could be home-based as long as he attended regular meetings. He'd reduced Chloe's nursery hours, and worked around his baby daughter. Jade came home less and less, until a few months later she left for good, telling Logan that 'she wasn't a natural mother' and that Chloe was better off living with him, promising she would visit regularly and put some money in his bank towards Chloe's keep. Obviously, Jade's idea of 'visiting regularly' wasn't the same as Logan's, as she only turned up every few months and didn't always make it for Chloe's birthday or Christmas. Logan was still waiting to hear if she intended to visit this Christmas. She was just as irregular with her maintenance money. A year after Jade had left, Logan had moved to Cornwall, wanting Chloe to live in a house with a garden to play in, and near the sea rather than an apartment in the city. He'd met Hannah and Lee, and Hannah had offered to look after Chloe whenever he had to attend a meeting, while Annie Mackintosh, the friendly next-door neighbour, babysat now and again if he wanted a couple of hours out in the evening. Chloe was now a happy, settled six-year-old. But she missed her mother.

'I'm sure she'll try,' he reassured Chloe. 'You know how busy Mummy is, she'll make it if she can.' Angry as he was with Jade's careless attitude towards Chloe, he was determined not to badmouth her to their young daughter. Chloe feeling loved and wanted by her mother was far more important than his irritation towards his ex.

'Not Christmas Day though, Daddy. I want us to go to the LH party on Christmas Day. It's the bestest part of Christmas. 'Sides, we have to go 'cos we have to take our cake.'

'We're definitely going to the LH Christmas party,' Logan told her. 'Mummy will probably come to see you on Boxing Day.'

Chloe looked relieved. 'Can I lick the icing bowl?' she asked.

'You can.' Logan grinned and ruffled his daughter's hair

Oscar, who had been watching them from the corner of the kitchen, stood up and trotted over, wagging his tail too.

'You can't have any, Oscar, it'll make you ill. Won't it, Daddy?' Chloe said.

'Yes it will.' Logan took his mobile out of his pocket. 'I'm just going to make a phone call, poppet. I'll be back in a minute.'

'Okay.' Chloe was used to Logan having to make calls and knew she had to keep quiet while he did, but this wasn't a work call to a client. He wanted to call Jade again and find out what her plans for Christmas were. If they didn't include a visit to Chloe he would let rip, and he didn't want Chloe to witness that.

To his surprise Jade answered on the second ring. 'Ah, Logan, I was about to phone you.'

'You were?' He tried to keep the sarcasm out of his voice. He hadn't heard from Jade for over six weeks.

'Yes, I'm flying over for a few days next week to visit my parents so I'm going to pick up Chloe on Boxing Day and take her there overnight. Can you make sure she's ready for about ten a.m.?'

Logan was momentarily stunned. Jade had never taken Chloe overnight before. His next reaction was irritation; it was typical of Jade to phone up and dictate the terms without bothering to consider that he might have plans.

'Logan? Are you still there?' Jade repeated, an edge to her voice now as if ready to snap if he protested.

He pulled himself together. 'Yes, I'm still here. You took me by surprise, that's all. Look, you can't demand to have Chloe overnight just like that. She hasn't seen you for months. You need to see her more often and give me time to prepare her. This is a big step for her.'

'Well, my parents are having a family gathering and they want Chloe to be there to meet everyone. They haven't seen her for such a long time. You're not going to be awkward about this, are you?' She was on the defence now. 'She's my daughter too and you have her for Christmas Day.'

Logan took a deep breath, forcing back the retort that he wished Jade would remember that Chloe was her daughter more often. And it was typical of Jade to expect him to fall in with her demands. It was Christmas time, for goodness' sake! Chloe had only met Jade's parents once, about two years ago. They were strangers to her, although they did send her presents and cards for her birthday and Christmas.

'It's out of the question,' he told her firmly. 'You're welcome to come and see Chloe for a couple of hours on Boxing Day but you need to form a regular relationship with her before I'm going to allow you to take her away overnight. And I need more than a few days' notice.'

'But—'

'No buts. We're in Boxing Day if you want to pop in and see Chloe. Goodbye, Jade.'

He ended the call, trying to mask his annoyance, and puzzlement. Jade had never wanted to spend much time with Chloe before; she'd pop in for the odd hour every few months and that was it. Why had she suddenly decided that she wanted to take her for an overnight stay at her parents'?

Chloe looked up as he came in. 'Was that an awkward customer?' she asked, perceptive as ever.

'It was Mummy. She's going to try and see you on Boxing Day.' He worded it carefully in case Jade didn't turn up. She'd let Chloe down before.

Chloe's face lit up. 'Really? Will she bring me a present?'

It always hurt Logan how pleased Chloe was to see her mother, not because he resented that but because Jade was so indifferent to her.

'I'm sure she will. But don't get too excited, poppet. She might not be able to make it. Now let's get this Christmas cake iced.'

His hands were covered in icing when the landline rang a few minutes later.

'I'll get it!' Chloe had the receiver off the hook before he could protest. He'd always told her not to answer the landline in case it was a work call.

'Hello,' Chloe said politely. 'This is Chloe. Daddy is busy right now.' Then her face lit up. 'Mummy!'

Jade? She never used the landline. Logan quickly washed his hands. What did she want now?

'Really? To see Nanny and Grandad? Oh yes!' Chloe was practically jumping up and down with excitement.

Damn Jade. She'd phoned up and told Chloe all about it and now Chloe was looking forward to it.

'Mummy is going to take me to see Nanny and Grandad on Boxing Day and I'm going to sleep in the bedroom Mummy slept in when she was a little girl,' Chloe told him excitedly.

'Let me speak to Mummy, poppet.' Logan held his hand out for the phone. 'Can you let Oscar out into the garden and watch him for a bit, please.'

As soon as the little girl had gone out of the room he snapped, 'What the hell do you think you're doing telling Chloe you're going to take her to stay with her grandparents? I told you that you couldn't.'

'You're being unreasonable. Chloe wants to come. You've got no right to stop me, Logan. I am her mother!'

'And Chloe is in my care. I'll talk to her about it and call you back later.' Logan finished the call before it turned into an argument.

'Oscar wants to come in now, Daddy!' Chloe came bounding in, the dog at her heels. She looked at his face. 'I can go with Mummy, can't I?'

Logan crouched down so he could read Chloe's expression better. 'Are you sure you want to? You haven't been away from home overnight before.'

Chloe's face lit up. 'Yeah! I can't believe that I'm having a sleepover at Nanny and Grandad's. Wait until I tell Ella.' Ella was her best friend at school. She clapped her hands excitedly, then the sparkle in her eyes was replaced by a frown on her forehead. 'But what about you? Won't you be lonely without me?'

It was typical of Chloe to worry about him. She so obviously wanted to go with Jade, how could he say no? Jade's parents lived in Bristol so it wasn't that far away. He could drive up and get Chloe if she wanted to come home. He had to fight back his own feelings and let her go.

'I'll miss you, poppet, but you know how busy I always am. You can have a super time while I get some work done, then we can do something special when you come back home. How does that sound?'

'Brilliant!' She grinned. 'I can't believe I'm going to sleep in Mummy's old bed. Can I pack my polar bear pyjamas?'

As he watched his little daughter's face light up he knew that he couldn't refuse her. Well, Jade had better not let her down or she'd get a piece of his mind. Chloe was old enough to understand now and it was time that Jade made more of a commitment towards her. And he hoped Jade wouldn't be accompanied by one of her male friends either. She might be committed to her work, but she hated to be without a man in her life and from what he could gather, there had been a string of them since they'd split up. Not that he'd exactly been a monk himself, but he'd kept his dating life away from Chloe, only seeing his women friends when Annie could babysit. Chloe was his top priority. He wanted her to feel secure and there was no way he was going to introduce another woman to his precious daughter and risk Chloe getting attached to her only for the woman to leave when she got fed up. It was him and Chloe now, and that was the way it was going to stay.

Then he realised he hadn't told Chloe about the new party arrangements. He hoped she wouldn't be upset; she was really looking forward to the party and she loved Hannah, Lee and the twins. He doubted if it would be as much fun this year without them, although he was sure Hannah's sister would do her best. Still, Chloe would get to meet her other friends and it was better than spending Christmas Day alone.

He sat down and beckoned Chloe to sit by him. 'I need to talk to you about the party, poppet. It's going to be a bit different this year.' He explained what had happened.

Chloe looked worried. 'Are the twins very ill?' she asked.

'They are quite poorly but they'll be better soon. They'll be home just after Christmas. And Hannah's sister is coming down from Birmingham to run the LH party.'

Chloe looked up at him, surprised. 'She must be very kind to do that,' she said.

'Yes, she must be,' Logan agreed. 'Now go and put your coat on, poppet, and get Oscar's lead for me, we need to get going.'

'I bet Hannah's glad she's got a sister to help her,' Chloe said, as she returned with her coat. 'I wish I had a sister.'

'You don't need one, you've got me,' Logan told her, bending down to help her with the buttons. He held out his pinky finger. 'Me and you forever, remember?

Chloe linked her pinky finger with his. 'Forever,' she said.

Chapter Four

The drive down to Cornwall brought back so many memories from Saffy's childhood, when they'd all packed into Mum's old Ford Escort with Mum's friend Jackie and her daughter Emily, and driven down to the caravan they rented for two weeks every summer. They'd always been pretty fortunate with the weather and had spent the days building sandcastles on the beach, flying kites, paddling and hunting for sea creatures in rock pools. The evenings were spent happily in the club on the campsite where Mum and Jackie relaxed with a couple of drinks while Hannah, Emily and she had soon made friends with the other children and spent the evening playing and dancing. Sometimes Mum and Jackie had got up and danced too, giggling and messing around. It was the only time Saffy remembered really seeing her mum relaxed. Most of the time her face was tight, pale and worried.

Hannah had always said that one day she was going to live in Cornwall, so when the supermarket Lee worked at opened a couple of branches down there and asked Lee to manage one of them they had both jumped at the chance. Saffy guessed it was Hannah's memories of Mum dancing and giggling at the campsite club that had made her organise a Christmas party for the single families. Hannah always wanted to make things better for people, had done even as a child, rushing to make a cup of tea for Mum when she came in from work, getting Saffy to help her tidy up. She'd always been bossy too.

Saffy suddenly felt nostalgic for those long-ago holidays and wished she'd driven down while it was still light so she could see the ocean clearly at the Avonmouth Docks in Bristol, and watch the coastline come into view as she drove through Cornwall. She'd have a walk along the beach one of the days before she went back, she promised herself. Take Oscar – if dogs were allowed on the beach, that was.

❄

It was gone ten when she finally arrived in Port Breok, where Hannah lived. Colourful lights lit up the darkness, twinkling at the windows of the houses, suspended across the street from one side to the other, and glistening on Christmas trees in front gardens. Reindeers and Santa Clauses adorned the rooftops of several houses and a huge Christmas tree sparkled with multi-coloured lights in the middle of the green. This was a town that seriously loved Christmas. No wonder Hannah loved it here; she loved Christmas too.

Only now Hannah was thousands of miles away, worrying over the twins and wishing she was home. In one of her many messages Hannah had said there was parking space around the back of the house so Saffy followed the instructions her sister had given her and a couple of minutes later parked up by the garages. She reached over for her coat on the back seat, leaving her luggage in the back of the car until she'd fetched the key from Logan. Opening the note folder on her phone where she'd pasted the most important information Hannah had sent her, she scanned for Logan's phone number and address. Here it was, Daisy Cottage, and Hannah said it was directly opposite Liwus Helyk.

Saffy got out of the car, pulling up the collar of her long camel coat and tied the belt – God, it was freezing! Then, slipping her hands in her pockets to keep them warm, she walked around the corner and along the pavement to Daisy Cottage. It was quite a large, thatched cottage, set back from the road and surrounded by a low wall – as most of the houses in the street were. Fairy lights flickered inside the window frame and a cheerful holly wreath hung on the door. There was no sign of any daisies but then it was winter – she guessed the front lawn would be covered in them during spring and summer. She unlatched the gate and walked down the path, wondering if she should have phoned Logan first. She had her finger on the bell ready to press it when the door opened so swiftly she almost fell onto the tall, fair-haired – and very sexy – guy standing in front of her.

'Whoa!' He reached out to hold her shoulders, steadying her, and her body zinged to attention. 'Sorry. I didn't mean to open it so quickly but I've been watching out for you. I didn't want you to ring the bell in case it woke my little girl up.'

Saffy looked up straight into deep blue eyes that held a slight glint, as if his body had reacted to her in the same way. She tore her glance away from the enticing eyes, down to the attractive stubble on his cheeks, almost subconsciously taking in the trim body clad in faded blue jeans, white T-shirt, jumper and bare feet – did this guy have ice for blood? – then realised he was still holding her and quickly stepped back. He immediately released her. 'You're Logan?'

'I am. And you're Hannah's sister, Saffy?'

'That's me. I've come for Oscar and the key, please. Sorry to disturb you so late.'

'Not a problem.' He took a key from his pocket and handed it to her. Then she heard a soft whine and a gorgeous white and black spaniel poked his head through Logan's slightly open legs.

'Hey, boy, you'll have me over.' Logan stepped aside and grabbed the dog's collar so he couldn't run off.

'He's adorable!' Saffy said, bending down to stroke the springer spaniel, who responded by wagging his tail enthusiastically. 'And he's grown so much! He was only a puppy when I last saw him.'

'Yes, Hannah said it has been a while since you came down.'

That sounded almost judgemental! Saffy shot him a questioning look and was taken aback by the disapproving look on his face. It was almost as if he was telling her off. Had Hannah been complaining about Saffy's lack of visits? Well, it was none of his damn business.

She stood up and coolly met his gaze. 'Well, I'm here now. So if you can pass me Oscar's lead I'll take him over to Hannah's and leave you to get on with your evening.'

'I've got it here, waiting for you. You'll have to be firm with him, he can be a bit scatty and runs off, chasing anything.' Logan reached out with his free hand to take the lead off the banister and clipped it onto Oscar's collar then handed the lead to Saffy. 'I've promised Hannah I'll be on hand if you need anything so call me if you need help.'

'Thank you, but I'm quite sure I'll manage. I'd hate to trouble you any further.' She took the lead from him and marched off with Oscar.

All she wanted to do was get inside, have a hot drink and go to bed, Saffy thought, as she walked around the back of Hannah's house again to get her luggage from the car. Too late she realised how difficult it would be to take the suitcase, hand luggage, presents and the odds and ends she'd brought down for the party while holding Oscar on his lead. Especially as Oscar was now sniffing around like mad and obviously wanted to go for a walk.

'I'll take you for a walk tomorrow, Oscar,' Saffy promised, tying his lead to a post so she could open the car boot. She decided to just take her suitcase – thankfully a four-wheeler she could easily push along – and handbag; she could get the other things out of the boot tomorrow.

She locked her car then set off back to Hannah's house. The sound of the wheels of her suitcase rolling over the pebbles echoed through the dark, empty street. There were a few lights on in the windows of neighbouring houses, and the Christmas lights sparkled in the darkness, but Hannah's house, which she was now standing outside, stood in silent darkness. A large, pebbledash cottage set back from the road with a small front garden surrounded by a low narrow wall, it looked bigger than she remembered. Last time she'd visited it had been bustling with life, Mum and Jon had been there too, friends, neighbours, and Hannah and Lee so proud of their twins. It had been a happy time.

Oscar started to whine, as if he was anxious to be home. Saffy put the key in the lock and stepped inside the cottage into the long hallway, carpeted with a deep red and grey patterned carpet. Three doors lined the left wall and a staircase, covered with the same carpet and with a polished mahogany banister, was directly opposite, towards the back of the hall. She remembered that the staircase led to the guest bedrooms; the family quarters were the two bedrooms at the back. She let Oscar off the lead, lifted her suitcase inside and closed the door, her eyes immediately resting on the photos lining the right wall. Most of them were of the twins and seemed to be fairly recent. The twins looked so cute and had grown so much. They were only babies when she last saw them. She felt a pang of guilt. She should have found the time to come down and see them all more. What if something happened to them? Hannah said Miles had complications. She shook the thought from her mind. They would be okay, measles could be dangerous but – according to the website she'd quickly Googled yesterday – most children recovered fine with no side effects at all.

She shivered. It was freezing. Hannah had said she'd left the heating on a really low setting so the pipes wouldn't freeze. She'd better turn it up. She opened the door of the front lounge where Hannah had told her the central heating control was and felt for the light switch, flicking it on. This time the carpet was beige patterned, and the large room was furnished with a comfy dark green leather Chesterfield suite consisting of a three-seater, two-seater and a chair, with a dark green rug over the carpet in the centre of the room, and a long sideboard along one wall. A TV sat in the far corner and there was an open fire and surround in the middle of the main wall facing. Running along the length of another wall was a huge unit full of photos, books and ornaments. On the wall were more photos, including a large frame of assorted family photos. Centre place was one of Saffy, Hannah and Mum taken at the twins' christening, Saffy noticed with surprise. A pile of toddler paraphernalia was neatly placed in the far corner by the window. It looked comfy, a family room.

She went to close the curtains – thick green velveteen – across the diamond-patterned leaded bay window. She hated curtains left open when it was dark outside.

Thank goodness Hannah had central heating and she didn't have to light that fire, she thought, heading over to the thermostat she'd spotted on the wall in the far corner of the room. It was set to seven degrees at the moment, which she knew was the freeze setting. She pressed the button to turn it up. Nothing happened. She tried again. Still nothing. It must be on auto and she couldn't remember what Hannah had said she had to do to turn it to manual. She took her phone out of her pocket and scrolled down to Hannah's messages, found the one she wanted and followed the instructions. Seven degrees still flashed on the screen.

Damn. It wasn't working.

Well, all she could do was wrap up warm and go to bed with a hot drink. Thank goodness she'd brought her onesie with her. She'd sort out the heating in the morning.

Chapter Five

By the time she'd made a cup of coffee she was absolutely shivering. There was no way she could go to bed when it was this cold. She'd get pneumonia.

Suddenly a text came through from Hannah. *Are you at LH now, Saffy?*

Oh no, she'd promised to tell Hannah when she arrived. *Yes, arrived about half an hour ago. I've got Oscar but can't seem to turn the heating up. What do I do?*

A few minutes later Hannah texted back. *If you go over to Logan's and sit with Chloe in case she wakes, he'll come over and do it for you. Leave Oscar in the house, he'll be fine.*

Damn, Logan rescuing her was the last thing she wanted. *No need to disturb Logan, I'll sort it out in the morning,* she messaged back.

Hannah's reply was instant. *Saffy, I've got enough to worry about without the thought of you suffering from hyperthermia on my conscience. Logan is waiting for you. Please go now.*

There was nothing else for it but to go over to Logan's house. Saffy shut the door on Oscar, who was now sprawled out by sofa, snoozing, and stepped out again into the bitter night air, the cold biting at her face. The temperature really was plummeting. Logan was waiting on his doorstep, the door pulled to but not shut behind him, now wearing a thick dark brown sheepskin jacket and trainers on his feet. He didn't look very pleased.

'I'm really sorry to bother you but this wasn't my idea,' she said defensively.

'No problem. Go in and get warm. Chloe shouldn't wake but if she does tell her you're Hannah's sister and she'll be fine,' he said when she reached him, stepping out of the doorway as she stepped in. Hands thrust deep into his jacket pockets, he hurried across to Liwus Helyk. She wiped her feet firmly on the mat before going inside and closing the door behind her. Maybe she should wait here. It didn't seem right to go into the lounge or kitchen; that would look like she was making herself at home.

'Who are you and where's my dad?'

Saffy looked up to see a young girl with tousled dark brown hair and sleepy blue eyes peering over the banister at her.

'Hello, you must be Chloe. I'm Saffy, Hannah's sister. I'm staying at LH,' she said. 'The heating isn't working so your dad has gone to fix it for me.'

Chloe considered this for a moment. Then she started walking down the stairs, a cuddly white polar bear tucked under her arm.

'Are the twins better?' she asked, plonking herself down on the bottom step.

Saffy sat down on the step beside her. 'Almost. They'll be home a day or two after Christmas.'

Chloe sighed. 'I wish they were home for Christmas. The party won't be the same without them.'

'Me too.' Saffy swivelled around to face the little girl. 'I'll do my very best to make in a nice party,' she promised.

'Will Daddy be long? I had a bad dream.' Chloe's mouth trembled a little.

Please don't cry! Saffy thought in horror. She was hopeless with kids and had no idea what to do if they cried. Desperately, she tried to think of something to say then her eyes fell on the polar bear in Chloe's arms. 'I've got a polar bear like that. I always cuddle him when I have a bad dream and it makes me feel better.'

The little girl's eyes widened. 'What's your polar bear called?'

'Snowy,' Saffy told her. 'I had him when I was little. My dad bought him for me.' The first Christmas after he'd upped and gone to live with his new girlfriend. It was the last present she'd ever had from him.

Chloe's eyes widened even more. 'Snap! My polar bear is called Snowy too. Does your polar bear look like mine?' She held out the bear so Saffy could get a better look at it. 'Are they twins?'

Before she could answer, the door creaked open and a blast of cold air swept over them as Logan came in, rubbing his hands together. 'All fixed,' he said. He knelt in front of Chloe. 'What are you doing out of bed, poppet?'

'I had a bad dream, but I'm okay now 'cos Saffy told me she's got a polar bear just like Snowy, and he's called Snowy too, and she cuddles him when she has a bad dream.'

'Did she?' Logan shot at thankful look at Saffy. 'Well, let me get my jacket and boots off and I'll take you back to bed.' He started to unzip his jacket.

'Can Saffy take me?' Chloe pleaded. 'I want to show her my polar bear duvet.' She stood up and held out her hand to Saffy. 'Do you have a polar bear duvet?'

Saffy stood up too. 'No, I don't but I'd love to see yours.' She turned to Logan. 'If that's okay?'

He nodded slowly. 'Sure, if you don't mind.'

'No problem at all, it's a fair exchange for you fixing our central heating.'

Well, I'd better take off my boots then. She unzipped them – wishing she was wearing something more elegant than black and red polka dot socks – placed them on the mat then took Chloe's hand in hers and walked up the stairs with her.

Chloe was clearly a very big fan of polar bears. There were several posters of polar bears on the walls, a big polar bear on the end of the bed, and the pale blue curtains and duvet cover were decorated with them too. It reminded Saffy of her own obsession with unicorns when she was a child. Her mother had looked everywhere for unicorn curtains to no avail, so had bought some fabric pens for Saffy to draw her own unicorns on some pink curtains. Saffy had loved them.

'Hey that's cute,' Saffy said. 'I haven't seen polar bear curtains and duvet covers before.'

'Daddy asked Marta to make them for my birthday,' Chloe replied as she pulled back the duvet cover and climbed into bed. 'Do you want her to make some for you too?'

It seemed that Logan would do anything to make his little girl happy. Although she didn't seem to be spoiled, because she had come back to bed without an argument and was already snuggling down, clutching Snowy. 'Actually, I've just bought some new curtains so I don't need any more,' she said.

'Okay. Night,' murmured Chloe.

'Night. Sleep tight,' Saffy repeated the words her mother and Hannah had always said to her when they'd tucked her into bed.

When Saffy went back downstairs, Logan was standing in the kitchen doorway, sipping coffee from a big mug with 'Best Daddy' written across the front and looking a bit friendlier. 'Want one?' he asked.

As much as she would love a mug of coffee, she was shattered and wanted her bed more. 'Thanks, but I'll get back. It's been a long day.'

'Okay. Well if you get any more problems, anything at all, then phone or message me. Hannah and Lee are good friends of mine and I promised them I'd do everything I could to help you.'

'Thanks.' She looked up and then wished that she hadn't because she was staring straight into his eyes, eyes that were bluer and deeper than any she'd ever seen before. They seemed to have that glint again and she couldn't tear her gaze away. It was a struggle to keep breathing normally and she was sure he could hear her heart thud-thudding in her chest.

He didn't blink. It was as if their eyes were locked together and he could see right into her soul. 'I guess it's us who should be thanking you, for giving up your Christmas to rescue ours.'

She stood up. They were face to face now, so close she could feel his warm breath on her face and still his eyes held hers. Somehow she tore her gaze away. 'I'm happy to help,' she said, determinedly keeping her voice steady. 'See you tomorrow.'

❄

Logan watched as Saffy strode down the path in her black leather stiletto-heeled boots and expensive long camel coat. His first reaction when he'd opened the door to find her almost falling into his arms was *wow*! Hannah was attractive, but Saffy was a knock-out, with her high cheekbones, big brown puppy eyes, perfect bow lips and cute tousled hair. She also seemed to have a gorgeously curvy figure from what he could make out from the skinny jeans, knee-length boots and baggy jumper she was wearing underneath that coat. And when she'd looked at him with those stunning deep brown eyes he'd felt mesmerised. Then he'd reminded himself that he'd been attracted to Jade at first, until he'd found out how self-centred she was, and from what Hannah had told him, Saffy was the same. Too busy with work and her social life to have any time for her family. He wondered how Hannah had even managed to persuade her fun-loving sister to give up her Christmas and come down to Cornwall to run the Christmas party. From what Hannah had said about her, he'd have thought she'd have refused point blank and just told her to cancel it.

He went inside, closed the door and went upstairs to check on Chloe. She was fast asleep, clutching Snowy. He sat down on the side of her bed and watched her sleeping. She looked so peaceful. He loved her so much and hated to think of her being away from him over Christmas. Was he doing the right thing? Was a night away too much for her?

She needed a relationship with her mother and had been so excited about going to stay with her Nanny and Grandad, but Jade had only ever taken her out for a couple of hours at a time before and her sudden interest in their little daughter surprised him. He leaned over and kissed Chloe softly on the forehead then went back downstairs, poured himself another coffee and sat down at his laptop. Half an hour or so should finish it off, then he could devote the next few days to Chloe, make sure her Christmas was special. He just hoped Jade would make Boxing Day special for her too.

❄

Saffy could already feel the warmth as she stepped into the house. *Thank you, Logan,* she whispered silently.

She let Oscar out through the kitchen into the back garden, then made herself a mug of hot chocolate and looked around the kitchen. Oscar evidently slept here as his dog basket was next to a huge cream and black Aga. Saffy looked at it anxiously. Is that what she had to cook Christmas dinner on? Please let it be a gas or electric one; she didn't think she could cope with coal or wood. She walked over and looked at the hob, noticing with relief that it was gas. That shouldn't be too difficult – it would basically be the same as a gas cooker but bigger. It had two ovens by the look of it. She opened the larger oven door – it was massive, plenty big enough for a giant turkey – which is what they were going to need to feed thirty-five! She'd cook something on the Aga over the weekend, make sure she knew how it worked.

The kitchen was huge. Wall to ceiling cupboards covered one side, with a large fridge-freezer and a larder on the other side. There was a double sink, a dishwasher – she was relieved to see – and a washing machine. In the middle was a wooden table and six chairs. It all looked really homely. She imagined Hannah, Lee and the twins sitting around the table having their meals, Hannah coaxing the twins to eat, Lee wiping up any mess they made. It would be noisy but happy. She opened the doors of the other room; a large dining room with several tables and chairs and a huge dresser with crockery on display. This must be where Hannah served breakfast for the guests.

Along the hall was a washroom and under the stairs a cloakroom with coats and shoes. Behind the mahogany staircase were the two doors to the family rooms.

Oscar started barking so she went back into the kitchen to let him in. He went straight to his basket and lay in it, wagging his tail. 'Goodnight, Oscar,' she whispered, stroking his head. He licked her hand then closed his eyes. He really was a lovely dog.

Saffy walked up the winding staircase to check out the guest rooms, hoping one of them was made up ready to sleep; she didn't fancy struggling with sheets and duvet covers this late at night. Luckily the first room she tried was. It was a double room, prettily decorated in pastel floral wallpaper and with a gorgeous lacy bedspread and matching curtains, and an en suite in the corner. She walked over to the window and peered out into the street but it was too dark to see the Atlantic now. The light came on in the bedroom of the house opposite – Logan's house – and she watched, transfixed, as Logan walked across the room to the window and looked out into the street. For a moment it seemed as if he was staring right at her and she held her breath. She could almost feel his gaze. *Don't be ridiculous. He can't even see you, your room is in darkness*, she told herself.

She turned away and closed the curtains before turning on the light and getting undressed. But as she climbed into her bed a few moments later the memory of Logan's arms around her as she'd almost fallen into him earlier flashed across her mind. It had only been for a second but it had felt so good. Too good.

He doesn't like you and you don't like him, she reminded herself. *And he's got a child.* An image of Chloe, sitting on the stairs clutching her cuddy polar bear, flashed across her mind. Chloe was so young and vulnerable. And Logan clearly adored her. She wondered where Chloe's mother was. Hannah hadn't said the Logan was a widower, and she was pretty sure that her sister would have volunteered that information. So it seemed that Chloe's mother had walked out on them. What kind of woman did that? It took a special kind of guy to bring a child up alone, she thought. Many women, like her mother, did it, but in her experience it was the men who usually left. Like her father.

Chapter Six

Should we message Hannah's sister and see if she wants us to bring anything?
Do you think her sister will just want us to eat and go?
Have you met Saffy? She hasn't got any kids, has she? Do you think it will all be too much for her?

❄

Logan scrolled through the messages from the other single parents again. They were all panicking about the party. Hannah had written a group message, tagging in everyone on her party list, explaining what had happened and everyone had sent their best wishes for the twins, thanked her for making alternative arrangements, praised her sister for coming to the rescue – then promptly started another group without Hannah to discuss the implications of this news. The general consensus seemed to be panic that the party wouldn't be as good as previous years. Logan hadn't noticed the thread, he'd opted out of message notifications to his mobile because it was so time-consuming, so Marta, one of the mums, had alerted him to it.

It had taken Logan half an hour to get through all the messages, assure them that everything was under control and that Saffy seemed pleasant and he was sure she could cope. He finished by telling everyone he wouldn't have time to respond to any further messages as he was busy – like them – with Christmas preparations, then left the group so he wouldn't have another string of messages to read when he logged on again. He had a feeling there would be a load more through the day. And no doubt Marta would keep him in the loop.

No sooner had he logged off than his phone rang. It was Marta. Damn, she'd be on the phone ages and he had such a lot to do. Still, he might as well answer and get it over with, otherwise she might turn up on his doorstep. She only lived around the corner and he knew she'd seize on any chance to call. They'd shared a kiss under the mistletoe at last year's Christmas party, which had evidently meant more to Marta than it had to him, and ever since she'd taken any opportunity to message him or call by. She was probably hoping they'd have a repeat performance this year, maybe even take things further, but it wasn't what he wanted. He liked Marta, but not in that way and even if he did, he wouldn't have a relationship with someone who lived in the same village. He kept his dates out of sight of Chloe, and far enough away for it not to be awkward when he ended things.

'Hi, Logan, it's such a shame about the twins isn't it? Have you heard how they are?' the familiar soft voice asked.

'I don't know any more than Hannah put in her message,' he replied. 'I'll contact her later and get an update.'

'We're all a bit worried about the party. It's nice of Hannah's sister – Saffy – to take over but will she be able to cope? It's a lot for her.'

'I'm sure it will be fine, it's only for a few hours and we can all muck in.' Logan glanced at the clock on the kitchen wall. Nine-thirty. He needed to get cracking. He had a couple more presents to get for Chloe and he needed to pick up the bike he'd bought her as a main present. Annie had said he could keep it at her house until Christmas

Eve so that Chloe didn't find it. Then he had to go to the carol service at Chloe's school.

'I've got to go now…'

Marta wasn't about to be fobbed off that easily. 'How about I call for you to go to the carol service and we can discuss it more then?'

He held back a sigh. Marta was so persistent. 'I'm going shopping first so I'm not sure what time I'll get there. See you at LH on Christmas Day, Marta.'

'Okay. See you Christmas Day,' she said, the disappointment clear in her voice.

He hoped he wasn't going to get phone calls and messages all day. He had to admit that he was wondering himself how the party would turn out. Hannah was so warm and efficient, she made everyone feel at ease, and Lee always seemed in command of every situation. Whatever happened, the two of them worked together. Just like they were probably doing right now, in Tenerife, he imagined.

Well, all they had was Saffy, and he had to admit it was kind of her to give up her Christmas and take over so that the party wasn't cancelled. However it went, it was better than no Christmas party at all.

❄

'Woof! Woof!'

Saffy's eyes fluttered open. It sounded like a dog was in her flat. It couldn't be, she must be dreaming. She rubbed her eyes and opened them, feeling a stab of shock as she took in the floral wallpaper and lacy curtains that definitely weren't hers…

'Woof! Woof! Woof!' The barks were louder, more impatient and she suddenly remembered that she was at Hannah's house, and it was her sister's spaniel, Oscar, who was barking. She glanced at the clock on the bedside table – ten o'clock! He probably needed to go out. She jumped out of bed and raced down the stairs. 'Coming, Oscar!'

The dog bounded up to her, his tail wagging with joy, and covered her face with slobbery wet kisses. 'Hello, boy. You're a sweetie, aren't you?' Saffy stroked his head as she eased him down gently. 'Come on, I bet you need to go out in the garden for a bit.'

She looked around for something to put on her feet and grabbed her boots, zipping them up over her bare feet and onesie, then her coat, opened the back door and let Oscar out. He shot up the path and she stepped out too, pulling her coat closer around her to ward off the cold morning air. The garden was mainly lawn with pots of plants dotted everywhere, as well as a couple of flower beds. There weren't many in flower now but she bet it would look beautiful in the spring. Hannah's doing, she was sure; Hannah had always tended their small garden when they were children. A memory of her older sister walking in from the garden, her arms full of beautiful flowers she'd just cut from her flower bed, ready to put in a vase for when Mum came home, flashed across her mind. Hannah had always been thoughtful. That's why, despite her bossy ways and the fact that she didn't seem to think Saffy was capable of doing anything right, Saffy loved her. And why she'd let her guilt-trip her into hosting the party.

She walked along the path to the huge willow tree, the one that gave the cottage its name. The branches were bare now. It had been summer when she'd been down for the christening and the willow had looked beautiful, amongst a garden bursting with colour. Maybe she would visit again in the summer.

Right now though she needed to get showered, dressed, take Oscar for a walk and then check exactly what Christmas decorations Hannah had and what further supplies she needed. She called Oscar to her and they both went back inside.

Hannah had messaged to ask how she was getting on, telling her that Lily now had a fever too, and giving Saffy instructions on how to look after Oscar – apparently Logan was coming over later to take him for a walk. She obviously didn't trust Saffy not to lose him. Hannah also reminded her to buy a Christmas tree. Saffy read the message with irritation – honestly, why did her sister have to tell her everything a dozen times? She knew what she had to do. And she didn't need Logan to take Oscar for a walk, she could do it herself. The less she saw of Logan the better. He might look hot but inside he was an iceberg. Well, to her anyway, she thought, remembering the look of love on his face when he'd spoken to Chloe.

By the time Saffy had showered, dressed, fed Oscar, had breakfast and checked her emails it was almost midday. Oscar finished his food then sat down beside her, wagging his tail.

'Sorry, Oscar, I don't have time to take you for a walk this morning. I've got to go shopping,' she said. 'I'll take you around the block before I go out but that's the best I can do.' What she would have liked to do was have a walk along the seafront, see the harbour and the beach and check out the little shops there, but she knew that most of them would be closed as it was out of season and she needed to get the essentials first. She could have a walk around tomorrow or at the weekend. The priority was making sure that the Christmas party went well. She wanted to do her sister proud – and prove to Hannah that she could make a success of it.

She was planning on getting some holly and ivy, so she could make a real wreath for the front door, rather than hang up an artificial one, and also wrap it around the banister. She was determined to make Liwus Helyk look really festive.

Hannah had said that the turkey and vegetables were ordered, but what about the Christmas cake, pudding, crackers? Saffy went through the well-stocked cupboards and found four huge Christmas puddings but no Christmas cake. Then she recalled that in one of her hundreds of text messages, Hannah had said Logan was bringing that.

Her list written, she got a poop scoop and bags from the outhouse, as per Hannah's instructions, put Oscar's lead on him and set off for a walk around the block. As soon as she locked the front door behind her Oscar shot off across the road, taking Saffy with him. 'Oscar! Stop!' she yelled, trying to yank at his lead but the spaniel ignored her and bounded over to Logan's house, nearly pulling Saffy over in the process. And just as Logan walked out of his garden. *Great.*

'How are you doing, boy?' Logan asked softly, patting his head.

Saffy somehow managed to regain her balance but she felt a total idiot. 'I guess he's pleased to see you,' she said, hoping her face wasn't as flushed as it felt.

'He's a bit of a handful. It might be better if you wore more sensible shoes when you take him for a walk in future. You could take a nasty tumble in those if he bounds off,' Logan said, glancing down at Saffy's high-heeled boots then up at her long camel coat. 'And you'll get that coat all covered in dog hairs.'

Sensible shoes? She didn't think she possessed a pair. And she didn't like the patronising tone in his voice. 'I'm dressed like this because I'm going shopping,' she replied stiffly. 'I'm taking Oscar for a walk around the block first.'

'I was on my way over to take him for a walk. Hannah messaged and asked me to, she was worried you'd have enough to do.' Logan held out his hand for the lead that was still firmly wrapped around Hannah's wrist.

Worried I'll lose Oscar, more like, Saffy thought crossly. Well she wasn't going to be bossed around by her sister or Logan. She was quite capable of taking a dog for a walk, for goodness' sake.

'I can handle it, thank you,' she replied firmly. 'Come on, Oscar.' She jerked at the lead and pulled the dog along. *Please come with me,* she thought, *don't show me up!*

Oscar took a last look at Logan then trotted happily over to Saffy – and promptly bounded off down the street, pulling her behind him. She fought hard to keep her balance and walk in a dignified way until she was out of Logan's sight. Then she clung on for her life as Oscar reached the end of the street and hurled around the corner to the back of the house where he sat down by the back gate, panting happily. She felt like Oscar had taken her for a walk, not the other way around!

Saffy leaned against the gate, trying to catch her breath. Honestly, Oscar was adorable but he was hard work. She had been wondering whether to take him to the shops with her but decided it was best to leave him at home. The last thing she needed was the crazy dog running off when she had her arms full of shopping.

She intended to buy things from the local shops, rather than go to a shopping centre. She always tried to support local shops, it was the ethos of buycreative.com, and she also thought it couldn't hurt to see if there were any local craftsmen that would be suitable 'partners', as Ajay called them. She'd consulted Google Maps and knew that the village centre was only ten minutes' walk and that there was a selection of small shops there.

She left Oscar sleeping in the kitchen and set off. The village was very quiet, almost like a ghost town, and didn't look as cheerful in daylight without the Christmas lights sparkling. She guessed everyone was out at work, school or shopping and it would be livelier later on. She hadn't realised how steep the hill was to the shops though and was out of breath by the time she reached them. There was a supermarket, a greengrocer which, she was pleased to see, also sold holly and ivy, a chemist… then she spotted a craft shop. Gorgeous homemade Christmas decorations hung in the window, and there was a selection of small wooden toys on display. Just what she was looking for. She stepped inside and gasped in awe. It was like stepping into a Santa's grotto. Exquisite decorations hung everywhere; chiming bells, cute Santas, snowmen and reindeer, wooden doll's houses, rocking horses and farms. This was exactly what she was looking for to join buycreative.com. She walked over to the counter to talk to the woman behind the till.

Chapter Seven

Logan watched in amusement as Oscar hurtled down the street, pulling Saffy behind him. From what Hannah had said about her sister he'd expected Saffy to come down at the last minute and try to hand over as much as she could to him, not arrive five days beforehand and be determined to do it all herself. Well, leave her to it; he had shopping to get and could actually do with not taking Oscar for a walk first. He'd call over later, when Chloe came home from school and offer to take Oscar over the dunes. Chloe would love that too. He'd promised Hannah he'd help Saffy and he intended to keep that promise. Even if she was stubborn, pigheaded, standoffish… and gorgeous. Not that he was attracted to her. She was *definitely* not his sort.

He drove to Launceston knowing that with the selection of high street shops and smaller outlets he'd be able to get what he wanted for Chloe there. Two hours later he'd got everything on his list, and a couple of things that weren't on it, bundled it all into his van –including the purple and silver bike that was to be Chloe's main present – and set off home.

As he drove down the hill, near the local shops, Logan was surprised to see Saffy trudging along, a bulging bag of shopping in each hand and rolls of Christmas paper tucked under her arm. Why hadn't she taken her car and gone to the big shops in Launceston, like he had?

Suddenly, the wrapping paper slipped out from under her arm and rolled away. Saffy trotted after it, her long coat flapping, the shopping bags bobbing up and down in her arms, almost tripping over in those ridiculous heels. A man saw her, stopped and picked up the paper, tucking it under her arm. She smiled her thanks, a dazzling smile that lit up her face, then continued on her way. Logan pulled up and lowered the window down.

'You've got quite a bit of shopping there. Want a lift?' he asked. 'I'm heading your way.'

A look of relief swept over her face. 'Yes please!'

He got out of the van and took the bags from her, placing them in the back. 'We'll have to hurry, though. I've got a carol service to go to.'

'Thanks for stopping.' She walked around the car and got into the passenger seat. 'I love carol services. Is it at the local church?'

'No, it's at Chloe's school. Come along if you want.' Then he wondered why he'd offered – of course she wouldn't want to go to a school carol service. 'Although I'm sure you have far too much to do.'

'Actually I'd love to come. But I have to take my shopping home first and let Oscar out. Will I be making you late?'

Another surprise. Well, he had to go with it now, he'd made the offer. 'Not if you're quick. I have to put these presents away too, before Chloe sees them.'

'Leave them at Hannah's if you want and I'll bring them over later, when Chloe's asleep?' she offered.

It made sense, they were running short of time now. 'If you're sure? I've got a bike in the back too.'

'It's the least I can do when you've fixed the heating for me and you're giving me a lift home.'

'Why didn't you take your car and go to the big shops?' he asked as they turned into the street where he and Hannah lived.

'Because I like to support local traders and craftsmen,' she replied. 'Let's park at the front, we'll only be nipping in for a few minutes.'

'Fine by me. I'll unload the car, you let Oscar out. Deal?'

'Deal.'

It took a bit longer to unload the car – thanks to the holly Saffy had bought getting wrapped around the bike wheels – and Oscar took his time 'doing his business' so the carol service had already started when they dashed into the hall, and all the seats were taken. 'Sorry,' Saffy mouthed as they stood at the back.

Luckily Chloe's class hadn't come into the hall yet so Logan mouthed back, 'It's fine.'

Then Chloe's class came in and his daughter beamed with delight when she spotted him and Saffy. She waved and they both waved back. Saffy seemed to really enjoy the carols, clapping loudly when they'd finished. He was surprised by her enthusiasm. She even waited with him in the playground for Chloe. He guessed she was bored in Hannah and Lee's house by herself.

'Did you like it?' Chloe asked, as she came running out of the gate to them.

'It was amazing.' Logan swung her up into the air then put her back down again.

'Did you like it too?' Chloe asked Saffy.

'I loved it. "Little Donkey" is one of my favourite carols, and I could hear your voice above everyone else's. You're such a good singer.'

Chloe looked delighted. 'Is Saffy coming to our house?' she asked.

'No, she's got things to do,' Logan said quickly.

Chloe looked crestfallen.

'Cheer up, we're going to take Oscar for a walk along the dunes before it gets dark. You'd like that, wouldn't you?'

The smile was back on the little girl's face. 'Oh yes. Will you come too, Saffy?' she asked, turning to look at her.

'Saffy's too busy—' Logan started to say but Saffy cut him short.

'I'd love to come. Call over when you've changed out of your school uniform. Oscar and I will be ready.'

❄

What had possessed her to agree to take Oscar for a walk with Logan and Chloe? Especially when she had the wreath to make, the decorations to unpack and a thousand and one other things to do, Saffy thought as she let herself into Hannah's cottage.

Because she was sick of him answering for her, that's why. Honestly, he was as bad as Hannah, always bossing her about. Well, Oscar was Saffy's sister's dog, and if she wanted to take him for a walk along the dunes, she would. It was Logan who was tagging along, not her.

She needed something a bit more sensible to wear though. She couldn't trudge along the dunes in these boots and coat, which was why she'd bought a pair of flat ankle boots from one of the local shops. And Hannah should have a coat she could borrow.

She opened the cubby hole under the stairs and rummaged through the coats hanging there. The only suitable thing she could find was a yellow duffle coat. Very Hannah but definitely not Saffy, and it was a bit big. She shrugged; it was far more practical that her long coat, and who cared what Logan thought? It wasn't as if she was trying to impress him.

She poured herself a glass of Coke and sent a quick text to Hannah to ask how the twins were and telling her that everything was fine.

Then she put on the coat, her new flat boots, put the lead on Oscar, picked up the keys and put them in her pocket just as the doorbell rang. Logan and Chloe, no doubt.

Oscar barked and bounded up the hall, almost pulling Saffy with him. As soon as she opened the door he was out, skipping around them happily and getting Chloe tangled up in the lead.

'Stop it, Oscar!' Saffy said, trying to pull him back but Oscar ignored her.

'Shall I take him? He's a bit of a handful,' Logan offered.

'It's fine. I can handle it, thank you.' She hated the way Logan always assumed she needed his help. Well, she didn't. Not all the time anyway. She was perfectly capable of handling Oscar.

The dunes were wild, just as Saffy remembered from her childhood holidays. Big sandy mountains with clumps of coarse grass here and there. Only it had been sunny back then and now there was a biting wind. Saffy pulled up the hood of the duffle coat as she watched Oscar running around, happily chasing the sticks Chloe was throwing for him. She wondered if Hannah brought the twins here in the summer.

'Can we get to the beach from here?' she asked Logan.

'Yes, if you walk a bit further but it's a bit of a steep hill down and it'll be dark soon.'

'Is there anywhere I can just see the beach then?' Saffy asked.

'Sure, you'll get a good view of it if you stand on the top of that mound.' He pointed to what looked like a small hill a little ahead to the right.

Saffy made her way to the top of the mound and looked down at the deserted sandy beach below. The sky was almost dark grey, and the steel blue sea was crashing wildly against the shore. It looked desolate and wild, but she bet it was lovely in the summer. Memories of their summer Cornish holidays with white clouds floating in a summer sky and a cobalt blue sea gently lapping the golden sand flashed into her mind. She imagined Hannah, Lee and the twins having picnics on the beach, paddling in the sea. Just like she, Mum and Hannah had done.

She shivered as the cold wind blew through her and glanced at her watch. Half past four; it would be dark soon.

'Ready to go?' Logan shouted from below, where he'd been keeping an eye on Chloe and Oscar. 'It's a bit cold for Chloe.'

'It's a bit cold for me too,' she said. 'Yes, let's go home. I need a hot chocolate.'

❄

Logan watched as Chloe skipped up to Saffy and slipped her hand in hers. Saffy looked down at her and they both smiled, then walked back over the dunes together. Chloe was a happy, friendly little girl and took to people easily, especially women. She was looking for a mother figure, he was sure. After all, she hardly saw her own mother. She adored Hannah, and as Saffy was Hannah's sister she perhaps looked on her as a substitute. But Hannah and Saffy were completely different. Hannah was capable, reliable, organised, a mother and a good one at that, someone who took people under her wing. Saffy was… he hesitated as he tried to figure out exactly what Saffy was like. Right now, skipping along with Chloe, dressed in that big duffle coat and what looked like new ankle boots, she looked a different person to the smart, elegant woman who had turned up yesterday in her expensive coat and skyscraper boots.

And she was surprisingly good with Chloe.

Suddenly, as if sensing him staring at her, Saffy turned. 'Come on, slow coach!' she shouted, laughing.

The winter sun caught her face, illuminating the twinkling laughter in her eyes, her parted red lips as she laughed, her wind-blown hair. She looked alive. Fun. Beautiful. And he felt his heart stir.

Chapter Eight

Saffy spent the evening making a holly wreath and decorating the mahogany banister with holly, weaving it in and out the balustrades and along the rail. It looked very festive when she had finished, even if not exactly *Vogue*-glam. Tomorrow she would go out and buy a Christmas tree, she decided, then get the decorations down from the loft. She might not know much about entertaining children, and decorating trees wasn't one of her talents, but she was determined to make the house look like a magical grotto when the families came in on Christmas Day.

The ring of her mobile startled her. Was it Hannah? Were the twins worse? Heart in her mouth, she reached over and picked the phone up from the table. To her surprise, Robbie's image was flashing on the screen. She pressed the 'accept call' button. It'd be good to have a chat with him.

'Hello, Robbie. Lovely to hear from you.'

'I need the address to your sister's house. Can you text it to me?' Robbie said, sounding rather breathless. 'I'm in a taxi on the way there.'

What? For a moment she thought she'd misheard. 'You're on your way?' she repeated.

'Yes, I've just got off the train. I remembered you said it was in Port Breok but I need the house number and street. Be quick!' He ended the call.

Her mind buzzing, wondering why Robbie had travelled all the way down here, Saffy keyed Hannah's address and sent the message to Robbie. He said he'd just got off the train, so he must be about ten minutes away. And he was obviously intending to stay. Perhaps he had a couple of days off work and had decided to spend them by the seaside. Well, it would be great to have some company.

She'd have to make a bed up for him, though, she thought, dashing upstairs. She'd put him in the room overlooking the harbour, where she'd stayed last time. She soon found the airing cupboard, where there was a supply of clean sheets and duvet covers and had just made up the bed when the doorbell rang.

'Coming!' she shouted, racing back down the stairs. Oscar was already at the front door, barking.

Saffy grabbed hold of Oscar's collar and opened the door with a smile. 'Robbie, this is—' She stopped as she registered his clearly upset face and the large suitcase by his feet –much too big for a weekend stay, even by Robbie's standards. 'What's happened?'

'Me and Duncan have had a massive bust-up. It's over. Finito. So I thought I'd come down to Cornwall with you and help you run the Lonely Hearts party for your sister.'

Saffy looked at him, stunned. 'But I thought you were going to propose…'

'I did. That was the problem…' Robbie looked as if he was about to burst into tears. 'I can stay here with you, can't I?'

'Yes, of course.' Saffy let go of Oscar, who immediately bounded into the front garden, and she gave Robbie a big hug. He looked so upset. 'Come in and tell me all about it.'

Robbie stepped in with his case and Saffy looked around for Oscar. Then she realised that the front gate was swinging on its latch. Robbie must have left it open. Where was Oscar? Hannah would never forgive her if she lost him, or he got run over…

'Oscar!' she shouted, running out of the garden and looking up the dark, empty road. 'Oscar!'

'He's over here!' Logan called.

Saffy looked over and saw Logan crossing the road with Oscar on a lead beside him.

'Oh thank goodness, I thought I'd lost him!' she said, relieved.

'It's a miracle you didn't, or that he wasn't run over,' Logan snapped. 'I was about to come over for Chloe's presents – she's fast asleep in bed so I wanted to take the bike to Annie's so Chloe doesn't discover it – when I saw the taxi pull up and your boyfriend get out. I decided to go back inside, give you a bit of time together then Oscar came charging over the road to me. It's a good job I have a spare lead.' He took Oscar into the garden then let him off the lead and Saffy quickly closed the gate. 'Better remind him to close the garden gate in future,' he said curtly. 'Hannah and the twins will be devastated if anything happens to Oscar.'

Saffy was about to tell him that Robbie wasn't her boyfriend but stopped herself. It was none of his business and he had no right to be so damned rude. Oscar wasn't his dog.

'Thanks. Do come in and get Chloe's presents,' she said stiffly. She pointed to the open front door. 'Would you like me and Robbie to help you carry them over?'

'No thanks, I'll manage.' Logan nodded briefly as he walked past Robbie into the house and was out again in less than five minutes, the bags containing the presents hanging over the bike handlebars. Robbie rushed to open the gate for him and Logan marched past him without a word.

'Well, he's a bit of a dish,' Robbie whispered as Logan wheeled the bike across the road to the house next door to Daisy Cottage without so much as a backward glance. 'Moody though.'

Rude, more like, Saffy thought. 'Over Duncan already, are you?' she asked.

Robbie's eyes clouded over. 'It'll take me years to get over that man but I won't be spending them wallowing, that's for sure.' He held his head up and put his shoulders back. 'There're plenty more men who'll appreciate me.'

'Duncan appreciates you. You two are made for each other,' Saffy said gently. 'Come on, I'll make you a coffee and you can tell me all about it.'

So, over three cups of coffee, laced with brandy, Robbie told her how he'd seen a gorgeous ring in the jeweller's window yesterday and had bought it on impulse. He pulled it out of his pocket and showed her – it was a slim gold band with a row of three dazzling diamonds. Then this morning he'd decided he couldn't wait until Christmas and had proposed. But Duncan had looked so horrified when Robbie went down on one knee in front of him, holding out an engagement ring, that they'd ended up having a massive argument.

Saffy listened, stunned. 'I'm so sorry, Robbie. Are you sure Duncan was turning you down? Perhaps you just took him by surprise?'

'It wasn't surprise on his face, it was horror! Marrying me is clearly the last thing he wants.' Robbie looked as if he was about to burst into tears.

'That's rubbish, I've seen the way Duncan looks at you. He adores you. You're both made for each other. You can't fall out over this. You need to talk to each other. Maybe he's not quite ready to take such a big step yet.'

'A big step? We've been living together for years. I would have thought marriage was the next step. It's obvious that he doesn't see us as a forever couple.'

Saffy put her hand over Robbie's and squeezed it reassuringly. She hated seeing him so upset. 'I'm sure you've got it wrong. Duncan probably needs time to take it in. I bet he'll be on the phone in a minute to tell you he's sorry and that of course he wants to marry you.'

'He doesn't know I'm here,' Robbie said miserably. 'He stormed out so I packed while he was gone and left him a note to say it was over. And I've turned off my phone so he can't contact me. Not that he'll want to. I bet he's glad to get rid of me.'

Saffy groaned. Robbie could be really stubborn sometimes. 'Why have you done that? He could be trying to contact you right now, to explain.'

'I bet he isn't.' Robbie picked up his mug. 'Anyway, there's no explaining this away. The look on his face said it all. Duncan and I are over.' Robbie set his mouth in that determined way Saffy knew so well.

'Robbie, it's Christmas. You guys can't split up at Christmas.'

'Too late. We already have. And I don't want to talk about it any more.' Robbie took a long swig of his coffee. 'And I'm not going to let it spoil my Christmas so I've decided to come down to Cornwall and help organise a fantastic party for those lovely families.'

'But what about your own Christmas party? You'll be letting all your guests down.'

Robbie glared at her. 'Honestly, Saffy, I've lost my partner, my home, my future and all you can say is that I'll be letting our Christmas guests down.' He sniffed. 'They're all Duncan's friends anyway and knowing him he'll still host the party and spend the whole day bitching about me.' He put his mug down. 'Now what's the plan of action for the Lonely Hearts Hotel Christmas Do?'

'Lonely Hearts Hotel?' Saffy repeated.

'Good name, isn't it? The initials of your sister's place, and they're single parent families, so are "lonely hearts". It's got a catchy ring to it.'

She smiled. Trust Robbie. Even when he was upset his marketing mind was still working. It was such a shame he and Duncan had fallen out; they were so right together. She was sure that they'd make up though. Duncan would probably phone tomorrow and Robbie would be back home. There's no way they would spend Christmas Day apart. But it was good to have Robbie's company tonight.

'I've been making a holly wreath and was about to hang it on the door,' she told him, showing him the wreath. 'Then tomorrow I'm going to get the decorations down from the loft, see what's there, order a Christmas tree and take a walk along the harbour...'

'That all sounds good to me. We're going to give those lonely hearts a day to remember.' Robbie yawned. 'Do you mind if I turn in now, hun? I'm shattered.'

'Sure. I've made a bed up for you. It's got a lovely view over the harbour, not that you'll be able to see much now.' She stood up. 'Want me to make you a hot chocolate? If you have any more coffee you'll be awake all night.'

'No thanks, I feel like I've got gallons of liquid swishing inside me as it is. Just lead the way to my chamber.'

❄

Logan looked out of his window over at the bedroom window opposite, the one it seemed Saffy was sleeping in, as he'd seen the light on and curtains drawn the past couple of nights . As they were now. Saffy and her boyfriend were probably about to go to bed. Together.

Well, it was none of his business if they were but Saffy could have mentioned that he was coming. Not a hint of it all the time they were at the carol concert or walking on the dunes. Hannah hadn't mentioned it either, so Saffy couldn't have told her. He guessed her boyfriend hadn't been able to come earlier, he was probably working, and he'd followed her down so they could spend Christmas together. Robbie, she'd called him. And by the way she'd greeted him she was very pleased to see him. So pleased that she hadn't even noticed Oscar shoot out of the gate and across the road. If there had been a car coming… Logan shuddered at the thought. Hannah, Lee and the twins adored that dog; they'd be devastated if anything happened to him.

He should have guessed Saffy would have a boyfriend, though. She was the sort of woman that always did. And Robbie was the ideal partner. Tall and handsome, with his chiselled features, cropped blond hair and designer clothes. They made the perfect magazine cover couple.

He thought back to Saffy on the dunes, wearing that bright yellow duffle coat and laughing as if her sides would burst. She'd been like a different person then. She was a real dichotomy, all elegant and self-assured one minute and then switching to the endearing girl-next-door the next.

Well, he was glad she had a boyfriend. He'd been starting to like her. More than like her. And a woman like Saffy was the last thing he needed in his life.

Chapter Nine

Bang! Crash! 'Bloody hell!'

Saffy woke with a jolt. It took her a couple of minutes to identify the voice that had sworn so loudly as Robbie's. And what was that crash? It sounded like it came from the kitchen. She hoped Robbie hadn't broken anything or injured himself.

She was out of bed, into the hall and racing down the stairs in a flash, glad she was wearing her onesie – it was freezing.

'Robbie! Are you okay? What's happened?'

She anxiously peered around the half-open kitchen door, hoping she wasn't going to be confronted by a pile of broken crockery scattered all over the floor. To her relief it was only a few saucepans and a frying pan. Robbie, clad in black Hugo Boss pyjama bottoms and a grey and black striped T-shirt, stood facing her, wet tea towel clapped theatrically to his forehead.

'It's a miracle I wasn't knocked out!' he said dramatically. 'I can't believe your sister kept the pots and pans all piled up in a high cupboard like that. I reached up to grab the frying pan and they all came crashing down onto me. I've got a bump the size of an egg on my forehead. Look.' He took off the tea towel, revealing a big swelling on his forehead. 'Now I'm going to have to go around like this all Christmas!'

'Put some frozen peas on it.' Saffy stepped over the pans on the floor to reach the freezer, opened the door and pulled open the trays one by one until she found a bag of peas. 'Here you are. Now hold the bag over the bump and go and lie down on the sofa for a bit. I'll make you a cuppa.'

'Thanks, hun. I do feel a bit shook up.' Robbie wrapped the frozen peas in the tea towel, placed it back over the lump then shuffled out.

Saffy filled up the kettle and plugged it in, then picked up the pots and pans, checking to see if they were dented – none of them were, thank goodness – and put them back in the cupboard. Brr! It really was cold. She checked the radiator – yes, it definitely was on. The forecast was for snow over the weekend and it was certainly cold enough.

Glancing at the kitchen clock she saw that it was nine-thirty. She hadn't meant to sleep so late again, there was such a lot to do today. She made two mugs of tea – adding extra milk and two sugars to Robbie's – then took them into the lounge where Robbie was now sprawled out on the sofa, the towel-wrapped bag of peas firmly pressed onto his forehead.

'I didn't realise it was so late,' she said, putting the two mugs down on the coffee table and sitting down on the chair opposite Robbie. 'I must have zonked out.'

'Lucky you. I couldn't sleep most the night, I must have finally dropped off about five.' Robbie yawned. 'I'm knackered.'

Saffy reached for her mug and cupped her hands around it to warm them. She'd have to go and turn the thermostat up in a bit. 'I'm guessing you couldn't sleep because of Duncan?'

Robbie swung his legs off the sofa and sat up. 'Obviously because of Duncan. I'm devastated. Totally broken. I thought I was going to spend the rest of my life with that man.'

'I'm sure he regrets how he acted now. Have you turned on your phone yet to see if he's messaged you now he's had time to think about things?'

'I've told you, we're over. Finito.' Robbie took the bag of peas away from his forehead. 'Has the lump gone down a bit?'

Saffy hesitated as she looked at the massive lump in the middle of his forehead. It didn't look like it had gone down at all but Robbie was so vain, she knew if she told him that he'd hide himself in his room all over Christmas.

'It hasn't, has it?' Robbie sprung up to look in the mirror. 'OMG, it's horrendous!'

'Keep the frozen peas on it, it'll go down soon,' Saffy reassured him.

Suddenly the bell rang and they both turned towards the window.

'Whoever it is, don't let them in! I can't possibly let anyone see me looking like this!' Robbie exclaimed.

'It's probably the postman. Who else would call this early?' Saffy went over to the window, pulled aside the corner of the still-closed curtains and peered out. She was horrified to see Logan standing on the doorstep, a big box of what looked like vegetables in his hands. Chloe was standing beside him. Saffy instinctively pulled back but it was too late, Chloe had seen her and gave a friendly wave. Not wanting to ignore her, Saffy waved back, then stepped away, out of sight. She'd expected Logan to bring over the veg on Christmas Eve, not today. He'd probably be too busy with his own stuff then though. But why so early!

'It's Logan and his daughter, it looks like he's brought the vegetables for Christmas dinner,' she said. 'You'll have to answer it. I'm not dressed.'

'Absolutely not! No way! Not with my head like this.'

She had no intention of letting Logan see her in her polar bear onesie and with bed hair and no make-up. There was only one way to make sure Robbie did it. 'Robbie, if you don't answer the door I'll message Duncan myself and let him know you're here and that you're pining for him.'

Robbie glared at her. 'You wouldn't!'

Saffy folded her arms. 'Try me.'

'That is total blackmail!' Robbie got to his feet, pressed the towel-wrapped frozen peas firmly to his head and strode to the door, muttering, 'Call yourself a friend.'

Saffy heard Chloe ask what Robbie had done to his head, then Robbie launch into a detailed explanation, followed by the soft murmur of Logan's voice. *Stop talking and hurry up and go,* she thought. She was dying for a shower and to get dressed. Then, to her dismay, Robbie said loudly and clearly, 'You'd better come in.'

Saffy stepped back in horror. He was actually inviting Logan in! How could he when he knew she wasn't dressed, showered, made-up? She was in absolutely no state to see Logan who'd looked drag-to-bed gorgeous in his dark brown jacket and jeans.

'Carry it through into the kitchen, will you?' Robbie said in an extra loud voice.

Okay, chill, he was letting Saffy know that Logan was just carrying something into the kitchen and then going. Although if Robbie had taken the bag of frozen peas off his head he could have taken the box from Logan and brought it through himself.

She sat back down on the sofa, watching the door warily.

'I'll bring the turkey over on Monday. Hannah asked me to pick it up. I'll leave you to it now, I can see that you aren't dressed.' She could hear the disapproval in his tone. He probably thought they'd been at it all night. Well, what business was it of his if they had? She could hear their footsteps walking towards the kitchen. Five minutes and they'd be gone.

'I'll let Saffy know,' Robbie replied.

'Can't we say hello to Saffy, Daddy? I want to show her Snowy's new jumper.'

'I think she's busy, poppet. We'll see her later.'

'But she's in there. She waved to me out of the window.'

Saffy froze in horror as she heard small footsteps run along the hall then saw the door handle turn.

There was no escape – she had to bluff this out.

She put her mug down on the table and quickly ran her fingers through her messy hair, wishing she'd at least washed her face and brushed her teeth.

'Saffy!' Chloe burst into the room, holding out Snowy, who was wearing a bright red jumper. 'Look! Snowy has a new jumper to keep him warm in the snow!'

That's lovely, Chloe,' Saffy said, smiling at the little girl and praying that Logan wouldn't follow her in to the lounge. Too late – he was standing in the doorway. Or should that be 'filling the doorway'. She hadn't realised quite how tall he was – and those shoulders!

'Morning, Saffy. Sorry to disturb you so early.' Why did he always sound as if he was judging her and finding her wanting? His eyes drifted over her and she felt her cheeks flame. Great, now she was blushing. How she wished she'd got out of bed half an hour earlier. Then she'd be showered and dressed. It was Saturday morning, and lots of people wore onesies, she reminded herself.

Yes, but polar bear onesies with ears and a tail? She'd been amused when Robbie and Duncan had given it to her for Christmas last year but right now she wished that she was wearing something more glamorous.

Chloe was staring at her, eyes wide. 'Daddy, Saffy's got a polar bear onesie just like I want. It's got ears. Look.'

'So it has.' There was no mistaking the twinkle of amusement in his voice and she was sure his lips were twitching. He was enjoying her discomfort, damn him.

She forced herself to meet his gaze. 'You'll have to excuse my… er… attire.' Attire! God, she sounded so pompous. This was bloody awful.

'Your onesie is so cool. Does it have a tail?' the little girl asked curiously. 'I want one with a tail.'

'Don't pester Saffy, Chloe, we need to go, we have a lot to do. And I'm sure she and Robbie have a lot to do too,' Logan said firmly.

Oh, what the hell! There was no rescuing the situation now so she might as well have a bit of fun. 'Yes, it does.' She got up, turned to face Chloe and wriggled her bum to show her the little white tail. 'See.'

Chloe clapped her hands in delight. 'See, Daddy, you can get them with tails. I told you!'

Logan's grin stretched from ear to ear but Saffy ignored him and concentrated on the little girl. If she didn't look at Logan she might not feel such an idiot. 'Polar bears are cute, aren't they?'

Chloe nodded. 'That's why they're my very favourite animal.'

'They're Saffy's favourite animal too, that's why we bought her the onesie last Christmas,' Robbie added, then clamped his mouth shut as if he wished he hadn't said anything and walked out of the room.

'We?' Logan repeated, looking surprised.

'Robbie and his boyfriend, Duncan… they've just split up which is why he's come down to Cornwall to join me,' Saffy whispered. 'He's heartbroken.'

'I can hear you,' Robbie called from the hall.

'Do they love each other?' Chloe whispered, eyes wide.

Saffy nodded. 'Yes and I'm sure they'll make up soon.'

'I can still hear you and no we won't!' Robbie shouted.

'That's so sad,' Chloe said sympathetically.

'It is, especially at this time of year.' Saffy could feel Logan's eyes on her. She didn't want to look at him. She felt such a mess but what the hell, in a couple of days' time she'd return home and he'd never see her again.

'Thanks for bringing the veg,' she said.

'No problem.' He shivered. 'It's a bit chilly in here, isn't it? Has the heating knocked itself back to "freeze" setting?'

'I don't think so. I checked the radiators and they're still hot.'

He walked over to the thermostat. 'It seems fine but I'll turn it up a bit,' he said, adjusting the dial. 'While I'm here let me show you what to do if the boiler kicks out. It's quite an old one and it's a bit temperamental. You don't want to be without heating or hot water in this weather.'

Okay, so suddenly he was being friendly again. What was it about him that he blew so hot and cold? Well, she could do with knowing about the boiler but she wasn't going to let him follow her and watch the perishing tail on her onesie wagging. 'Lead the way,' she said.

Half an hour later, after explaining how to get the boiler to start again if it kicked out and going through the contents of the box of vegetables he'd brought with him, Logan and Chloe finally left. 'Oh, I'll bring the cake along tomorrow. I haven't finished decorating it yet,' he added.

Saffy looked at him, puzzled. 'Decorating it? You mean you're making it?'

'Yes. Didn't Hannah tell you?'

'She said you were bringing the Christmas cake, I presumed you were buying one. How cool. I can't wait to see it.'

'Why? Because a man made it?' Logan demanded.

What was this guy's problem? 'I'm not that sexist. Duncan is a good cook, as is my stepdad. I just love Christmas cake.'

'We're going to buy some more decorations for it today. Daddy said I can choose some of them,' Chloe told her.

❄

Well, Logan obviously loved his daughter; she seemed to be the only one who could melt his frosty exterior, Saffy thought, watching through the window as they walked down the garden path, hand in hand. She wondered what had happened to Chloe's mother. Did she see Chloe regularly? Surely no one would turn their back on an adorable little girl like that.

Her father had though. He'd walked away from her and Hannah to move in with another woman and her son when Saffy was only four. He'd had another daughter with his new girlfriend, then left her too. Then he met someone else and was now living in Australia with his third family. He'd wiped her and Hannah – and probably his other daughter, who they'd never met – out of his life as if they had never existed.

Chapter Ten

As soon as Logan left, Saffy headed for the shower. Half an hour later, dressed in jeans and a warm sweater, with light make-up and her hair held back with a couple of clips, she felt ready to face the day.

Robbie was already in the kitchen, assessing the crockery and cutlery situation. 'Well, your sister seems to have plenty of supplies,' he said.

'She runs a B&B,' Saffy reminded him. 'There's more crockery and cutlery in the dresser in the other room too.'

'All good on that front then. So what's the schedule? Check the decorations then buy the Christmas tree or go for the Christmas tree first? We're leaving it a bit late,' he added. 'There's only three more days before Christmas and it might be difficult to get a tree tomorrow or Christmas Eve.'

'I know. I think get the tree first. Hannah said she had plenty of baubles and lights. I'll check if she's got a Santa outfit though, that would be a nice touch.'

'I'll wear it. I like being Santa,' Robbie said.

'If you and Duncan aren't back together by then,' Saffy said. 'I'm sure he'll message you soon.'

Robbie crossed his arms across his chest. 'No he won't. He'll be busy planning the Christmas party and enjoying his single life.'

'Don't be silly. He'll be just as miserable as you. Why don't you text him? Let him know where you are?' she suggested.

'No way. It's not up to me to make the first move,' Robbie said, flicking his head. 'Now let's take a quick look through your sister's Christmas stuff and see if there's a Santa outfit.'

There wasn't. As Saffy had guessed, there were plenty of baubles, lights, crackers, tinsel, chair covers, tablecloths, place mats – everything you could need for a party. But no Santa outfit.

She jotted down a shopping list. 'I'll take Oscar for a quick walk around the block, then we'll be off,' she said.

She was hoping desperately that Logan wasn't about as she set off along the street with Oscar. Fortunately, he wasn't, and the spaniel was very well-behaved for once. When she returned she left Oscar chewing a bone in the kitchen while she and Robbie set off in the car to find a real Christmas tree and a Santa outfit.

❄

'It's such a shame about the twins, isn't it? Have you heard how they are?' Ariane asked as she joined Logan in the queue in the butcher's. Ariane had moved into the village a few months ago and she and Logan had formed a bit of a friendship since her daughter, who was in Chloe's class, had taken Chloe's school bag home by mistake. She'd been so apologetic when she returned it that he'd invited her to stay for a coffee. When she'd confessed to being a bit lonely, he'd mentioned it to Hannah and she'd immediately invited Ariane to the Christmas party. Hopefully, it would help her get to know the other families and make friends. Logan knew what it was like to be on your own. When Jade first walked out on them he went days without seeing anyone apart from Chloe.

'I haven't heard from Hannah today but Saffy said she's hoping to be home on Boxing Day,' he said.

'It's lovely of his sister to come down and run the party for her. To be honest, I would have really struggled if I had to provide Christmas dinner at such short notice. I hadn't budgeted for it. And it's the first Christmas me and the kids have been on our own.'

'You're not the only one in that position,' Logan told her. He was lucky; he earned a good living from his work as an architect, and every now and again Jade sent some money towards Chloe's upkeep. His mother had told him he should insist Jade made regular payments, but his pride wouldn't let him. He wanted to provide for his daughter, and luckily still could, but he knew many of the parents struggled. It made him angry that so many men fathered children and then walked away, barely paying a penny for their upkeep, or bothering to check that their children had everything they needed. The LH Christmas party not only provided everyone with a fun Christmas Day, it was a chance to make friends and form a support group, back-up for when one of the children – or even a parent – was ill. One couple from last year's party were now happily living together. He hoped that would happen for Ariane too. Sometimes Logan was the only man at the party but this year Geoff would be there. Geoff's wife had died a few years ago and his son was about eleven or twelve. Geoff was a nice bloke, and Logan hoped he and Ariane would hit it off together. They were well suited.

❄

Saffy and Robbie found a huge tree and arranged for it to be delivered Sunday morning. They also managed to buy a Santa outfit with an inflatable tummy that made Robbie look like a fat, jolly Santa, an inflatable Santa and reindeer and some craft materials for the children to make things with on Christmas Day. It was such a lovely festive atmosphere in Launceston that they spent far longer around the shops than they meant to, stopped at a pub on the way home to eat and it was gone eight when they finally returned home. Poor Oscar looked really forlorn and dashed to meet them, wagging his tail, as soon as they stepped in the front door. Saffy fussed him then let him out in the garden.

'I don't know about you but I'm shattered,' Robbie said. 'How about we take the dog for a walk and then I'm off to bed.'

He looked pale, and his eyes were heavy. *He's devastated about Duncan*, Saffy thought.

'Have you turned your phone on to see if Duncan has messaged you?' she asked.

'It's a waste of time. I told you, he's glad to be rid of me,' Robbie told her.

'Of course he isn't. He's being stubborn, like you. And he must be wondering where you are. Why don't you message him and let him know you're down in Cornwall with me?'

Robbie shook his head. 'I am not making the first move. And if you don't mind, Saffy, I don't want to talk about it any more.'

So they took Oscar for a walk then both headed for bed. Saffy glanced over the road to Logan's house and saw that his curtains were still open. Was he catching up on work while Chloe slept? she wondered. She watched the bedroom window for a few minutes, wondering if Logan would walk in and turn on the light, as he'd done the night she arrived. Finally, she closed the curtains and got ready for bed, feeling foolish for waiting for him to appear. It took a while for her to drop off to sleep though; her mind kept drifting to Logan. There was something about him that attracted her. *He's grumpy, bossy and opinionated,* she reminded herself as she drifted off to sleep.

❄

Robbie was red-eyed when he came down the next morning, and Saffy was sure he hadn't slept a wink. He sat down at the table looking as if he were about to burst into tears.

'I was so excited about this Christmas. I never thought it would turn out like this.' He sniffed and a couple of tears rolled down his cheeks. He furiously brushed them away with the back of his hand. 'I thought Duncan and I were forever. I really did.'

'You are! And I know he's just as upset as you are. Stop being stubborn and turn on your phone. I bet he's messaged you.'

Robbie sighed. 'If I must.' He took his phone out of his jacket pocket and switched it on. The screen lit up as it kicked into life. There was a succession of pings as text messages flashed onto the screen.

Saffy waited anxiously as Robbie eagerly scrolled through what was evidently a long list of messages. 'Well?'

Finally, he tore his eyes from the screen and looked at her. 'They're all from friends wanting the gossip on why I've walked out on Duncan. Evidently, he's cancelled the party and told everyone it's because I've left him. But there's nothing from Duncan. Nada.'

'He's probably hurt like you are. Make the first move. Send him a message.'

'I am not making the first move!'

'You're both as stubborn as each other,' Saffy told him. 'You both adore each other and you know it.'

'Looking totally horrified when your partner proposes to you is not a sign of adoration, Saffron,' Robbie told her. 'I've got to face it.

We're finished.' He got up. 'My Christmas is ruined, but at least I can help you make sure the lonely hearts have a spectacular Christmas.'

Saffy's heart went out to him as she saw tears well in Robbie's eyes again. He and Duncan both loved Christmas. They celebrated it in a big way. A huge real Christmas tree always stood outside their house, decorated with a different theme each year, and a smaller one just as beautifully decorated inside. There was a stocking of presents each at the end of their bed, a big party. This year Robbie had planned on proposing; it should have been such a special moment but somehow it had gone drastically wrong and he and Duncan would be celebrating Christmas apart if she didn't do something.

After breakfast Robbie asked to take Oscar for a walk, so as soon he left, Saffy phoned Meg.

'How's it going, hun?' Meg asked.

'The party prep's going okay but Robbie's dead miserable. Duncan hasn't even been in touch. Have you heard from him? I can't believe it's really over for those two. They're so good together.'

'No and I wasn't sure whether to message him or not. You know what Duncan can be like.'

Yes she did. Duncan could sulk for England, while Robbie was so stubborn that he'd cut off his nose to spite his face, to use one of her mother's favourite expressions. Neither of them would take the first step – well, not any time soon anyway, and that would mean Christmas would be ruined for them both.

'We've got to get them back together, Meg. It's Christmas Eve tomorrow. They'll be miserable without each other.'

'I know but what can we do?'

'I'll think of something. I'm not going to stand by and watch them split up over this.'

As soon as she'd finished the phone call to Meg, Saffy sent a message to Duncan. If he cared about Robbie, and she was sure he did, then he would reply.

Chapter Eleven

The Christmas tree arrived just as Robbie and Oscar returned. They had a bit of a struggle getting it inside, and into Hannah's tree stand. It was so big it took up a whole corner of the lounge.

'Now that's what I call a tree,' Robbie said as they both gazed at it.

'It's fantastic, isn't it? Just what we need to make it look really festive. I want LH to look like a Christmas grotto,' Saffy said enthusiastically.

'Sounds good to me.' Robbie nodded. 'Shall we get started decorating it?'

'You bet!' She'd already got the box of decorations, lights and tinsel ready. Decorating the tree was one of her favourite things to do at Christmas.

She was in the middle of winding red and gold tinsel around the branches of the tree, whilst Robbie was standing on the step ladder they'd found in the shed, stringing trimmings from the ceiling, when the doorbell buzzed.

'You'll have to get that, babe, I'm in a bit of an awkward position,' Robbie said, stretching out his arm to tack the end of the glittery Christmas garland to the corner of the ceiling.

'I expect it's Logan with the cake,' Saffy said, going to answer the door, red tinsel draped around her neck and two baubles dangling from her fingers.

Sure enough, Logan was standing on the doorstep, snowflakes covering his brown jacket, holding a large plastic box containing what she thought must be the cake. Chloe stood beside him, wrapped up in a purple, fur-trimmed, hooded coat, scarf and gloves.

'You look like a Christmas fairy!' Chloe giggled. 'You've got tinsel in your hair too.'

'And you two look like snow fairies.' Saffy smiled. She looked at the thin layer of white covering the ground. 'I hadn't noticed that it was snowing.'

'It started about an hour ago and it seems that it's sticking,' Logan told her.

'Daddy said we might have a white Christmas.' Chloe's eyes were dancing with excitement. 'We can build a snowman and have a snowball fight and go sledging.'

'Snow! Did you say it was snowing?' Robbie shouted from the lounge. 'OMG! It is! How fab-tastic!'

Saffy grinned at the obvious delight in his voice. Putting up the Christmas decorations had certainly cheered him up. 'Robbie likes the snow,' she said to Chloe. 'I bet he'll be building a snowman too.'

'We could have a competition – who can build the biggest snowman,' Chloe suggested.

'We'll need a lot more snow for that,' Logan said, shuffling the container he was holding a little. 'Shall I take this through into the kitchen for you?'

'Sorry, yes, please bring it through.' Saffy stood back to let Logan and Chloe in. It would be rude to just take the cake off him without looking at it and thanking him properly.

'You both look frozen. Fancy a hot drink while you're here? I was about to put the kettle on,' Robbie said, striding ahead into the kitchen.

Saffy stared after him. Why had he invited Logan to stay for a drink? She really didn't want to spend any more time with Logan than she had to; he so obviously didn't like her. Besides, they had the tree to finish decorating. Mind you, she was dying to take a look at the Christmas cake.

They all followed Robbie into the kitchen, where Logan put the cake down on the table.

'We've got a special decoration this year – for you,' Chloe said. She grabbed Saffy's hand. 'Come and see.' She led her over to the table.

'Shall I do the honours?' Robbie asked.

Logan nodded. 'Be my guest.'

'Ta da!' Robbie pulled off the lid to reveal the most gorgeously decorated Christmas cake that Saffy had ever seen. It was a huge square, the white icing piped to look like snow, and the top was covered with cute decorations. The icing around the edge was a bit wonky in a couple of places; she guessed that was Chloe's doing.

'I helped decorate it,' Chloe said proudly. 'And I helped choose the decorations too. We bought one especially for you. Can you see it?'

Saffy scanned the array of decorations. There was a sleigh with a Father Christmas – no, hang on, that was a Mother Christmas! She shot a glance at Logan, who winked.

Chloe giggled. 'That's you, Saffy, because you rescued our Christmas. There's something else you'll like too.'

Saffy turned her attention back to the cake. There were tiny houses, a frozen pond and – a polar bear! She smiled as she pointed to it. 'Did you choose the polar bear too?' she asked Chloe.

'Yes. It's for us, 'cos we like them.'

'It's lovely. It looks…' She stopped awkwardly.

'Professional,' Logan finished for her.

She winced. 'That sounds condescending, doesn't it? But yes, really professional. You could sell this.'

'I do sell my cakes. I make them to order for birthdays and special occasions. Obviously, I haven't charged for this one.'

Double wince. Why had she presumed he was an amateur? 'Sorry.'

'No need to apologise. Thank you for the compliment.' He nodded towards the cake. 'There should be enough for everyone, I hope.'

'Plenty,' Robbie agreed. 'And it's totally gorgeous. We'll put it in pride of place in the dining room so everyone can see it.'

'We will, but for now, let's put it in the larder so that Oscar doesn't get hold of it,' Saffy said. She put the two baubles she was still holding down on the table, opened the top cupboard of the larder and put the cake inside.

'Can I go and look at the Christmas tree?' asked Chloe.

'Sure you can.' Saffy picked up the baubles again and handed them to Chloe. 'You can put these on for me, if you like.'

'Yes please!' Chloe clasped the baubles in her hand.

'I'm going to finish hanging that trimming up,' Robbie said, filling up the kettle. 'Bring the coffee in, will you, hun? Come on, Chloe, let's get decorating.'

Chloe eagerly followed him out of the kitchen.

Honestly, could he make it any more obvious that he was match-making!

Logan looked at Saffy thoughtfully as she spooned coffee into three mugs. 'How are you coping? Do you need help with anything?'

Saffy leaned back against the worktop and pushed a strand of hair from her eyes. 'I don't think so. We'll decorate the tree and the lounge and dining room today, then I'll bring the presents down and put them under the tree tomorrow. Then we'll prepare the food tomorrow evening and maybe cook the turkey overnight. I'm saying we, but I'm not expecting Robbie to still be here on Christmas Day. I'm pretty sure he and Duncan will make up by then. That is if they both stop being too pigheaded to speak to each other.'

'No communication between them then?' Logan kept his voice low too.

'I'm working on it.' The kettle came to the boil so Saffy turned around and poured the boiling water into the three mugs then added milk and sugar. 'What about Chloe? Shall I warm her up some milk?' she asked, looking over her shoulder at Logan.

'Milky tea with one sugar will be fine, thanks.'

Saffy opened the food cupboard to see if there were any biscuits, found a packet of chocolate ones, then put them on the tray along with the mugs and, leaving Oscar chewing a bone in his basket, carried it into the other room.

Robbie had finished putting up the trimming now and he and Chloe were busy hanging baubles on the tree – Chloe in a rather haphazard fashion. Saffy smiled; the little girl looked like she was having fun.

'It's looking pretty in here now, isn't it?' she said as she put the tray down on the coffee table. 'Take a break for a few minutes, you two, and help yourself to a drink and biscuits.'

'Auntie Hannah always has red and gold.' Chloe hung a red bow on the end of a branch. 'But we have all colours, don't we, Daddy?' she asked as Logan walked into the room. 'We have a rainbow tree.'

'We sure do. The brighter the better in our house,' Logan agreed.

Chloe sat down on the sofa, reached for one of the chocolate biscuits and took a big bite out of it. 'I bet your tree is silver and really sparkly. You look a sparkly kind of person,' she said to Saffy.

'It's a big white one, and I've got silver and blue baubles on it with lots of lights. I put it up on the first of December,' Saffy confessed. 'I know it was a bit early but I couldn't wait.'

Chloe grinned. 'We put ours up last week and I helped hang the baubles.' She turned to Robbie. 'Do you have a Christmas tree?'

'Oh yes, we always have a massive real tree and we decorate it in a different theme every year. This year it's red and tartan…' Robbie welled up, put his cup down and hurried out of the room.

'Oh, Daddy, he's so sad,' Chloe said. 'Were you sad when Mummy left?'

'It was a long time ago, poppet,' Logan said easily.

So Chloe's mum had walked out on them. *How long ago?* Saffy wondered. *Had Logan been so devastated he'd decided to never have a relationship again*? His expression gave away nothing of how he was feeling and she didn't like to pry. Besides, he didn't look the sort of guy who would have trouble finding a replacement; more likely he would have them queuing at the door. Still, it was none of her business.

'I'm sure Robbie and Duncan will make up, lots of couples fall out sometimes,' she said to Chloe. 'Now do you want to help me finish decorating the tree or do you have to go somewhere with your dad?' She turned to Logan. 'Chloe can stay and help me if you have some jobs to do.'

'Really?'

She saw the relief on his face.

'I do have a couple of last-minute presents I need to wrap. I'll come and collect her at…' He glanced at his watch. 'Six–thirty, if that's okay?'

'Perfect, longer if you want.' Chloe was a well-behaved, helpful little girl so she was sure she wouldn't be any bother.

❄

'That's very kind of you,' Robbie said when he discovered that Saffy had agreed to look after Chloe for a couple of hours. 'And, of course, it was nothing to do with making sure you saw Logan again today, was it?'

'What? Of course not!'

'I've seen the way you look at him, Saff, and how he looks at you. There's definitely chemistry between you.'

'Don't be silly.'

Robbie wagged his finger at her playfully. 'Protest all you want but I know two people who fancy each other when I see them. Good job we've got some mistletoe in the garden, isn't it? I'll go and pick a sprig.'

Saffy stared after Robbie as he went out into the back garden, obviously to get some mistletoe. She didn't fancy Logan at all, And she was sure he didn't fancy her.

Did he?

Chapter Twelve

Logan couldn't believe he'd left Chloe with someone he barely knew, but Saffy was Hannah's sister – and Chloe had really wanted to stay, and would enjoy decorating the tree. Besides, Saffy was great with her. And so was Robbie. He hadn't really been looking forward to the Christmas party thinking that it might be an awkward, forced affair this year, not like the usual relaxed, fun day with Hannah and Lee, but now…

Saffy had surprised him. He hadn't expected her to be so warm and friendly. Or to be so attracted to her. He smiled as he thought of her in that polar bear onesie. She'd looked so cute – and so irresistible when she'd waggled her bum like that. He remembered Hannah saying that Saffy was almost thirty but showed no sign of settling down, laughing that her little sister had always liked to be free, and had given their mother a few hair-raising moments in her teens. Logan had instantly thought that Saffy was like Jade, expecting her to be self-centred and standoffish. Mind you, Jade had seemed warm and friendly at first, he reminded himself.

But Jade would never have worn a polar bear onesie and let a six-year-old help her decorate the Christmas tree. Jade was always immaculately dressed and considered the Christmas tree as another accessory that had to be perfectly decorated and matching, without a bauble out of place.

Logan fetched the last of Chloe's presents and carefully wrapped them up, adding the pretty ribbons and bows that Chloe loved, and placing them under the Christmas tree. He would fetch the bike from Annie's and wrap it up when she was in bed. He didn't want to take advantage of Saffy's generosity but there were a couple of emails he could do with replying to and it was easier to do it if Chloe wasn't around. He went into the third bedroom that doubled up as his study and fired up his computer.

❄

Robbie had collected a few sprigs of mistletoe and hung them just inside the front door and over the other doorways. 'That'll get folks in the Christmas spirit,' he said with a wink at Saffy.

Saffy stuck her tongue out at him and Chloe giggled. 'You two are so funny!' she said.

Saffy smiled at her. The little girl seemed to be really enjoying herself and so did Robbie. At least it helped keep his mind off his heartbreak. She still couldn't believe that he and Duncan had split up, and all because Robbie had proposed. It was such a shame. Well, if she had anything to do with it they would soon be back together again.

'Shall we take a look through the box and see what other decorations we can find?' Robbie asked. 'We want it to look really festive, don't we?'

'Don't forget the inflatable Santa and reindeer we bought,' Saffy said. 'Chloe might like to blow them up with you.'

'Oh yes!' Chloe clapped her hands in delight. 'I'm the bestest blower-upper!'

'I'll leave you to it then and go and give Hannah a ring to see how the twins are,' Saffy said. She went into the kitchen and checked if she'd had a reply from Duncan first. She had. She swiped her finger across the screen to read it.

Robbie's the one who's left. And at Xmas too. I've had to tell everyone the party is cancelled tomorrow. How do you think I feel?

Saffy paused. Duncan had a point. How could she explain in a text how hurt Robbie was? She'd have to phone him. She selected Duncan's number.

'I don't know why Robbie doesn't call me himself instead of getting you to do it,' Duncan said, as soon as he answered. 'Or hasn't he asked you to do it and you're just interfering?'

'He doesn't know I'm calling you and I'm not interfering, I'm helping. Robbie's really upset, Duncan. He thought you and him were forever.'

'*He's* upset!' Duncan snorted. '*He's* walked out, left me in the lurch over Christmas, and is down in Cornwall partying with you. How the hell do you think I feel?'

'He proposed to you, Duncan, and you turned him down. He's heartbroken.'

'I did not turn him down,' Duncan snapped.

'Oh… so you accepted then?'

'No, but—'

'Robbie said you looked horrified and didn't reply.'

'Yes, I was bloody horrified. Because I've bought him a ring and was going to propose on Christmas Day, that's why. And I didn't reply because I didn't know what to say. I was totally stunned.'

Saffy was stunned too. Duncan had been planning on proposing to Robbie? Someone else might have whipped out their ring and proposed too, laughing over it being a double proposal, but not Duncan. He'd have been really miffed that Robbie had stolen his thunder. That's why he'd reacted the way he did.

'Then tell Robbie that and he'll be back like a shot. He left you because he thought you were horrified at the thought of marrying him. He's heartbroken, Duncan.'

There was silence on the other end of the phone.

'Duncan, are you still there?'

'Yes. Okay, so I can see that I might have given Robbie the wrong impression but that doesn't change the fact that he's walked out on me at Christmas. We had fifteen guests coming to dinner on Christmas Day and Robbie has upped and gone. He should have talked to me. If he cared about me at all he would have talked to me.'

'I thought you had a big row?'

'We rowed because Robbie jumped to the conclusion that I didn't want to marry him and got all arsey. You know what he's like.'

'He proposed to you. You didn't reply. What's he supposed to think?' she pointed out. 'And I bet you got arsey too. Robbie said that you walked out.'

She knew what Robbie and Duncan were like when they had a row; they were both too hotheaded, they threw insults about then both retreated to have a good sulk. It was usually a couple of days before they made up. This time, though, it was bigger than a normal row and she was genuinely worried they wouldn't make up. Because Robbie was convinced Duncan didn't love him.

'I went for a walk to calm down. I decided to come back, explain why I was put out and accept his proposal but he'd gone. And he hasn't bothered to contact me since.' It didn't sound like Duncan was about to back down.

Saffy hesitated. How was she going to fix this? She could see both sides.

'Have you cancelled the party?' she asked.

'Of course I have.' There was a sniff the other end of the phone. Was Duncan crying? 'I'm heartbroken. How can I throw a Christmas party when me and Robbie are over?'

'Duncan. Do you love Robbie and want to marry him?'

Another sniff. 'Yes, but I wanted to be the one who proposed.'

'For goodness' sake, what does it matter who proposes? You can both propose! Look, drive down to Cornwall now, propose to Robbie and you can both be home for Christmas, together.'

'I'm not making the first move. Robbie left me,' Duncan said stubbornly. 'And don't you dare tell him that I was going to propose to him. I've told you in confidence.'

'If you don't do this you've probably lost Robbie for good,' Saffy said sternly. 'Is that what you want?'

No reply.

'Think about it, don't let your stubbornness ruin the best thing that's ever happened to you. You and Robbie are meant to be together, and you know it,' she said. 'Tomorrow is Christmas Eve. Do you really want to spend Christmas apart?'

There was a click as Duncan cut her off.

Well, she'd done all she could. Would Duncan swallow his pride and come down to Cornwall? If he didn't, could she talk Robbie into going back *without* telling him about Duncan's proposal? Although Duncan had asked her not to mention it, she had not actually *promised* she wouldn't.

Honestly, relationships! And her friends wondered why she didn't want to get serious with anyone. It was too much heartache.

She texted Duncan the address of Liwus Helyk then gave Hannah a call. There was no reply so she sent her a message asking how the twins were and telling her not to worry, everything was all under control for the party, briefly mentioning that Robbie had come down to help with the party too, then she went back inside. Robbie and Chloe were in fits of giggles, still attempting to blow up the Santa and reindeer, which were now both half-inflated and bent into awkward shapes.

'We... need... an... air... pump,' Robbie said, collapsing into a chair, out of breath. 'How are the twins?' he asked when he'd finally recovered.

'I couldn't get hold of Hannah so I sent her a message,' Saffy replied. She picked up the wobbly Santa. 'Maybe Logan has an air pump. I'll WhatsApp him.'

She sent Logan a quick message, and he immediately replied that he'd be over for Chloe in ten minutes and would bring the air pump with him.

'Right, let's get working on this room then,' Saffy said, picking up a bunch of tinsel. 'It needs far more sparkle and glitter.'

They all set to work, winding tinsel around the Christmas tree, picture frames and across the window ledge. By the time they'd finished they'd turned the lounge and dining room of Liwus Helyk into a magical grotto. Outside looked magical too. The snow was still coming down and was forming a soft, white carpet everywhere.

'This is going to be the bestest Christmas ever,' Chloe said, her eyes sparkling.

Saffy saw Robbie's eyes cloud over. This would be the worst Christmas ever for him and Duncan if she couldn't get them to make up. She had to get Robbie to turn his phone back on. What if Duncan was trying to contact him?

There was a tap on the window and they all turned to see a snow-covered Logan peering through. 'Daddy looks like a snowman!' Chloe chuckled.

Saffy quickly went to the front door to let him in.

He shook the snow from his jacket and wiped his feet on the mat, then held out the carrier bag. 'I've brought the pump I use to inflate the air beds when we go camping. It should do the trick.'

'Thanks, Robbie and Chloe have blown them up a bit but they ran out of puff,' she said as they walked into the lounge.

Suddenly her phone pinged. Was it Duncan saying he was coming down? She glanced at the screen; it was Hannah. She opened the message. Lily's temperature had dropped, thank goodness, Miles's ear infection was clearing and if they carried on improving they would be able to come home on Boxing Day. Hannah thanked Saffy again for holding the fort. 'The twins are almost better and they might all be home on Boxing Day,' Saffy told the others.

'Are you going back home then?' Chloe asked.

'No, I'm going to spend a couple of days with Hannah and the twins, then go home on Friday.'

To Saffy's surprise Chloe flung herself at her, wrapping her arms around her waist. 'I'll miss you,' she said.

Wow! She didn't usually have this effect on kids. Saffy glanced up and saw Logan watching her. For a moment their eyes locked and she felt a frisson of… something.

She patted Chloe's head gently. 'I'll miss you too,' she said, her eyes still locked with Logan's. 'But don't worry, I'm here for a few days yet.'

Chapter Thirteen

It was still snowing when Saffy got up the next morning. She opened the curtains and gazed at the winter wonderland scene in front of her. True, the snow was still only fine but it was smattered over the ground and trees, making everywhere look really magical. If only it would snow some more and stick. She would love a white Christmas.

She showered, dressed and went downstairs. Logan would be popping in with the turkey today and she didn't want him to catch her in her polar bear onesie again.

She was eating a slice of toast and marmalade and sipping coffee when Robbie came storming into the kitchen.

'I can't believe it! I don't know how he could do this to me!' he shouted, brandishing his phone. 'Two days I've been gone. Two days, that's all it takes for him to wipe me out of his life.' Robbie sank down at the table and plunged his head in his hands. 'I can't believe I've been so stupid as to waste four years of my life on That Man.'

Saffy stared at him. 'What is it? What's he done?'

Robbie raised his head, red-rimmed eyes glistening in his blanched face. He looked devastated. 'Well, I checked again to see if Duncan had left me a message. He hasn't, BTW.' He swallowed. 'Then I checked out his FB page and he'd blocked me. I thought, okay, what's he up to that he doesn't want me to see?'

Saffy waited anxiously. This didn't sound good.

'So I checked in with my other FB account.'

'You've got another account?'

Robbie shot her an incredulous look. 'Honestly, Saff, everyone has a second account so they can check out what the people who block them are saying about them.'

'I don't.'

'That's because you're hardly ever on FB,' Robbie replied impatiently. 'Anyway, I checked out his page and he's completely erased me. All our photos, any reference to me at all, gone. And he's put a message on there saying that I've walked out on him so the Christmas party is off. That's why everyone was messaging me. And, of course, all our so-called friends have left comments saying how sorry they are, so he's made me look like the total bad guy.'

Saffy chewed her lip. No wonder Duncan had been so off on the phone. It looked like he was just as hurt as Robbie.

'It's only because he's upset. You've walked out on him at Christmas time, Robbie. And he would have to tell everyone the party is off and why wouldn't he?'

'Whose side are you on? How come I'm the bad guy all of a sudden, when I proposed to him? I declared my love forever and had it shoved back in my face.' Robbie sat back, arms folded across his chest, chin jutted out.

She'd upset him now. Maybe she should come clean, let Robbie know she'd spoken to Duncan?

'He didn't turn you down. He was put out because…' She paused. Was she doing the right thing? She didn't want to make the situation worse – if it could be any worse. Robbie and Duncan weren't speaking to each other and Robbie was convinced Duncan didn't love him. She couldn't let him keep believing that. And she hadn't promised Duncan she wouldn't tell Robbie, had she?

Robbie's eyes narrowed. He unfolded his arms and leaned forward. 'You've spoken to Duncan, haven't you? You've contacted him when I specifically asked you not to?' he accused.

Saffy held up her hands, palm outwards. 'Okay, yes I have. Someone has to try and sort this mess out.'

'So, what did he say?' Robbie demanded. 'Why exactly was he so horrified that I proposed to him after four years of living together? Four years when he'd told me day after day that he loved me?'

Saffy drew a deep breath. She had to tell him. He had a right to know. 'Because *he* was planning on proposing to *you,* that's why. He's bought you a ring and was going to propose on Christmas Day.'

Robbie's mouth opened and shut like a fish gasping for air.

'What. Did. You. Say?' he stammered, incredulous.

'Duncan loves you and wants to marry you. He was going to propose to you on Christmas Day,' Saffy repeated with a smile. 'So you see it's all just a big misunderstanding.'

Robbie pushed the chair back, got up and paced around the kitchen. 'Then why did he let me leave?' he demanded, turning to face Saffy. 'And why hasn't he contacted me to explain?'

'He's upset, like you are. You are the one who walked out, remember?'

A conflict of emotions danced across Robbie's face; surprise, pleasure then disbelief. 'It doesn't make sense. If Duncan wants to marry me, why didn't he accept my proposal?' he said, shaking his head. 'You should have seen his face when I proposed. He looked horrified.'

'Because you spoilt his surprise. Not because he didn't want to marry you.'

'You mean he finished with me because I proposed first?' Was that anger she could hear in his voice? Had she made the situation even worse?

'He didn't finish with you, did he? You're the one who packed your bags and walked out,' she reminded him.

'Yes, because of how he acted when I proposed!'

'You know what Duncan is like. He was planning on proposing to you, but you got in first so I guess he was a little bit miffed.'

'So miffed that he's let us break up?' Robbie shook his head. 'It's Christmas tomorrow, our first Christmas apart since we got together. If Duncan really loved me he would have phoned me to explain. I wouldn't have come down to Cornwall to be with you then. We could have made up, had Christmas together.' Tears sprang to his eyes. He turned around, ripped off a sheet of tissue from the kitchen roll and blew his nose.

Saffy felt for him. 'Look, why don't you go home and sort it out? There might be a train today. Or you could catch a taxi.'

'Why should I?' Robbie folded his arms across his chest. 'No way am I going crawling back. It's up to him to put this right. Okay yes, I was the one who walked out but he let me think that he didn't want to marry me just because he wanted to be the one who proposed. That's a terrible thing to do. I don't think I want to be with someone who's got that much pride.' He levelled his gaze at Saffy. 'I'm better off without him.' He walked dejectedly out of the room.

Saffy sighed as she heard Robbie go up the stairs, obviously to his room. It looked like she had no chance of getting Robbie and Duncan back together for Christmas but at least now Robbie knew that Duncan did want to marry him, instead of believing that he didn't love him. She'd have to try to get them to make up when she returned home.

Robbie remained upstairs all morning. Saffy thought it best to leave him to think things over; she had lots to get on with.

The morning whizzed by and she suddenly noticed that it was gone twelve. Time to prepare lunch. She wanted to practise cooking in the Aga before trusting herself to cook the turkey tomorrow so had bought a couple of pork chops. She turned the dial to heat up the big oven – no good testing the small one if the turkey needed the larger one – peeled some potatoes to roast and prepared some sprouts.

An hour later it was all cooked and she and Robbie were sitting at the table eating it.

'That was delicious. Thank you,' said Robbie as he scraped the last bit of potato off his plate. 'I feel bad that I was upstairs sulking and left you to do it all by yourself.'

'I don't mind, I wanted to familiarise myself with the Aga before tomorrow,' she told him. 'But feel free to ease your guilt by loading the dishwasher.'

'Consider it done.' Robbie pushed his chair back and picked up the plates.

He'd just finished loading it up when the doorbell rang. Oscar barked and ran into the hall.

'That must be Logan and Chloe with the turkey. Do you mind if I go upstairs? I'm not much company at the moment.'

'Sure.' Saffy went to answer the door. 'Thanks so much,' she said, taking the huge carrier bag from Logan. 'Do you want to come in for a coffee or do you have too much to do?'

'A very quick one would be great, thanks, then we're off to visit Annie. We always spend a couple of hours with her on Christmas Eve. She spends Christmas Day with her daughter and family,' he added.

'That's lovely.' Saffy put the kettle on, then opened the carrier bag Logan had just put on the table and took the turkey out. It was huge. Bigger than she'd ever seen before. Still, it needed to be, to feed all the people. She put it in the bottom of the fridge then turned around to see Logan making the coffee.

'I hope you don't mind. I often do it for Hannah,' he said.

'No, of course not.' She looked at Chloe, who was sitting by Oscar's basket stroking him. 'Would you like a drink, Chloe?'

'No thanks.'

'Is there anything you want help with?' Logan asked. 'Organising this party is a lot for you at such short notice. I'm happy to do anything I can.'

'I think we're okay, thank you. We're going to get as much as we can prepared this evening,' she said. 'To be honest, it's not so much cooking the meal I'm dreading, it's entertaining everyone afterwards. Hannah said she and Lee always organised some games, and I'm a bit hopeless at that sort of thing, but I've got a few things for the kids to do so hopefully it will all be okay.'

'I'm sure it will be fine. There's enough adults to help too, we won't leave you to deal with it all.' Logan looked around. 'Where's Robbie?'

'Upstairs.' She glanced at Chloe, who was still stroking Oscar and quietly told Logan the latest development. 'I've spoken to Duncan and tried to persuade him to come down and patch things up so they can spend Christmas together, but…' She sighed. 'They're both as stubborn as each other.'

'Look, why don't you and Robbie come over to mine for a drink tonight? I've got mince pies and mulled wine.'

She'd like that. She wasn't relishing spending another evening with brooding Robbie. Back at home she'd be out partying, she thought wistfully. Well, she'd have to make up for it on New Year's Eve. 'Thanks, can I let you know? I've still got stuff to get ready.'

'That's fine, I don't go to bed until late. Don't worry if you can't make it.' He smiled at her. 'I think it's wonderful that you've given up your Christmas to help your sister out and put on a lunch for all us "lonely singles". I bet you're usually out partying all over Christmas.'

'I am,' she admitted. 'But I don't mind. Hannah would do it for me – and it'd be horrible to let everyone down at Christmas,' she said. 'Our mum brought us up on her own, I remember how hard it was for her.'

'It's not easy being a single parent, and most of us don't plan it to be that way. Unfortunately, relationships break down. Did your parents' split really affect you? Is that why you haven't settled down and had kids yet?' Logan asked. Then he looked mortified. 'Gosh, that was a really rude question. I'm sorry.'

The question threw her for a moment. She stared at him, not sure how to answer. 'It's fine. I'm not against settling down, it's just not for me…' she stammered.

'A career woman, eh?'

Now he sounded disapproving again. Well, it wasn't any of his business. 'I guess you could say that.'

Thankfully the doorbell rang, preventing any further awkwardness. Then a chorus of 'We Wish You A Merry Christmas' rang out.

'Carol singers!' Chloe shouted, getting up and running to the door, closely followed by Oscar.

Saffy was delighted too. She'd always loved it when the carol singers came around to the house when she was a child; as she'd got older she'd even joined them, but as she now lived in an apartment block she was never visited by carol singers. She and Logan both went to the front door where Chloe and Oscar were already waiting, and Logan grabbed Oscar's collar and shut him in the kitchen while Saffy opened the door. A group of carol singers were standing on the doorstep – a mix of young children and adults – singing away heartily. When they launched into a rendition of 'Jingle Bells', Chloe joined in at the top of her voice. Logan and Saffy exchanged smiles then joined in. Then Robbie came to the door and he sang along too. After 'Jingle Bells' came 'Away in a Manger', 'O Little Town of Bethlehem' and finally another chorus of 'We Wish You A Merry Christmas'.

It all felt very festive and Saffy, Logan and Robbie gave a generous donation. The carol singers' faces lit up and they chorused, 'Thank you so much!' and 'Merry Christmas!' before going on their way.

'I guess we ought to be going too,' Logan said. 'I've still got quite a bit to do at home.'

'Of course. Thanks for all your help,' Saffy told him.

'I don't want to go yet.' Chloe pouted.

Saffy bent down so that her face was level with Chloe's. 'We have lots to do, sweetheart. Remember that Santa is coming tomorrow with your presents.'

Chloe looked thoughtful. 'Will Santa still leave Lily and Miles's presents even though they aren't here?'

'Sure he will. He knows they'll be back soon,' Saffy answered. 'They'll have to celebrate Christmas a little later.'

'That means they'll have two Christmas. One in Tenerife and one here,' Logan added. 'Now come on, poppet. We'll see Saffy and Robbie tomorrow.' He took Chloe's hand in his. 'See you later.'

As she stood in the doorway watching them both walk off through the fluttering snow, Saffy felt a stirring of a longing that she'd buried five years ago when the consultant had told her she was unlikely to ever have children. The stomach pains she'd suffered from throughout her teenage years had turned out to be endometriosis. By the time it was discovered, one of her ovaries had been destroyed. She'd told herself that she didn't mind, having children wasn't the be all and end all; that she had lots of things she wanted to do with her life. Besides, she'd never met anyone she wanted to settle down and raise a family with, so what did it matter? But now, watching Logan and Chloe walking off together, the little girl clutching his hand, and looking up at her father as he spoke to her, Saffy felt a sense of loss. There seemed such love between them. A love she would never know.

Chapter Fourteen

Saffy was beautiful. It was a shame she was going back home at the weekend because he'd really like to get to know her more. There again, maybe it was a good job she wasn't staying any longer because getting too friendly with Saffy wasn't a good idea. Chloe already adored her. Logan had promised himself that he would never get serious with anyone, never let Chloe get to know any of the women in his life because he didn't want her to get hurt when they eventually walked away. And Saffy would definitely walk away. It was obvious that her career was the most important thing to her, like Jade. So she certainly wouldn't want to take on another woman's child.

Saffy was just here for Christmas, a touch of sparkle and fun in their lives and then she'd be gone. Which was a good thing. It didn't give Chloe time to get too attached.

He'd miss her, though.

'Daddy, my hands are cold now.' Chloe was tugging at his sleeve.

'So are mine, poppet. Let's go inside, get these wet clothes off and have a mug of hot chocolate, shall we?'

He ran a warm bath for Chloe, with her favourite pink bubbles and then, all cosy in her pyjamas, she sat on the sofa with a mug of hot chocolate and a brownie, watching a cartoon.

Logan poured a drop of brandy in his hot chocolate and sat down beside his daughter, wrapping his arm around her shoulder and pulling her close. 'All right, poppet?' he asked, kissing her on the forehead.

'All warm and cosy now.' She snuggled into him. 'I'm glad Saffy and Robbie came to do the party tomorrow, Daddy. I like Saffy, she's really nice. Robbie is too, but he's a bit sad. It's a shame to be sad at Christmas.'

'Yes it is.' Logan's mind cast back to their first Christmas in Port Breok. He was feeling rather lonely and out of the scene now he was working mainly from home and was wondering how he was going to make Christmas special for Chloe, who was only a toddler. Then he'd bumped into Hannah and she'd invited him to the Christmas Party and from then on he'd been embraced into the social circle of the village. The LH party was now the highlight of his and Chloe's Christmas. Some familiar faces showed up every year, Marta and Toni, for a start, but others moved on to relationships during the year and new faces came instead.

His mind drifted to Sonja, Toni's best friend. Dark-haired, voluptuous and sultry, she'd made a beeline for Logan that first Christmas and he'd been flattered. She was attractive and very sexy, there was no doubt about that, and had no intention of settling down with a man again, she'd been very firm about that. Before long, they'd started having a fling. It had been fun, but Sonja had changed her mind and begun to want more from their relationship. The fall-out when Logan had finished it made him resolve never to get together with anyone from the village again. A pact he'd stuck to. Sonja had moved away and things settled down but Toni had never really forgiven Logan for driving her best friend away and the atmosphere was still cool between them. They'd learnt to avoid each other and be polite when they were forced together but it was still an awkward situation.

Chloe murmured and he glanced down to see that she'd fallen asleep, her long lashes fanned out on her cheek, her chest rising and falling as she snored softly. He gently eased his right hand under her legs and lifted her up as he got to his feet. She stirred sleepily and snuggled in close as he carried her up the stairs and into her bedroom. He pulled back the duvet and gently placed her in bed, then covered her up again. 'Night, poppet,' he whispered as he kissed her on the cheek.

Chloe sighed contentedly and turned over onto her side.

As he watched her sleeping Logan wondered for the thousandth time how Jade could have left her. How she could go for weeks, months even, without seeing her.

And he vowed that while he had breath in his body nothing and no one would ever harm his little girl. He was all she had and he was never going to let her down.

❄

As soon as Logan and Chloe had gone, Saffy and Robbie set to getting the lounge ready for the party. They pushed the sofa and chairs against the walls to make more space for the games, leaving one armchair by the window for Santa. Saffy found a red throw to cover it, then consulted her list to check where Hannah had put the presents for the guests. Ah, the green guest room. She took the sack up with her, filled it with presents and then placed it on the 'Santa' chair to make sure Oscar didn't lie on it and cover it with hairs.

'I think you should try on the Santa costume in case we need to do some last-minute alterations,' she told Robbie, handing him the bag it was in.

'Fair enough.' He went upstairs to get changed and came down a few minutes later dressed in the Santa outfit. Saffy hardly recognised him with the long white wig, beard, moustache and the huge inflatable belly.

'You look very authentic,' she said, smiling.

As Robbie went upstairs to change back into his normal clothes, Saffy consulted her to-do list. All that was left to do was prepare the potatoes and vegetables for tomorrow. She'd start those now.

Robbie came back down and helped. Then she got the turkey out of the fridge, relieved to see that it was self-basting. She put slices of bacon over the top then covered it in tin foil and put it back in the fridge.

'I don't know whether to cook it tonight on a low heat or get up early in the morning and put it in,' she said.

'I'll do it. I'll set my alarm for six, I won't be able to sleep anyway,' Robbie told her. 'You have a couple of hours' rest before the party starts.'

'Are you sure?' Saffy asked. 'I don't mind getting up and doing it.'

'Positive. I'm going to get an early night anyway. I'm whacked.'

'Logan asked us to pop around this evening for mince pies and mulled wine. Shall we go? It might cheer you up?'

'I'm not sure I'd be much company,' Robbie said. 'But you go. You don't want to be stuck here with miserable me. And like I said, I'll be going to bed soon anyway.'

He looked so desolate that Saffy's heart went out to him. 'Duncan's being stubborn, like you. Phone him. Tell him I've told you everything. Please, Robbie. What you guys have got together is too good to throw away.'

Robbie shook his head. 'The first move has to come from him. I was the one who proposed.' He poured himself a brandy and swigged it back in one gulp. 'I'm sorry, Saff. I don't want to spoil your Christmas but right now I just want to go to bed. I'll pull myself together for tomorrow, I promise.'

Saffy patted his arm. 'It's fine. You go to bed, it's been a long day. Actually, I'm whacked too so I won't stay at Logan's long.'

'Thanks, hun.' Robbie got up and walked slowly out of the kitchen.

Damn Duncan, he could have at least sent him a message after she'd spoken to him and told him how heartbroken Robbie was, Saffy thought angrily. Poor Robbie.

❄

Logan tidied up the kitchen, lit a log fire in the living room, dimmed the lights and got out the mulled wine to warm up, not wanting to think about why he was making so much effort for Saffy – and Robbie, of course. *I want a pleasant evening, that's all*, he told himself; it wasn't often he got adult company and he wanted to make the most of it.

The mulled wine was ready, the mince pies warm from the oven and the fire roaring impressively but there was no message from Saffy to say they were on their way. He glanced at the clock. Ten past nine. He felt a sharp pang of disappointment. She wasn't coming. It was stupid of him to ask her, she had so much to do before tomorrow and had been working hard since she'd arrived. She must be shattered. He was about to turn the coffee off when there was a gentle knock on the door followed by the ping of a WhatsApp message. *It's me, Saffy.*

Feeling unexpectedly elated he went straight to the door and opened it. Saffy was standing there alone, dressed in her long camel coat and Hannah's strawberry-patterned wellies, fluffy snowflakes fluttering down over her and clinging to her windswept hair. He looked over her shoulder. 'Where's Robbie?'

'He doesn't feel like company, he's too upset about Duncan,' she said, stepping inside. 'Sorry I'm late – and treading snow into your house.' She sat down on the bottom step and tugged at her right wellie.

It didn't budge. She tugged again, biting her lip and grimacing with the effort. 'Hannah takes a size smaller than me so they're a bit of a squeeze but the snow will ruin my boots.'

'Here, let me help you.' Logan knelt down and tugged hard at the wellington. It popped off with such force it sent him flying backwards onto his bum.

Saffy giggled then clapped her hand over her mouth. 'Sorry. Are you hurt?'

She looked gorgeous when she giggled. 'I think I might have a big bruise on my bum tomorrow,' he told her. 'So put me on the comfiest seat, won't you?'

'I'll put a soft cushion on there for you,' she promised him.

'Thanks. Now let's try the other wellie – and I'll be more prepared this next time.'

That one came off much easier. Saffy stood up and sniffed appreciatively. 'That mulled wine smells lovely.'

'Take off your coat, then go into the lounge and make yourself comfy – second door on the left. I'll bring you a glass in. Do you want a mince pie, too?'

She nodded. 'Please.'

'With cream?'

Her eyes widened. 'Double yes.'

When he walked into the lounge a few minutes later with the tray containing the two glasses of mulled wine, a jug of cream and a plate of mince pies, Saffy was sitting on the mat, her back against the sofa with her legs stretched out, warming her feet on the fire.

She grinned up at him. 'I hope you don't mind, my feet are a bit cold.'

'Feel free.' He put the tray down on the coffee table and squatted down on the rug beside her, handing her a mulled wine.

She cradled the glass in her hands. 'Sorry I turned up alone, and so late. Robbie's really upset and has gone to bed.'

'I don't mind at all.' He couldn't think of anything else he'd like to be doing right now other than sitting in front of the fire talking to Saffy. 'Have Robbie and his boyfriend been together long? Do you think they will make it up?'

'Four years.' She took a long sip of her wine, as if savouring the taste, then took a bite of her mince pie before turning to smile at him, a blob of cream smeared endearingly on her top lip. 'I hope they do. It was all a big misunderstanding really. They really love each other but they're both so stubborn.'

'Quite the little matchmaker, aren't you?' Logan teased. He leaned over and wiped the cream off her lip with his finger, then wished he hadn't because the feel of her soft skin on his finger sent a spear of desire shooting through him. He gasped as Saffy's eyes widened. It seemed as if time stood still as they both sat there, gazing into each other's eyes.

God, she was gorgeous.

Kiss her.

Oh God, he wanted to. Wanted to so much that his whole body shivered with longing but he held back. What if she didn't want him to? What if it went all awkward? What would happen tomorrow then? How could he go to the party if he'd made things uncomfortable with Saffy? Then Chloe would be upset. He couldn't ruin his daughter's Christmas because of his own selfish desires.

He pulled himself together. 'Sorry, I didn't mean to startle you, you had a bit of cream on your lip.' He held out the cream for her to see then grabbed a tissue from the box on the coffee table and wiped it off – but what he really wanted to do was lick it off. He swiped away the image of licking her lips and threw the tissue into the fire. 'Will

Robbie be okay for the party tomorrow?' he asked, when he could speak calmly again.

She nodded. 'He's upset, of course, but he wouldn't spoil Christmas Day for us all.' She took another bite of her mince pie. 'These are scrummy. Did you make them yourself?'

Her praise made him feel ridiculously proud. 'Yep, I like cooking. I find it relaxing.'

'You're good at it too. What work do you do?' She finished the mince pie and slowly licked her fingers, seeming completely unaware of how sensual it was and the effect it was having on a certain part of his body.

'I'm an architect. I'm based mainly at home now so that I can take care of Chloe. Hannah or Annie look after her her while I go to meetings, although I try to arrange most of them within school hours.'

'Hey, I'm impressed. What sort of projects do you work on? Commercial or private?' Saffy asked, taking another sip of her wine.

'Private mainly. I'm designing a bungalow for a couple who want to retire by the coast at the moment. The company I work for deals with a variety of projects though and I'm sometimes called in to help on a commercial one.'

He put another log on the fire, and it roared into life. 'So what do you do for a living?' he asked. 'I don't think Hannah's ever mentioned it, although she said you love your job and are very career-orientated.'

Saffy wrinkled her nose. 'That doesn't sound like a compliment, coming from Hannah! But yes, I do love my job. I work for buycreative.com – an online retail firm that brings creatives together and gives them more selling power whilst providing customers with a choice of beautifully made, unique goods.' Her face lit up with enthusiasm as she talked.

'Are you office-based?' he asked. 'What exactly do you do?'

'We have a big office in Birmingham city centre. At the moment, I'm part of the digital marketing team which means I input marketing data and look for ways to improve sales. It's not all desk-based, I have meetings with partners – that's what we call our team of creatives – and with the product and marketing team. But what I want to do is become a business development manager and find new creatives to add to their list of partners. There's a vacancy in that department coming up soon which I'm hoping to get. I've seen a couple of people who I'd love to join us while I've been here.'

'I like the ethos of that,' he said. 'It's hard for a small trader to make it on their own.'

They sat in front of the fire for the rest of the evening, talking, laughing, sharing stuff from their lives and Logan thought it was one of the best evenings he'd ever spent in his life. This was turning out to be a very special Christmas.

Chapter Fifteen

It was after midnight when Saffy finally returned to Liwus Helyk. She opened the door and listened in surprise. Robbie was whistling! She was expecting him to be fast asleep in bed. Did that mean he and Duncan had made up? Perhaps Duncan had thought about what she'd said and phoned Robbie to explain and apologise.

She stopped as she heard the deep rumble of a familiar male laugh. Duncan! He must have driven down after she'd spoken to him. So he had listened to her. And by the sound of it he and Robbie had definitely made up. Thank goodness for that. She made as much noise as she could taking off her coat and wellies, to alert them that she was there and sure enough, Robbie popped his head around the kitchen door. 'Hello, hun, you've been ages. Have you been enjoying yourself so much you couldn't tear yourself away?'

'A good job I was,' she replied. 'It gave you two a chance to talk.'

'How did you know Duncan was here?' Robbie asked, all wide-eyed innocence.

'I heard him laugh, although your beaming face would have given it away.' She smiled. 'I'm so pleased you've got back together.'

'More than that.' Duncan popped his head around the door too, then in unison both men held out their left hands and wriggled their ring fingers. A thin gold band with a star sapphire gleamed on Robbie's finger, and a gold band with a row of three diamonds in the middle sparkled on Duncan's finger. 'We both proposed to each other,' Duncan said, with a grin. 'We're officially engaged.'

'Wow! Congratulations! This calls for a group hug!' Saffy held out her arms and enveloped them both in a big hug. 'I'm so pleased. This is the best Christmas present ever.'

'Thanks to you for making us both see sense,' Duncan told her, as they unhugged.

'Someone had to!' she teased.

'And before we go to bed, we want you to join us in a toast to our engagement. Duncan brought a bottle of champagne down with him – a bit presumptuous of him, I must say!'

They all laughed as Duncan took a bottle of champagne out of the fridge, popped it and poured three glasses.

'To Robbie and Duncan!' Saffy said as they chinked glasses.

'To us!' Robbie and Duncan both said together.

Thank goodness they'd made it up; she loved a happy ending, Saffy thought as she climbed into bed half an hour later, leaving the reunited lovers still downstairs, after checking with Robbie that he was still okay to set his alarm and put the turkey in the Aga in the morning. 'I'll do it,' Duncan told her. 'You have a lie-in. You deserve it for getting two stubborn men back together!'

Her mind flitted to Logan. Getting married hadn't been a happy ending for him, had it? It had been for Hannah and Lee, though, and she hoped it would for Robbie and Duncan too.

As she drifted off to sleep she thought that this Christmas was turning out to be way, way better than she had expected.

❄

When Saffy had gone, Logan poured himself a Scotch and sat down at the kitchen table. This was the first time he'd been so attracted to a woman since he met Jade at a party, eight years ago. It was her laugh that had attracted him first. He'd heard it as soon as he'd walked into the room, a rolling peal of tinkly laughter, and had immediately glanced over to see who it was. Jade was sitting amongst a group of people, but she was holding the floor, regaling them with some amusing tale. Her dark brown hair was cut elfin-like around her face, enhancing her cut-glass cheekbones; her eyes were twinkling, her beautiful face animated. He stood watching her for a few minutes, thinking he'd never seen anyone so alive, so beautiful. Then, as if she'd sensed him staring at her, she'd turned her head in his direction, their eyes had met, acknowledged each other, and she'd waved him over to join them. He'd gone, of course. That night he and Jade had left together for his flat, woken up in bed the next morning and spent the day together. That was it. They were a couple.

Jade was fun, witty, engaging and they'd spent the next six months happily together, living at his place half the week, and hers the other half. It worked. It suited them both perfectly. Until Jade discovered she was pregnant. Having a child wasn't part of her life plan, she had said tearfully. He'd tried to reassure her that she wouldn't be a single parent; that he would be there for her. He'd asked her to give up her flat and move in with him, and she had for a while, during her pregnancy, and the early months of Chloe's life. But Jade didn't want to be a parent at all. And to be honest, ultimately there wasn't enough love between them for her to want to stay with him and she'd walked out.

At first he'd thought Jade had just wanted a break for a few days, that she'd be back, but as the days went into weeks he realised that she really had gone for good. It seemed as if she had left Chloe too and that he was now solely responsible for their little daughter. One day, out of the blue, Jade had announced that she wanted to visit Chloe. He'd agreed, sure that once she saw their adorable baby daughter again she'd want to keep regular contact but no, after a couple of hours she'd waved goodbye and that was the last they saw of her for another couple of months. Yes, there had been the odd 'how is Chloe' text in between, and she put some money in their bank account now and again, but that was it as far as Jade was concerned. Her daily life didn't involve Chloe.

And now she was back again but instead of wanting to see Chloe for an hour or two, as she usually did, she wanted to take her for the whole day and night. What's more, Jade wanted Chloe to spend time with her grandparents too. It was as if she was finally admitting that Chloe was her child, finally felt ready to be part of her life. But was he ready to let her be?

He sipped his drink, the bite of the liquid warming his throat as he swallowed it and thought about tomorrow.

He was looking forward to seeing Saffy again. Looking forward to it too much.

He was drawn to Saffy, just like he'd been drawn to Jade, but he wasn't going down that path again. Saffy might seem warm and caring but, like Jade, she didn't want a family, so it was a good job she was only here for a few days. Chloe wouldn't have chance to get too close to her and miss her. And neither would he.

He would go to Liwus Helyk tomorrow and enjoy the party but that was it. Then it was goodbye Saffy and on with his life.

Chapter Sixteen

Duncan's singing broke through Saffy's sleep. She reached for her phone and swiped the screen to life to see the time. Eight-thirty! She shot up in alarm. God, she'd overslept! She had less than five hours before the guests arrived and there was so much to do: the dinner to cook – had Duncan remembered to put the turkey in? She flung the duvet back and got out of bed.

'Are you decent?' Robbie shouted.

You couldn't get more decent than her polar bear onesie; it covered her from top to toe. 'Yes, come in!' she shouted, feeling a bit guilty that she had overslept.

'Merry Christmas to you, Merry Christmas to you!' Robbie and Duncan sang in out-of-tune unison as they opened the door.

'And it's a white Christmas!' Robbie announced as he strutted in, carrying a tray with a plate of toast and three mugs, one of which she hoped was tea. Tea was her wake-up drink, then countless cups of coffee kept her going all day. Duncan was behind Robbie, carrying an armful of beautifully wrapped presents. They were both wearing Santa hats and Christmas jumpers. Duncan had certainly come prepared!

'Is it?' Saffy raced over to the window and opened the curtains. Sure enough, everywhere was covered with a thick white blanket of snow. 'That's fantastic!'

'Blooming brilliant. A perfect Christmas,' Robbie said, beaming.

'The turkey's cooking and everything's under control so get back into bed and eat this breakfast,' Duncan ordered.

Robbie placed the tray on the bedside table and handed Saffy the red mug. 'Tea for you,' he said.

'Thanks.' She peered at the liquid in the mug – medium brown, just as she liked it.

Duncan placed the presents on the nearby chair, then he and Robbie picked up a mug each and sat down on the side of the bed.

'Toast, anyone?' Robbie picked up the plate and offered it first to Duncan, then Saffy. They both took a slice.

'Well, I'm feeling very spoilt,' Saffy said, glancing at the inviting pile of presents. Were these all for her?

'Yes, they're all yours,' Duncan said, obviously noticing her glance. 'We've already exchanged our presents – some of them were a bit personal.'

'I'm glad you saved me from witnessing that then,' she said with a grin. 'I've got you two a present too. It's a joint one,' she added. Thank goodness she'd bought a present when she was shopping the other day, choosing something that would be suitable for Robbie on his own, or both of them, depending if they had made it up.

'No rush, open yours first.' Robbie scooped up a present, exquisitely wrapped with red ribbon and bows, and handed it to her.

Robbie had probably chosen the presents – he had the knack of finding quirky gifts – but the wrapping was down to Duncan, she knew. Presentation was everything to him; he always bought classy wrapping paper, with coordinating ribbons and bows. She was so pleased that she'd bought some beautiful gift paper from the Christmas craft shop she'd visited on Friday.

She put down her mug and carefully undid the ribbons, tugging at the paper to reveal expensive chocolate shoes in a cute handbag-shaped box, a gorgeous polar bear shaped scented candle, a purple pair of fluffy heeled slippers, a pretty notebook and pen set and the final one, a bottle of Jimmy Choo perfume. 'Thank you, they're lovely.' She leaned forward and gave both men a kiss on the cheek then wriggled out of bed over to the wardrobe, taking out a large box, wrapped in the gorgeous handmade holly gift-wrapping paper and placed it on the bed. 'I don't know which one of you wants to open it.'

'We'll do an end each,' Robbie said.

They were both delighted with the stainless steel ice cream maker she had bought them. Robbie set to putting it all together while Duncan was engrossed in the recipe leaflet included. 'Hey, there's some great desserts here we can try for our Boxing Day dinner party,' he said.

'Boxing Day dinner party?' Saffy repeated. 'When was that organised? Is it to replace the Christmas one?'

'Yes. We messaged everyone last night to tell them we were back together but couldn't get home until tomorrow morning – we didn't want to go and leave you to run the Lonely Hearts Christmas party by yourself,' Robbie said.

'So we suggested having a Boxing Day dinner party to make up for today's being cancelled and they all said yes,' Duncan added. 'We've got all the food in so it'd be a shame to waste it.'

'You're welcome to come too, but I thought you'd want to stay and see your sister, wouldn't you?' asked Robbie.

Saffy hesitated. It would be so tempting to go back with Robbie and Duncan but she hadn't seen Hannah, Lee and the twins for ages. She nodded. 'I promised Hannah I'd spend a couple of days with her.'

'You'll be back for our engagement party on Saturday, won't you?' Duncan asked.

'Gosh, you guys don't waste any time, do you? When was all this sorted out?'

'This morning. If you can't make it we'll postpone until next week. We need you there, you were the one who brought us back together,' Robbie said. 'There'd be no engagement without you.'

'I'll be there. I'll head back home Saturday morning at the latest,' Saffy promised. Then she remembered Robbie telling her that Duncan had a special theme planned for their Christmas Day party. 'Seeing as I can't come to tomorrow's dinner party can you tell me the theme – I promise I won't breathe a word to anyone.'

Robbie glanced at Duncan. 'Let's tell her.'

Duncan nodded. 'Okay. It's…' He paused for dramatic effect. 'Hollywood!' he announced. 'I've got the décor all planned and hired costumes for the guests.'

'We've got a big Hollywood sign, stars for people's seats, even a couple of Oscar statuettes for prizes,' Robbie told her. Saffy knew it would be amazing. Duncan planned everything right down to the last detail.

'That sounds wonderful. I'm so tempted to go back with you but I can't, not without seeing Hannah.'

'No stress. I've hired some gorgeous movie-themed costumes from a local theatre company and don't have to return them until the New Year so we can have the same theme for our engagement party if you like,' Duncan said.

'Yes please!' She'd look forward to that.

'Right, we'd better clear this lot then and leave you to get dressed.' Duncan put the cups and plate back on the tray and Robbie picked up the ice cream maker. They both looked so happy, Saffy thought.

'Why don't you two go off for a walk? You must want to spend some time together and I can handle this now. Everything's prepared, the turkey's in the oven – all I have to do is shower, tidy around and arrange a few games.'

'If you're sure. We'll be back in an hour or so,' Robbie told her.

'I'm positive. Go!' She flapped her hands at them. 'I don't want you both mooning around me all morning. But make sure you're back well before dinner. I don't want to be dealing with the cooking all by myself.'

'We'll be back,' Robbie promised.

As soon as they'd gone, taking Oscar with them, Saffy phoned Hannah to wish her Merry Christmas and ask her how the twins were – much better and definitely able to fly home on Boxing Day, Hannah told her, sounding more upbeat now that the twins were out of danger. They chatted for a while, then Saffy showered, dressed in jeans and a red top – she'd brought a more glamorous outfit with her for the party but didn't intend to change into it until just before the guests were due to arrive; knowing her she'd probably spill something all over it. The delicious smell of the turkey roasting wafted up the stairs, and she headed for the kitchen to check on it. It was cooking well and everywhere looked neat and tidy. She was glad that Duncan and Robbie were here – without them she'd feel a bundle of nerves right now. Keeping up Hannah's traditional Lonely Hearts Christmas dinner was such a responsibility.

She made herself a cup of coffee and sat down at the kitchen table to plan the day. She was trying not to freak out about the fact that in less than four hours' time ten parents and twenty-five children – all strangers apart from Logan and Chloe – would walk through that door and expect her to feed and entertain them. The adults would, hopefully, mingle and chatter to each other but kids got bored easily so it was the kids she wanted to concentrate on. Hannah had told her she'd got a selection of board games in the long cupboard in the dining room, but Saffy had wanted to come up with some ideas herself too so had picked up some crafty things for them to do while she was out shopping with Robbie. And she'd painted a big reindeer on a piece of white card, and a tail to pin on it – a variation of the Pin the Tail on the Donkey game. That should keep the younger kids occupied. She'd brought a packet of multi-coloured balloons down with her, remembering how much fun she and her friends had playing with balloons when they were young, and had wrapped a couple of parcels for Pass the Parcel. She went up to her case to get them but they weren't there. Drat, she remembered now, she'd left them in a carrier bag in the boot of her car. Pulling on her coat and Hannah's strawberry wellies again she set off through the snow-covered back yard to get them out of her car, then made her way back to the house. It wasn't until she reached the back door of Liwus Helyk that she remembered she'd left the house keys on the table in the kitchen. And her phone too. She was locked out. And she couldn't call anyone for help.

Damn. Now what did she do? Logan had given her his spare key to Hannah's house, so surely wouldn't have another one. Besides, she didn't want to keep being rescued like some damsel in distress. There must be a way she could do this herself.

She scanned all the windows to check if any were open. Normally she would think it was highly unlikely since it was so cold, but Duncan was a bit of a fresh air freak and liked to air his room no matter what the weather. Yep, the top window of his and Robbie's room was half-open. Now all she had to do was get up there, slip her hand through the open window, reach down for the latch on the side window and climb in. Heck, she sounded like a burglar! She hoped no one took her for one.

Luckily, Robbie and Duncan's bedroom was just above the low kitchen roof, so she could climb on that then haul herself up on the window ledge. Thank goodness she was wearing her jeans, but her long coat and Hannah's wellies weren't ideal for climbing in. She took off her coat and hung it on the fence, knowing she'd be cold but that it would be much easier to climb without it. She could do this.

She brushed the snow off the kitchen windowsill, then held onto it to haul herself up, first her right knee, then her left knee. Done. She gripped the handle of the window and pulled herself upright. If only they'd left the kitchen window open it would be much easier. So far, so good, but so perishing cold! She shivered. That was a mistake because suddenly her foot slipped and she almost lost her balance. She lifted it back onto the windowsill again and stood still for a movement, getting her balance. *Careful, Saffy*. The narrow windowsill was wet and her wellingtons big and clumsy. It all felt a bit precarious. She looked up at the kitchen roof. It wasn't that far to pull herself up. It would be dead easy if it wasn't covered in snow and she was wearing trainers instead of these cumbersome wellingtons.

You can do it! Gripping the window handle tightly with her left hand she reached up with her right hand and swiped along the roof, brushing the snow onto the ground below. Okay, there was still a lot of snow on there, but at least she'd cleared enough to give herself room to stand once she'd climbed up.

She took a deep breath then gripped the edge of the roof. Up, up and she was on the top! But bloody hell, it was cold! If only she hadn't taken her coat off. She shivered, hugging herself to keep warm while she considered her next step. She had to get up onto the bedroom window ledge, slip her hand through the half-open top window and release the catch on the side window then climb through. She wouldn't allow herself to think what would happen if she lost her footing on the snow-covered roof.

Carefully, one step at a time, she made her way over to the window. The kitchen roof was so slippery her feet were sliding under her; it took all her concentration to remain upright. And the windowsill was still a tantalising few metres away.

'Saffy! Stop!'

Logan's shrill shout took her by surprise. Saffy spun around, lost her footing, skidded and tumbled off the roof.

Chapter Seventeen

'Saffy!' Logan shouted and through the blur of her fall she was sure she glimpsed him racing towards her.

She was shooting down towards the ground and there was nothing she could do about it. She closed her eyes tight as the ground came racing up to meet her. *Oh God, please don't let me break my back or my neck or…*

Suddenly, strong arms grasped her, breaking her fall, and she was tumbling into the snow. Snow was in her hair, her eyes, her mouth, down her jumper. And those arms were still holding her, rolling in the snow with her. She was cold. And wet. Then she realised it was Logan who had caught her, and who was rolling in the snow with her. And the whole episode had been witnessed by Chloe and a woman she didn't know. Talk about feeling a total idiot.

They finally stopped rolling and she wriggled out of Logan's grasp, her body aching so much it would be a miracle if nothing was broken.

The woman and Chloe both ran over to them.

'Are you hurt?' the woman asked anxiously, her arm wrapped protectively around Chloe's shoulder.

Saffy was too winded to reply but Logan was already getting to his feet. 'I'm fine.' He knelt down by Saffy. 'Are you okay? That was some fall. Is anything broken?'

He gently helped her sit up, and watched, his face etched with concern, as she flexed her arms, then her legs. Nothing seemed broken, thank goodness.

'See if you can stand,' Logan said, holding out his hand for her to use as support.

She ignored it and slowly scrambled to her feet. All bones felt intact. She was a little stiff, and probably had a couple of bruises, but Logan – and the snow – had eased her fall. Her pride, however, was smarting.

'I think so, no thanks to you!' She glared at him. 'If you hadn't shouted like that and startled me, I wouldn't have slipped. I could have broken my neck.'

'But Daddy did catch you,' Chloe said tearfully. 'And he fell in the snow too.'

Back off, Saffy, you can't have a go at him on Christmas Day, especially in front of his daughter. Besides, look at him all covered in snow, even in his hair. And he must feel as bruised as her.

'Yes, he did, didn't he?' She sucked in her breath and avoided Logan's eyes. 'Thank you.' She brushed the snow off her clothes, trying to compose herself before asking, 'What are you doing here anyway?'

'Mrs Timms saw you climbing the roof and called me,' said Logan, indicating the woman standing with them.

'I live next door and have just come back from spending the weekend with my daughter and family. Logan had told me you were running the party for Hannah because the twins were ill and she couldn't get home,' Mrs Timms explained. 'When I saw you climbing onto the roof I guessed you'd got locked out so phoned Logan.'

'I was terrified you were going to fall and hurt yourself,' Logan told her. He took her coat off the fence and draped it over her shoulders. 'Here, you're shivering, wrap this around you.'

'So you came to my rescue but decided to shout at me, startling me so much I did just that!' she couldn't stop herself from retorting.

'I'm sorry, but the slightest movement and that chunk of ice would have dropped off onto you!' Logan pointed up to the roof. Saffy followed his finger and saw a huge clump of ice hanging over the roof on top of Robbie and Duncan's bedroom window. Why hadn't she noticed that before? 'It's a big piece and looks frozen solid. I was worried that if you dislodged it you'd be knocked out or slip.' Deep blue eyes searched her face. 'Are you hurt? You took quite a tumble.'

She shrugged. 'I'll live.' She paused. 'Er, thanks for catching me anyway.'

'No problem.' He ran his fingers through his wet hair. 'Why didn't you message me and tell me you were locked out instead of imitating a cat burglar? I told you to ring me if you need anything.'

'I don't have my phone on me. Besides, do you have another key to Hannah's house?'

He shook his head, 'Nope, sorry.'

'I thought not, so what would be the point of disturbing your Christmas Day? It's my problem and I'm the one who should solve it.'

'I'll climb up and get in through the window. My jacket and boots are a lot more suitable for climbing than yours.' Without waiting for her to agree, Logan trudged over to the house and heaved himself onto the kitchen roof.

'Daddy, be careful!' Chloe shouted.

'I'll be fine, poppet, don't worry.' He pointed to the broom in the corner of the yard. 'Could you pass me that please – and stay well clear.'

Chloe ran to get it and held it up to him. Logan grabbed it then walked slowly over the snowy roof to the bedroom window.

'What's going on? Why is Logan standing on the kitchen roof?' Robbie asked, as he and Duncan walked into the back yard with Oscar, who immediately ran over to the house and started barking at Logan.

'Because I'm locked out. I went to get something from the car and left my keys on the kitchen table.' She rubbed her arm; it was throbbing. All her left side was throbbing too where she'd landed in the snow. She guessed Logan must be feeling pretty sore too. She glanced over at him. He was standing by the open bedroom window now, brandishing the broom.

'Stand back!' he shouted.

They all stepped back as Logan whacked the large chunk of overhanging ice with the handle of the broom, quickly stepping aside as it crashed onto the roof a few centimetres away from him. Moments later he had his arm through the small top window and was turning the catch on the side window below. If he fell… She pulled her coat closer around her and held her breath as Logan eased the window open, then climbed inside. There was a chorus of applause from Duncan, Robbie, Chloe and Mrs Timms. Logan paused, smiled and gave them a mock-bow, before disappearing from sight. A couple of minutes later the back door opened and he was standing there, holding his boots in his hand – he'd obviously taken them off upstairs to avoid making a mess.

'Daddy!' Chloe ran over and flung herself at him. 'I was so scared. I thought you were going to fall too.'

'I'm fine, poppet.' He looked apologetically at Saffy. 'Sorry, my coat's dripped a bit on the carpet but it should soon dry.' He stepped aside. 'Anyway, you're in!'

'Thank you,' Saffy said stiffly. She couldn't help feeling piqued about him causing her to fall then taking over and playing the hero. She was sure that she'd have managed to open that window and climb inside herself if he hadn't come charging along on his white horse.

The smell of roast turkey wafted from the kitchen. 'I reckon that turkey's done,' Robbie said. 'Good job you got us back inside, Logan.'

'Well done, mate.' Duncan slapped Logan on the back.

Robbie glanced at Saffy and Logan then said brightly to Chloe and Duncan, 'I think we should all take Oscar inside and check on the turkey.'

They all walked down the hall into the kitchen. Leaving just Saffy and Logan. Staring awkwardly at each other.

Saffy forced herself to be gracious. 'Thanks for getting us back inside. And breaking my fall – even though you caused it. And I could have managed by myself,' she added.

His face was stony. 'Then I'm sorry I didn't leave you to it. I was brought up to look after women, to help if I saw them in any danger. I guess that's a bit of an old-fashioned view now.'

She crossed her arms and met his icy gaze. 'Nothing wrong with helping but maybe make sure the woman in question needs and wants help first? And try to avoid making her fall of a roof.'

'Daddy, the turkey's massive!' Chloe came running down the hall. 'And you should see how many potatoes they've peeled.'

Throwing Saffy one last furious look, Logan turned his attention to his daughter. 'That's because a lot of people are coming for Christmas dinner. In fact, we'd better get going and leave Saffy and Robbie to it. They've got a lot to do, and so have we.'

He sat down on the ottoman in the hall and put his boots back on. 'I'll see you at one-thirty.' He took hold of Chloe's hand and walked out without as much as a backward glance.

What an arrogant man, Saffy thought crossly. Just when she was starting to think he was okay he went and did something like this.

If there was one thing she hated, it was being told by a man that she needed looking after. Her mother hadn't had a man in her life for years, and had brought Saffy and Hannah up to be strong and self-reliant.

'Oh dear, have you two had a fall-out?' Robbie asked. 'He was only trying to help, Saff.'

'I'm going to get into some dry clothes,' Saffy said wearily. There was still lots to organise and that tumble had shaken her up.

❄

'Saffy looked very upset, Daddy,' Chloe said, holding Logan's hand as they walked over the road. 'I think she must have been frightened when she fell.' She looked up at him. 'You did shout at her really loud, that's why she slipped.'

He sighed. 'I know, poppet. I didn't mean to.' The sight of Saffy perched precariously on the windowsill, then hauling herself onto the roof right underneath that jagged chunk of ice had sent shivers of fear through him. He hadn't stopped to think, he'd just run towards her and shouted as loud as he could. He'd been horrified when she'd slipped, plunging down off the kitchen roof. And now she was angry with him.

He didn't blame her. He shouldn't have startled her. But God, she'd scared him.

He shivered. He was freezing. He guessed rolling in snow and getting your clothes wringing wet did that to you. Saffy must be freezing too. He needed a hot shower to warm himself up, and to get into some dry clothes. He wondered if Saffy was doing the same, and tried not to think of her peeling off those wet clothes…

'I'm going upstairs for a quick shower. I won't be long,' he told Chloe.

'Okay, Daddy. Can we play Hungry Hippos after?' It was one of Chloe's favourite games.

'Sure. I'll be ten minutes.' He was already mounting the stairs.

When he came back down Chloe was talking on the landline. 'It's Mummy,' she told him.

Jade. He guessed she'd phoned to wish them a merry Christmas but why had she used the landline again when he'd specifically told her she had to ring his mobile? He took the phone out of his pocket. No missed calls. It was as if she was hoping Chloe would answer.

Chloe was still chatting away animatedly, telling her mother what presents she'd had. Then she listened for a while, and he gathered from the few words she said that Jade was telling her what they'd be doing tomorrow.

'Daddy, Mummy wants to talk to you.' Chloe held out the cordless phone.

'Thanks, poppet.' Logan took it from her and put it to his ear.

'Merry Christmas, Logan.' Jade sounded bright and breezy. 'It sounds like Chloe has had a lot of presents.'

'Merry Christmas,' he repeated. 'I do what I can for her. Don't want her missing out.'

'Seeing as her mum ran out on her, you mean?'

He really didn't want to get into this now; it was Christmas Day. 'What did you want, Jade? And why didn't you call my mobile? I've told you I only use the landline for work.'

'I wanted to speak to Chloe and wish her a merry Christmas. She's my daughter. Is it so strange that I should want to speak to her?'

'Let's not do this, not today,' he replied, keeping his voice level.

'Fine.' She sounded almost conciliatory. 'Look, I know I've let Chloe down but I'm going to make it up to her.'

He'd heard that before. He didn't bother to reply.

'I'll be there at nine tomorrow, so please make sure she's ready. It's a bit of a drive.'

'It's snowed quite a bit down here, are you sure it's wise to travel? Why don't you leave it for a day or two for the snow to clear?' he suggested.

'I've checked, the main roads are clear and there's no travel warning so there's no reason to postpone. I'll be there tomorrow at nine. Enjoy your party.'

Logan tapped the phone against his chin and stared out of the kitchen window. He didn't like the thought of Jade driving in this weather, not with Chloe, but Chloe was really looking forward to her overnight trip. He took his mobile phone out of his pocket and checked the weather again. There was a possibility of more snow this evening. Well, if that happened he'd tell Jade that Chloe was staying here until it cleared. He wasn't going to risk them getting stranded in the snow somewhere, or Jade having an accident with Chloe in the car.

Chapter Eighteen

Liwus Helyk was a whirl of activity for the next couple of hours. On Duncan's insistence, Saffy had a soak in a nice, hot bath. Then she put some witch hazel on her bruises – she only had a couple, miraculously – and changed into the black leather trousers and glittery silver top she'd brought with her to wear on Christmas Day, far more suitable than a party dress when she had a load of children to entertain. She felt much better now, apart from her pride which was still dented. Meanwhile, Robbie and Duncan had been busy in the dining room and had already laid red tablecloths trimmed with white fur on each of the four large rectangular tables. Oscar had been shut in the lounge with his new Christmas squeaky toys to ensure he wasn't tempted to try to sneak some of the Christmas food. He had a special big bone to keep him busy in the kitchen once dinner was served.

'Feeling better?' Robbie asked, looking up from putting Santa and snowmen salt and pepper pots on every table.

'Much,' she told him. Then she noticed that the bump on his forehead had now gone down a lot. 'Hey, your bump has almost gone.'

'I told you witch hazel works a treat.' Duncan held up a selection of chair covers – Santa, elf and snowman. 'Any preference which ones you want on the kiddies' chairs?'

'Santa, I think,' Saffy replied.

'Yes, deffo the Santa ones for the kids,' Robbie agreed. 'I fancy an elf one.'

'I'll be a snowman,' Saffy said. She glanced at her watch. In just under two hours' time the guests would be knocking at the door. 'I'll do the chairback covers while you two finish laying the tables, if that's okay. We're a bit pushed for time now.'

'My favourite job,' Robbie said. He and Duncan fished into Hannah's decorations box, ooohing and aaahing over red stocking-shaped cutlery holders trimmed with white fur, red napkin rings, Christmas serviettes, and a Santa pulling a sleigh decoration for the centre of each table. Meanwhile, Saffy laid out the chair covers, table mats and place cards.

'That's great.' Saffy smiled. 'I don't know what I'd have done without you two. The table looks fantastic, and the turkey is almost done. Thanks so much for helping.'

'I guess it's a fair exchange for getting us back together again,' Duncan said. The loved-up look he and Robbie exchanged made Saffy really glad she had managed that. She hated to see any of her friends upset.

Logan had told her that Jade had walked out on him just before Christmas, she remembered. That must have been really hard for him, especially with Chloe to look after. She thought about how close Logan and Chloe were. He was a good dad. And maybe she'd over-reacted a bit about the falling off the roof episode. He was just trying to warn her about the ice, it wasn't really his fault that she'd lost her balance. Maybe she should apologise to him when he arrived? After all, he'd got wet too, and had come to help when it wasn't really his problem. And it was Christmas. A time for peace and joy and all that. Well, definitely not a time for falling out anyway.

'Where're the plates and cutlery, hun?' Robbie asked, breaking through her thoughts.

Saffy checked her list. 'Cutlery's in the big cabinet drawer in the dining room and the plates and cups are in the cupboard. I think Hannah uses the same ones every year.'

Between them they took out the cutlery, plates and glasses – there were plastic Christmas plates and beakers for the children – and laid the tables.

Half an hour later, the tables were all laid, the roast potatoes were almost cooked, Duncan was expertly slicing the turkey and the veg were about to be switched on. Saffy found a Christmas carol CD and slipped it into the DVD/CD player on the TV stand. She checked her watch. Quarter to one. Three quarters of an hour to go.

'I think we're all entitled to chill with a Buck's Fizz now,' Robbie said, pouring three glasses. 'Then I'd better get changed before the guests arrive.' He handed Duncan and Saffy a glass each. 'Merry Christmas!'

'Merry Christmas,' they all chorused.

Saffy took a swig of the sparkly liquid and felt herself relax. It was all going to be fine. Everything was ready, now all she had to do was make sure Hannah's guests had fun for the next few hours. Tonight it would all be over and she could put her feet up and chill.

'How are you feeling, Saff?' Duncan asked when Robbie went up to change into the Santa outfit. 'Would you like me to greet the guests with you when they arrive, give you a bit of moral support? I could hand them all a Christmas cocktail, get them in the festive mood right away.'

'Yes please,' Saffy replied gratefully. She really could do with some moral support right now. She so wanted this to go well, to do Hannah proud.

The doorbell ringing broke through her thoughts. The guests had arrived. 'I'm heading for the lounge now,' Robbie called. 'Give me a couple of minutes and let them in.'

'Shall we go to the door?' Duncan asked, picking up the tray of cocktails he'd prepared. He looked quite dashing in his bright red snowman Christmas jumper, fine black cords and a Christmas hat trimmed with white fur.

Saffy took a deep breath. 'Let's do this.'

As they opened the door, a chorus of 'Merry Christmas' rang out from the group of parents and children crowded on the doorstep, all dressed very festively and covered in snowflakes.

Saffy smiled at them. 'Merry Christmas. I'm Saffy, Hannah's sister, and this is Duncan, a friend of mine. Come in, all of you.'

She stepped aside and one by one they all stepped in, kissing first Saffy then Duncan on the cheek and introducing themselves as they did so. There were 'ooohs' and 'aahs' from the children as they looked around, wide-eyed, at the decorations and lights sparkling in the hall.

'Well, this all looks very jolly,' a pretty, auburn-haired woman dressed in a cream fake fur jacket and black boots said as she took the cocktail Duncan handed her. Saffy tried to remember her name. Marta, that was it. 'And so do you,' she said to Duncan.

'Thank you.' Duncan smiled at her. 'Do take a Christmas cocktail, everyone.'

'It's so kind of you to give up your Christmas for us,' Ariane, a fair-haired woman wearing black velvet leggings and a sparkly gold top, told Saffy.

'It's a pleasure,' Saffy told her. 'Would the children like to go through to the lounge and get a present from Santa? He's waiting for them.'

'Santa's here?' a little girl shouted. The children jumped up and down excitedly. 'Santa's here!'

One by one the guests arrived, and after taking off their coats and snow-covered boots, the children raced into the lounge to see Santa while the adults gathered around, drinking their cocktails and chatting happily. Several of them asked how Hannah and the twins were and everyone remarked how lovely it all looked.

It was going well. All except for one thing.

There was no sign of Logan and Chloe.

Was he still so mad at her about this morning that he had decided not to come?

Chapter Nineteen

Saffy's heart soared as the bell rang. Was it them?

'Sorry we're late, my parents phoned from Scotland to wish Chloe Merry Christmas just as we were about to leave,' Logan told her when she opened the door.

'It's fine. Do you want to go straight in to see Santa, Chloe?' she asked.

Chloe's eyes widened. 'Yes!' And she disappeared into the lounge.

Logan raised an eyebrow questioningly. 'Robbie?'

'Yes, and he's a very jolly Santa this morning. Duncan drove down last night and they've both made up.'

'I'm pleased to hear that.' Logan paused. 'Talking about making up…'

'I'm sorry,' they both said in unison and then laughed.

'Friends again then?' He held out his hand.

'Please.' She held out her hand too and he took it in his, holding it instead of shaking it, his eyes locking with hers, his touch leaving her skin tingling. She imagined what it would be like to feel that hand gently caressing her skin, touching, stroking…

'Do you see what we're standing under?' Logan asked. She followed his gaze and saw a sprig of mistletoe hanging directly above them.

'Shame to waste it.' Logan leaned forward and kissed her on the cheek, sending a surprising shiver of delight coursing through her. 'Merry Christmas.'

'Merry Christmas,' she whispered, her eyes on his, unblinking as he lowered his head and his lips came closer and closer. Then they were on hers, kissing her softly, and it felt so good…

'Sorry to disturb you both but Molly wants to go the loo.' The sharpness of Marta's voice brought Saffy back to earth. She looked up, startled, and Logan released her. Tight-lipped, Marta walked past them, holding her little girl's hand.

Saffy was quite taken aback by her response. For goodness' sake, it had only a Christmas kiss.

But what a kiss.

'I think we'd better go in and join the others, don't you?' Logan asked softly.

'Sure.' She pushed open the door to the dining room, which was a scene of some hilarity with two of the women sitting on Santa's knee asking him for a Christmas kiss. Duncan was roaring with laughter and taking photos.

Then Santa announced that he had to be somewhere else and waved goodbye to everyone, returning a few minutes later as Robbie in a green Christmas jumper with a reindeer on the front of it and black chinos, carrying a tray of soft drinks for the children. Duncan had been busy in the kitchen for the past quarter of an hour or so, doing the last-minute preparations for the Christmas dinner. He came out, wiping his brow with his Christmas apron. 'It's all ready to serve up,' he said triumphantly to Saffy.

'Thanks so much, you're a star,' she told him. Then she clapped her hands to get everyone's attention. 'It'd like to introduce you all to Robbie, Duncan's partner. I'm really grateful to them both for helping me organise this party for you all.' This was greeted by a round of applause and Robbie and Duncan took a bow.

'Now if you'd all take your drinks into the dining room and find your seats – there are place cards on the tables – dinner will be served in just a few minutes,' Saffy continued.

Robbie, Duncan and Logan all sat at a different table each, so they could mix with the guests, with Logan on the same table as Geoff, the only other male single parent at the party.

Saffy directed everyone to their seats, and they sat down, greeting each other, exchanging gifts, settling the children. 'You and your boys are sitting here, Toni,' she said to a tall, dark-haired woman wearing a long red dress. Toni looked over at Logan sitting in the seat next to her and stiffened. Saffy immediately sensed tension between them.

'I think Toni would like to sit with Marta on the next table,' Logan said easily. 'Perhaps Ariane wouldn't mind swapping seats.'

'Of course not.' Ariane immediately got up. 'Come on, kids.'

Okay, so something had gone on between Toni and Logan in the past. Had he slept with her? Saffy wondered as Ariane sat down, all smiles, next to Logan. She shrugged; it was none of her business and at least Ariane seemed happy to sit next to him.

As the dinner progressed and the wine started to flow, everyone seemed to relax and get along well.

'So how do you usually spend Christmas, Saffy?' asked Ariane.

'Oh you know, the usual single-without-kids stuff,' she said with a shrug. 'Lunch with friends, parties.'

'Sounds like heaven,' Ariane said. 'And to think you gave that up for us.'

Saffy smiled. 'It's a pleasure. This party means a lot to Hannah and Lee, they are both really upset that they can't be here.'

'How are the twins?' asked Ariane.

'Much better, they're coming home tomorrow afternoon. So, I'll be having another Christmas dinner on Friday, with Hannah and Lee, before I go home.'

They chatted easily, about children, jobs, boyfriends, all the women on the table joining in, sharing anecdotes about their kids, their exes, their lives in general. Saffy was so pleased that she'd agreed to host the party for Hannah. Looking around and seeing how everyone was enjoying themselves made it all worthwhile.

When the meal was over, several of the guests insisted on helping clear the table and load the dishwasher. 'We always do it for Hannah,' Marta said. Then Saffy took orders for dessert – Christmas pudding for those who wanted it, or mince pies or ice cream (or both) for those who didn't. She, Robbie and Duncan dished up and handed it out, then crackers were pulled, and the kids collected all the joke slips, reading them out repeatedly. It was a noisy, jolly affair.

When everyone had finished eating, Duncan tapped his glass with his spoon and stood up. 'If I can have your attention please.'

He was going to give a speech, Saffy thought with amusement as they all turned to look at him.

'First of all, I'd like to say how lovely it is to spend Christmas with you all. Christmas is a time for everyone to get together and celebrate.' He looked around and smiled at all the watching guests. 'Robbie and I are delighted to help Saffy keep up Hannah and Lee's tradition and host this dinner for you all.' He raised his glass. 'Merry Christmas, everyone!'

'Merry Christmas!' they all chorused, raising their glasses too.

Logan stood up then. 'Thank you. I'm sure we'd all like to thank Saffy for saving the day, Duncan for cooking such a marvellous dinner, and Robbie for "helping" Santa.'

This was greeted with a big round of applause, more raising of glasses and cheers.

Duncan stood up again. 'Secondly' – he paused for effect and looked slowly around the room to ensure he had everyone's attention – 'I would like to ask you all to join me and Robbie' – he looked at Robbie, who immediately stood up, glass in hand – 'in celebrating our engagement!'

Cheers and claps greeted this announcement as Duncan and Robbie proudly held out their hands, wriggling their fingers so everyone could see the rings sparkling there.

'How exciting! Let me have a look!' Marta got up from her seat and dashed over to them. Others joined her and soon Robbie and Duncan were surrounded.

Saffy smiled as she listened to the gasps of admiration and chit-chat. The ice was well and truly broken, thanks to Duncan and Robbie. She took a sip of her drink and started to relax as the warm liquid trickled down her throat.

'It's going well, isn't it?'

Saffy turned her head as Logan slipped into the seat beside her.

'Yes, thanks to those two,' she replied.

'Rubbish, you've made just as much effort, but yes – no one can resist an engagement, especially at Christmas time.' He was gazing seriously at her now. 'Look, I wanted to apologise properly about earlier. You know, the falling off the roof thing. I shouldn't have shouted so loud and startled you. I just sort of freaked out when I saw you up there.'

'It's okay. I know you were only trying to help, and you did break my fall. I guess I freaked out too, when I saw the ground racing up towards me…' She swallowed. 'Anyway, I shouldn't have been so rude.'

His eyes were holding hers and for a moment she thought he was going to kiss her again but Chloe tugged at his sleeve to ask for glass of water and the moment was gone.

Then she remembered Logan's Christmas cake; she should show it to everyone and thank him properly. She went to the kitchen to get it, where Oscar was now so happily chewing his Christmas bone he didn't even get up to greet her, merely wagged his tail. When she returned to the dining room with the cake she put it down on the dresser and clapped her hands to get everyone's attention.

'Logan has kindly made us this gorgeous Christmas cake, which we'll be cutting up later – although it seems a shame to spoil it.' She held it up so everyone could see it. 'Just look at this!'

'That's amazing!' Ariane exclaimed. 'Clever you, Logan!'

'They say men make the best chefs,' Geoff quipped and was good-humouredly shouted down.

Everyone congratulated Logan, who looked a bit bashful, then Duncan took the cake back into the kitchen to be sliced up later, and made another tray of Christmas cocktails, while Saffy organised some games for the children in the lounge.

There was a lot of laughter as the children played Saffy's Pin the Tail on the Reindeer game. Some of the adults joined in too, and were in fits of giggles when Robbie pinned the tail to the reindeer's mouth. Then Saffy got out the balloon pump and blew up an assortment of different coloured balloons for the children to play with. Several got accidentally popped but there were plenty more to ensure that each child could take one home. This was followed by Pass the Parcel for the younger children and board games for the older ones. It was so nice to see the parents sitting chatting while the children played happily together, Saffy thought as she watched them.

'Come on, Saffy, play Twister with me and Daddy,' Chloe urged, tugging at Saffy's sleeve. 'I'll show you how to play it if you don't know.'

Saffy looked dubiously at the white mat with its big coloured circles spread out on the floor. It was one of her and Hannah's favourite games when they were children and from what she remembered they often got twisted in all sorts of positions. She wasn't sure her leather trousers were up to it. And Twister was one of those games that was often more fun to watch than to play. Not to mention that she was still a bit sore after this morning's plunge from the kitchen roof.

'I think it might be a bit too energetic for Saffy,' Logan said, the challenge evident in his voice. 'I'll play with you.'

Challenge accepted. Saffy stood up. 'Not at all, we used to play Twister a lot when we were kids and I was the champ.'

'Really?' Chloe sounded very impressed. 'Daddy's hopeless at it,' she confided.

'I am not!' Logan protested, pretending to be offended.

Saffy grinned. This sounded like it might be fun.

Robbie was the referee. One game had just ended so Chloe ran over and touched his arm to get his attention. 'We're next!' she said excitedly.

Robbie looked Saffy up and down. 'In those trousers?' he asked, raising an eyebrow questioningly.

'They're very stretchy,' she replied, hoping they were.

'Well, if you're sure.' It was obvious he wasn't, which made Saffy even more determined.

'I am.'

'Right then, take off your shoes everyone, then Logan, you get this side of the mat, Saffy that side and Chloe, you're in the middle. When I blow my whistle, I'll start the spinner and the game begins. Right?'

'Right,' Saffy and Logan said in unison as they faced each other, one foot on the blue and one foot on the yellow circle. Chloe placed her feet on the two red middle circles.

Robbie blew the whistle then spun the spinner. 'Left foot yellow!'

And so it went on until Saffy and Logan ended up in a ridiculous position with Saffy bent over Chloe on all fours, like a crab, and Logan with one leg stretched out so far he wobbled and fell. Saffy won.

'You're right! You are the champion,' Chloe said. 'Can we have another game?

'I want to play,' a young lad said.

Logan wiped the back of his forehead with his hand. 'You can have my place. I need a drink.' He pointed his thumb at Saffy, who was beaming. 'See if you can beat the champ.'

Chapter Twenty

The party had gone much better than he'd expected, Logan thought, as he watched Chloe playing Twister with the lad and Saffy. Saffy looked so incredibly sexy in those black leather trousers that clung seductively to her – especially when she stretched out her legs like that. He couldn't tear his eyes away from her as she stood, legs open wide, trying to reach her next circle. An image of her bending over him, her sexy leather-trouser-enclothed crotch just centimetres from his eyes flashed across his mind. No wonder he needed a drink! Seriously, those trousers were so tight you'd have thought she'd been poured into them. He hoped they were stitched up securely.

There again…

'Gorgeous, isn't she?' Duncan sat down beside him. 'And one of the kindest people you'd ever meet. If I was into women she'd be the one I'd go for.'

'No boyfriend in the frame then?' Logan asked casually. Saffy had told him she had no intention of settling down and having a family but he presumed she had boyfriends.

'In between them at the moment. She's left a lot of broken hearts in her wake, has our Saff. She doesn't do serious. Married to her career.'

Like Jade.

Duncan turned to him. 'At least until someone comes along and makes her realise that there's more to life than work.' He got back up. 'Okay everyone, let's have a bit of dancing music, shall we?'

He'd been playing jolly Christmas songs but now switched to a more current playlist.

Everyone looked like they were having a good time. Geoff and Ariane were chatting, heads close together, with plenty of eye contact and laughter. Logan hoped this was the start of something special with them; they were both lovely, kind people but Ariane was rather shy and had taken some persuading to come to the party. It would be great to see them both together. Marta and Toni seemed to be hitting it off too. If Toni made another friend she might finally forgive him for Sonja leaving.

Saffy sat down by him. 'I know Hannah usually ends the party about now but everyone is having such a good time, I was wondering if I should rustle up a buffet. There's a couple of loaves in the freezer – they won't take long to defrost – and I'm sure I could find something to put on them. What do you think?'

'Good idea, do you want me to help you?' he offered.

'If you don't mind. We can leave Duncan and Robbie to entertain everyone, they're enjoying themselves.'

Logan grinned. 'They do tend to take over a bit, don't they?'

They slipped off to the kitchen, and soon Saffy had located and defrosted two loaves, which Logan set to buttering while she sliced some cheese and ham.

'Need any help?' Marta sauntered in and placed her arm loosely around Logan's waist. He gently eased himself away on the pretext of getting some more butter out of the fridge.

'We're all covered in here, thanks, but it would be really helpful if you carried the plates through into the dining room. I've pushed a couple of tables against the back wall ready.' He handed her a plate of ham sandwiches. 'Thanks.'

Marta looked disappointed but walked off with the plate.

'She's got the hots for you, hasn't she?' Saffy said. 'Don't mind me if you want to go and hang out with her.'

'No. She's nice enough and Chloe adores her but there's no spark there, not for me anyway.' He took a beaker out of the cupboard and turned on the tap. 'The trouble is I kissed her at the last Christmas party, nothing heavy, a Merry Christmas kiss under the mistletoe, but she took it for more than that and has been virtually throwing herself at me ever since.'

'And Toni? Did you kiss her under the mistletoe too?'

'No, I made the mistake of going out with her friend, Sonja, who wanted more of a permanent relationship than I did. She was pretty cut up when I ended it and she moved out of the village. Toni has never forgiven me for driving her best friend away.'

'Been there, got the T-shirt, guys don't take rejection any easier than women.' She thought of an ex who had hounded her for weeks, begging her to go back out with him.

'You've no one serious in your life then?' Logan asked.

'No.' *Not since Joe.* Joe, who told her he had loved her then spent the whole six months of their relationship trying to change her before dumping her when he found out she couldn't have children. 'And that's the way I want it to stay. How about you? Have you ever thought of getting married again?'

'I've never been married. Jade and I lived together.' He picked up a glass and filled it with water. 'And no. I have no intention of getting married. Chloe is my number one priority and I'm not bringing another woman into her life for her to be abandoned again.'

She wanted to ask him what had gone wrong, why Jade had walked out and left Chloe behind, but it wasn't really the topic for a jolly Christmas Day.

'My mum was the same, she refused to even date until I was in my teens. She's remarried again now though. She lives in France.' Saffy opened the fridge and took out a large pork pie.

'Hannah told me your father walked out when you were only four. That must have been tough,' Logan said sympathetically.

'It wasn't easy. Mum held down three jobs just to keep it all together and was constantly apologising for not spending enough time with us. Hannah was like a substitute mum to me.'

'And that's why you've given up your Christmas to help her?'

'Well to be honest, Hannah guilt-tripped me, but I'm so glad I did. Everyone seems to be having such a good time. Christmas can be lonely when you're a single parent.'

'It sure can.'

The tone of his voice made her turn and look at him. The blue eyes were clouded now, as if he too was remembering. *It must be tough for him to bring up Chloe alone*, Saffy thought. *Tough for every parent here. And Hannah, with her big heart, brought them all together on Christmas Day. That was the true Christmas spirit. Maybe some of the parents here have made lifelong friends. Maybe there has even been a wedding.*

She asked Logan if there had been but he shook his head. 'I think Hannah would love that to happen though. You know your sister, she's a romantic. Shall I cut up the cake?'

'Go ahead, you made it.' Saffy was now slicing cheese into cubes and popping it onto cocktail sticks.

Logan opened the top cupboard by the sink and took out the large cake knife.

'How did you know the knife lived there?' Saffy asked. 'I was looking for it for ages earlier.'

'I have been here quite a few times, you know,' he joked. 'And your sister is pretty safety conscious, she always keeps knives and anything dangerous away from the twins.' He deftly sliced the cake in half, then half again, and again, until he had lots of small slices. One chunk he left uncut. 'That's for Hannah and Lee,' he said, taking a plastic food container out of the cupboard and putting the cake in it. 'I'm guessing you haven't been down here for a while?'

'Not since the twins' christening.' She shrugged. 'You know how it is when you're working.' She opened a large tin of pineapple chunks and started to place each chunk on top of the cheese on the cocktail sticks.

Yes he did, he was busy with his career himself and hadn't seen his own parents, who lived in Scotland, for ages. Work and looking after Chloe seemed to take up all his time. Saffy didn't have a child though so it seemed a shame she couldn't spare the odd weekend to come down to Cornwall and visit her sister and nephew and niece.

❄

After the buffet, Saffy sat the children around the table and got out the craft things she'd bought, hoping it would wind them all down before they went home. The children loved making the Santa hands, which involved drawing around their hands then covering the fingers with cotton buds, and colouring in the hand to make a Santa's face, before adding a red tissue hat with a cotton ball pompom. Then they made pompom Christmas trees too and some sparkly masks, which they all immediately put on. Several parents joined in, and some of the masks were very flamboyant, with feathers, sequins and glitter all over them. Laughter filled the room.

'Well done, babe, you've totally nailed the Lonely Hearts Christmas Party,' Robbie told her. 'Your sister will be proud of you.'

'Well, that'll be a first,' Saffy replied. 'But I couldn't have done it without yours and Duncan's help.' She was so pleased that the party was a success, though.

It was gone eight before the guests started to leave, the children clutching the things they'd made and their Santa gifts, all hugging Saffy, Duncan and Robbie goodbye, thanking them and saying what a wonderful time they'd had.

Logan was the last to go. He helped tidy up a bit and then gathered together his things.

'It's been fantastic,' he told them. 'Thank you all for saving Christmas for us.' He held out his hand and shook Robbie's and Duncan's hands in turn. Then he leaned forward and kissed Saffy lightly on the cheek. 'Look, if you want to pop over for a nightcap later, you're all welcome. Chloe is exhausted and will be fast asleep in half an hour.'

Robbie and Duncan exchanged glances. 'Thanks, but we're travelling home really early in the morning and would like to spend the rest of the evening together,' Robbie said. 'But I'm sure Saffy will keep you company.'

'Meaning you two lovebirds want me out of the way,' Saffy retorted. But what the hell, she wasn't ready for Christmas to end yet and she didn't fancy playing gooseberry here. 'I'll come over in a couple of hours, when I've tidied up.'

'Can't you come with us now?' Chloe asked. 'I want you to see me in my polar bear onesie.'

Saffy shot a questioning look at Logan. He nodded. 'That's fine by me, unless you prefer to wait a while.'

'Please, Saffy,' Chloe begged.

'We'll help you finish the last of the tidying up, it won't take long,' Duncan offered. The way he and Robbie were looking at her they might as well have been begging too.

'Okay, give me half an hour and I'll be over,' she said.

Chapter Twenty-One

Chloe was bathed and ready for bed in her polar bear onesie when Saffy arrived. 'Look, Saffy, see my tail.' She turned around and wriggled her bottom.

'That's really cute,' Saffy told her. 'And I think that tail is a little bit bigger than mine.'

'Why don't you go and put yours on too, then we can be twins,' Chloe suggested.

'I don't think Saffy wants to go all the way back just to pick up her onesie, poppet,' Logan said, a twinkle in his eye. 'Would you like a drink, Saffy? Wine? Coffee with a drop of brandy?'

'Oh, yes please – coffee with brandy,' she replied as she tugged off her boots.

'Go and make yourself comfortable in the lounge. I've got a fire burning,' Logan told her.

'I've got a present for you.' Chloe held out her hand to reveal the Mother Christmas figure from the Christmas cake. 'I saved it for you because you're our Mother Christmas.'

Saffy was really touched. 'Thank you. I'll keep this to remind me of you and the fantastic party we all had.' She popped the red and white figure into her handbag.

Chloe slipped her little hand into Saffy's. 'Will you read me a story? I've got a new book about a polar bear who gets lost.'

'That sounds fun. Does he find his way home again?' Saffy asked as she walked into the lounge with the little girl.

'You'll have to read it and find out.' Chloe ran over to the coffee table and picked up a picture book with a polar bear on the front cover then brought it over to Saffy, who was now sitting on the sofa in front of the blazing fire.

'Get yourself comfy then,' she said and Chloe snuggled up close to her.

As Saffy read out the story, Chloe joined in eagerly with the phrase 'poor little polar bear far away from home', pointing at the pictures.

'I'm glad he got home safely,' Saffy said, closing the book just as Logan came in with two mugs of coffee.

'Can you read it again? Please?' Chloe begged.

'No, it's your bedtime now, Chloe. And Saffy's had a busy day organising a party for us all so let her relax for a while now.' He handed her a mug of coffee, put the other one down on the table and scooped Chloe up into his arms. 'Say goodnight to Saffy.'

'Night, Saffy!' Chloe blew her a kiss.

'Night. Sleep tight.' Saffy blew a kiss back.

She cradled the mug in her hands and settled back into the deep cushions of the sofa as Logan carried Chloe upstairs. It was so cosy and comfortable in here.

She thought back over the day as she watched the flames flickering behind the fireguard. It had all turned out far better than she'd expected. Everyone seemed to enjoy themselves, Robbie and Duncan were back together – and she'd had a good time too.

And she had shared a kiss under the mistletoe with Logan. He was a good kisser, and she reckoned he'd be a brilliant lover… she pushed the enticing thought of making love to Logan out of her mind. There was no way she'd go there, even if he wanted to. It would be far too complicated. And complications were something she definitely didn't want.

She took a sip of her warm drink, savouring the bite of the brandy. Now she could finally relax. Tomorrow morning she could maybe take Oscar for a walk along the harbour and beach. Then tomorrow afternoon Hannah would be back home, she could catch up with her sister and family then return home on Friday to her normal life. Saturday there was Robbie and Duncan's engagement party to go to, then their New Year's Eve party. And she'd got some potential partners to talk to Ajay about; if she showed him how much she'd enjoyed sourcing creatives he might give her the promotion. It was all good.

She'd miss Logan though. Very much.

'You look very content.'

Logan's voice startled her. She'd been so engrossed in her thoughts that she hadn't heard him come back into the room.

'I was thinking that today went well, didn't it? Everyone seemed to have a good time.'

'It was great, you did Hannah proud.' Logan picked up his mug and sat down next to her. 'Were you that worried about it? You seemed at ease with everyone and you played a great game of Twister. Chloe was impressed.'

She glanced at him. 'We used to play Twister a lot when I was young. Mind you, I was a lot more athletic then.'

Twinkling blue eyes looked into hers. 'You didn't do too badly – especially in those trousers. I thought you were going to split them a couple of times!'

'Me too,' she admitted. 'I wasn't sure what to wear, parent parties aren't usually my thing. These seemed a sensible choice at the time.'

'They were a great choice,' he said with a smile. 'I think people will be talking about this Christmas party for a while. Duncan and Robbie's engagement was an added bonus too.'

'I know, I'm so pleased they've patched things up.' She took another sip of her coffee, feeling the heavy dose of brandy relax her. 'Did you see how pally Geoff and Ariane were getting? I reckon we've got a budding romance there. Hannah will be pleased, she's such a romantic.'

'You must be too or you wouldn't have tried so hard to get Robbie and Duncan back together.'

She thought about it. 'I like to see people happy together and hate them to break up when they are both so obviously in love, but I wouldn't call myself a romantic. I don't think a relationship with someone is the be all and end all to a happy life. I think you can be perfectly happy on your own. There are other things that are important too; a career, travelling, friends.'

Logan nodded. 'Well, you've made a lot of people happy today, Saffy, including Chloe. As Chloe said, you were our Mother Christmas. Thank you.'

'You're welcome.' She really needed to drag her eyes away from his. She felt as if she was drowning in the blueness of them.

He leaned forward slowly and kissed her on the cheek, his eyes still looking into hers, mere centimetres away. Then his lips brushed, feather-light, over her skin as they moved slowly to her lips, resting tantalisingly on them in a delicate peck. He withdrew, his eyes still holding hers, as if to gauge her reaction, and she wound her arm around his neck, drawing him closer and then their lips locked as they kissed: deeper, longer, hungrier, as if they were savouring each other's very soul.

Suddenly Saffy felt an uncomfortable wet patch on her thigh. Damn! She'd spilt her coffee. She looked at the wet stain on her leather trousers in dismay then jumped up to check that it hadn't spilt onto the sofa too. Luckily it hadn't.

'Let me get you a cloth.' He took her mug out of her hand, put it down on the coffee table and went into the kitchen.

Why the hell did she have to be so clumsy? Now their special moment was ruined.

A good job too, she told herself, because where would they have gone from there? Hot as Logan was, there was no way she would have jumped into bed with him, not when his little girl was sleeping upstairs. Maybe he wouldn't have either, but things would definitely have been awkward if they'd gone any further.

Logan came in with two cloths, one damp and one dry. He handed them both to her. Feeling really self-conscious, she dabbed at the wet patch with the damp cloth then tried to blot it dry with the other one. She could feel Logan's gaze on her as she did so.

'If it stains, try shaving foam. I used that to get a coffee stain out of my leather jacket,' Logan told her. 'You need to wipe it all off afterwards, of course, but it's really effective.'

'Thanks. I'll take these cloths back into the kitchen.'

'It's fine, just put them on the coffee table.' Logan reached for the remote. 'Shall we see what's on the TV?' he said, switching it on. Then he sat down beside her and placed his arm casually around her shoulder.

Okay, he was probably regretting the kiss and wanted to get things back on to a casual footing. Which was fine by her, she didn't want to complicate things with a neighbour – and friend – of Hannah and Lee's. In fact, she had better get going in a few minutes; it had been a long day and she was pretty exhausted.

Which is probably why she ended up falling asleep with her head on Logan's shoulder.

When she awoke the room was in darkness, the fire glowing and Logan was snoring softly beside her. What time was it? She tried to look at her watch without waking him but he jerked awake and sat up.

'What time is it?'

'I was about to look.' She glanced at her watch. 'Gosh, it's past midnight.' She got to her feet. 'I'd better go,'

'Sorry.' He got to his feet too. 'I invite you around for company and end up falling asleep.' He reached for the table lamp and flicked the switch, the blast of light illuminating his still-sleepy face and making him look vulnerable. Her heart skipped a beat. This guy oozed sex appeal.

'We both fell asleep. I'm not sure if it was the drink or exhaustion. Probably both.' She grabbed her bag off the floor by the sofa.

'I'll get your coat.'

She followed him out into the hall, pulled on her boots, then slipped her arms into the coat he held out for her. 'Thank you for a lovely evening.'

He wrapped his arm around her neck and gently pulled her towards him, touching her lips in a sweet caress of a kiss. Wow! 'Thank you for a lovely day.' Then he slowly released her. 'Safe journey back on Friday.'

'Thank you.'

So this was it. This was goodbye.

He stood in the doorway as she made her way across the snow-covered street. She turned as she reached Liwus Helyk and saw that he was still standing there, watching her. He waved. She waved back. Then she opened the door and went inside.

Chapter Twenty-Two

The mixture of alcohol and exhaustion had lulled Saffy into a deep sleep, punctuated occasionally by replays of Those Kisses with Logan, and a sleepy awareness that people were talking downstairs – Robbie and Duncan no doubt getting ready – but nothing pulled her out of the comfort of a deep sleep. It was gone nine when she finally woke, listening to the silence of the house for a while, before pulling on her dressing gown over her onesie – it was cold – and padding over the room to the window, to pull back the curtains and look out, gasping as she saw the thick curtain of snow fluttering down. It was as if someone in the sky had opened a giant box of fluffy snowflakes and poured them out onto the ground below. It must be at least six centimetres deep. She hoped the guys had got home safely.

She went downstairs and switched on the kettle for a much-needed coffee boost. She made the coffee and sat at the kitchen table drinking it. Today felt such an anti-climax after yesterday, when Robbie and Duncan were here and the house was full of people, of laughter, of life.

Yesterday, when she and Logan had kissed. Three times. And fallen asleep on each other's shoulders as if it was the most natural thing in the world to cuddle up together on the sofa in front of the fire together. As if they were completely comfortable with each other.

And Friday she was going home and would never see him again.

There was still today. Hannah wasn't due home until this afternoon and Chloe was going away with her mother, so that would give her and Logan a chance to spend a little time alone. Should she invite him over?

He hadn't suggested meeting up, though, and he knew she was home alone. Maybe he regretted those kisses yesterday and didn't want to spend any more time with her.

Suddenly her phone buzzed. It was Hannah on a WhatsApp call. Saffy frowned. She should be on the flight now.

'Hannah. Is everything okay? The twins?'

'They're fine, fit to travel. But the flight's been cancelled because of the snow in the UK.'

'Oh no! Is it that bad?'

'There's no flights to Bristol at all today. The rep said if the snow eases we might be able to fly early in the morning.'

She could hear the desperation in Hannah's voice. This holiday hadn't been the restful break she and Lee had hoped for. 'I'm so sorry, Hannah. You must be longing to get back home again.'

'I am. How bad is it over there, Saffy? Are you all snowed in?'

Saffy walked over to the window and looked out into the back yard. Snow was piled up high against the fence and was still coming down.

'It's pretty deep. Robbie and Duncan left early this morning so should be home now, Duncan was driving an SUV so I'm sure they'll be okay. I'll message them in a minute to check they arrived safely.'

'I'm so sorry, Saffy. You're down there all by yourself over Christmas when you should be out partying. I feel awful.'

'Well, don't. I had a great time yesterday and I've got some work to do so that'll keep me busy. I'm absolutely fine.'

Saffy felt deflated as she ended the call. She'd been looking forward to spending a couple of days with Hannah, Lee and the twins. Instead, she was stuck here all day on her own.

Snap out of it, she told herself. *Get some breakfast and a shower then get some work done.*

❄

'I've told you, Jade, there's no way you're taking Chloe up to Bristol in this. It's madness. There's an amber weather warning and people have been advised not to travel.'

There was a pause the other end of the phone. 'I guess you're right. I'm just going to have to sit in this hotel room until the weather clears.' Jade sounded annoyed and he could imagine her pacing up and down. She liked to fill every minute of the day so would hate being in a hotel by herself. He had to admit though that he was relieved she wasn't taking Chloe today. He hated to think of his little girl being so far away from him.

'If the snow clears I'll come for her tomorrow then.'

He hesitated and Jade pounced. 'Logan, she's my daughter too and I want to spend some time with her.'

'Yes, okay, but only if the snow has cleared. And you phone me to check before you start out.' He had to think of Chloe in all this. She'd been looking forward to going with her mum and seeing her grandparents.

As if on cue, Chloe came down the stairs. 'Was that Mummy?' she asked. 'Will she be here soon?'

Logan scooped her up and gave her a 'good morning' hug. 'It's been snowing again, really heavily, so Mummy can't come today,' he said, leading her into the lounge and over to the big bay window so she could see out. 'If the snow clears a bit she'll come tomorrow. Sorry, poppet.'

Chloe stared out of the window, eyes wide with excitement. 'Can we build a snowman?' she asked. 'Mummy can see it when she comes tomorrow.'

'Sure, but let's have breakfast first,' Logan told her.

Chloe ran on ahead into the kitchen. 'Can I have chocopops?'

❄

Saffy read Robbie's message telling her that they'd only just got home, and the roads were really bad because of the snow. *It's a good job we arranged for the dinner party to start at seven,* he wrote. She wished she was going to Robbie and Duncan's party, instead of being stuck here alone. She hoped Hannah and Lee could get a flight back tomorrow or she wouldn't get a chance to see them at all.

She went over to the window and looked out at the flurry of snow. Then she spotted Logan and Chloe building a snowman in their front garden. They were laughing as they rolled up a big ball for the body and a smaller ball for the head. They heaved the head onto the body then wrapped a purple and pink scarf around his neck (probably Chloe's) and put a black cap on his head (which must have been Logan's). It reminded her of the times she and Hannah had built a snowman when they were young. Sometimes, if she wasn't working, Mum would join in too. Those were the best times. Mum would bring out her button tin and they would choose buttons for the snowman's eyes and make his mouth with a curve of smaller buttons, then use a carrot for his nose. One day, she and Hannah had made a snowman family, putting a headscarf on the snowlady and borrowing one of Mum's aprons. Then they'd made some smaller snowchildren, one of them wearing Hannah's hat, and the other one wearing Saffy's. She'd loved that snowman family, had made up stories in her head about them and wished that she had a proper family too, with a mum and dad instead of just a mum who was always busy and tired. Did Chloe wish she had a family too? she wondered. Did she hope her mum and dad would get back together again?

She watched as a snowball whizzed through the air and hit Logan on the back. He spun around and laughed at Marta and her two children, all togged up in hats, scarves, wellies and thick coats, throwing snowballs. Marta shouted something to him and then scooped up another snowball and hurled it; this one hit Logan on the shoulder. He whispered to Chloe, then they both grabbed handfuls of snow, smoothed them into snowballs and threw them at Marta and Tom, Marta's eldest. Logan's hit her smack on her arm. Chloe's hastily formed snowball landed just in front of Tom.

Soon they were out in the street, having a mad snowball fight. A couple of other children and their parents came out of their houses and joined in too.

Saffy opened the door and stood watching the fun. It had been ages since she'd had a snowball fight; she wished the twins were here so she could join in. Oscar trotted to the door and poked his head out, barking as if he wanted to join in the fun too.

She burst out laughing as a snowball hurled through the air and splattered on top of Logan's head and snow trickled down his face. Logan heard her, wiped his face with his scarf and looked over.

'Come and join us!' he called, waving.

She hesitated.

'Please, Saffy. You can be on our side!' Chloe shouted.

'Give me a minute!' she shouted back, dashing inside. She'd need to borrow Hannah's wellies again, and her duffle coat. She went to get them both from the cubby hole, then her eyes rested on a carrier bag full of scarves and mittens. Her leather gloves would get ruined; perhaps she should borrow a pair of those. Grabbing a red and white knitted pair that were only slightly too big, she patted Oscar, telling him she'd be back soon, and went out, slipping the door key into the tiny pocket at the front of her jeans – she didn't want to get locked out again – and crossed the road to join in the fun.

Splat! A snowball hit Saffy in the face.

'Got you!' Tom chortled.

'And I'm going to get you right back!' she laughed, scooping up a handful of snow.

She caught Logan's eye and grinned. His eyes were sparkling, his face glowing, his hair and stubble speckled with snow. He grinned back.

❄

'Well, that was fun, but now I'd better go and get dry,' Saffy said.

Logan didn't want her to go. Not yet. Hannah and Lee would be back soon and that would be it, Saffy would go home and he'd never see her again. Why did that make him feel so desolate?

'Want to come back for some mulled wine, warm yourself up?' Logan asked. 'I've got some mince pies left too. And I can provide a warm house and a towel to dry your hair with.'

To his delight, Saffy nodded. 'That sounds great, much better than going back to an empty house, apart from Oscar, of course.'

Chloe slipped her hand in Saffy's. 'I wish you lived with Auntie Hannah,' she said. 'I don't want you to go back home. I'll miss you.'

I'll miss you too, Logan thought as he watched Saffy smile down at his daughter. Chloe was clearly taken with her, and she seemed fond of Chloe.

'You'll see me again when I come down and see Hannah and the twins,' Saffy told her.

'Pinky promise?' Chloe held out the little finger on her right hand.

Saffy glanced at Logan.

'That is, if it's okay with your dad.'

He nodded.

'Pinky promise.' Saffy linked her little finger with Chloe's and then they walked over to Logan's house hand in hand. Logan walked behind them, resisting the urge to take Saffy's other hand. He had to fight this growing attraction he had for Saffy; there was no future in a relationship with her and a casual fling wouldn't work, what with her being Hannah's sister. Assuming she was attracted to him too. He had a feeling she was, though. She'd seemed to enjoy those kisses they shared yesterday.

Back indoors, they all took off their coats and wellies and headed straight to the kitchen.

'It's so lovely and warm in here,' Saffy said, standing with her back against the radiator. Chloe stood beside her.

'It should be. The heating's on day and night at the moment,' Logan replied, crossing the kitchen to take a saucepan out of the cupboard. 'Are you cold at Liwus Helyk?' he asked. 'Isn't the heating working properly?'

'It is but I don't like to have it too high when there's just me there, I don't want to run a big bill up for Hannah and Lee.'

Her answer surprised Logan. Not many people were so considerate when they were staying at someone's house, especially when they were doing them a favour.

'Run and change into some dry clothes, Chloe, while I make you some hot chocolate,' Logan said. 'Your trousers are soaked and I don't want you catching cold.'

'I don't want to catch cold either or I won't be able to go to Nanny and Grandad's with Mummy tomorrow,' Chloe said. She ran out of the kitchen and they soon heard her racing up the stairs.

'She seems to be looking forward to seeing her mum,' Saffy observed. 'It's nice that you've both been able to keep a civil relationship for her. A lot of couples don't manage that.'

Logan poured the mulled wine into a saucepan on the stove and added some cinnamon, gently stirring it as he considered his answer. 'Civil is the right word. Jade walked out on us when Chloe was only eight months old – not that she bothered with her much before then. She said that being a mother had never been part of her life plan. She has probably seen Chloe four or five times a year ever since and has never had her overnight. That's why Chloe is so excited. She adores Jade's mum and loves the idea of having a sleepover. She's never had one before.'

He made Chloe's hot chocolate, placed it and the two cups of mulled wine on the tray along with a box of mince pies and carried them over to the table. He pulled out a chair. 'Do you want to sit down or are you more comfy standing by the radiator?'

'I'll sit down and let the radiator spread its heat.' She pulled out the chair next to him. 'So you've looked after Chloe since she was eight months old? Never even been away for a night?'

'Yes to looking after her, no to never having been away for a night. I've had the occasional night away but Annie next door has always looked after Chloe here, so that she's been in her own home.' He opened the box of mince pies. 'Help yourself.'

'Thanks.' She took one.

'Have you heard from Hannah today?' he asked. 'How are the twins? What time are they home?'

'She phoned me this morning. Their flight has been cancelled because of the snow over here. She said that the staff at the hotel have been very kind but they all can't wait to come home.' Saffy took a sip of her wine. 'The twins are eager to open their presents, of course. Hopefully they will be able to fly back tomorrow. I really want to spend a bit of time with them but I need to be home for the weekend.'

'I'm sorry, it must be lonely for you in that house by yourself. It's awkward being in someone else's house, isn't it? You don't have your own things around you.' He bit into a mince pie, chewing it before asking, 'Did your leather trousers stain?'

'No, they're fine, thank goodness.'

'I'm done!' Chloe came running in wearing a clean pair of leggings. She scrambled into the seat next to Saffy. 'Don't you want to change into dry clothes too, Saffy?'

'Yes I do,' Saffy told her. 'In fact as soon as I've drunk this I'm going to go home, feed Oscar, and have a nice long soak in the bath.'

'With bubbles?' Chloe asked. 'Bubbles are my favourite.'

'Definitely with bubbles,' Saffy agreed.

Logan let his mind linger for a moment on the image of Saffy naked in the bath surrounded by bubbles, then he brushed the image away.

'Fancy coming back later and watching a film with me? You can bring Oscar too. Or do you want a quiet night at home?'

She hesitated for a second, then nodded. 'Thank you, it'll be good to have some company. Shall I make it about eight?'

'That's too late. I want you to play some games with me,' Chloe protested. 'Can Saffy come for tea, please, Daddy?'

Logan looked at Saffy and raised an eyebrow questioningly.

'Sure. It'll save me cooking.'

'See you about five-thirty then.'

Chapter Twenty-Three

Saffy sank into the hot creamy bubbles and closed her eyes. Heaven. Her clothes had got wet during the snowball fight and she should have come home and got changed right away instead of going over to Logan's for mulled wine and mince pies. Chloe had really wanted her to go with them, though. Saffy sank lower into the bubbles so they touched her chin. *Stop blaming it on Chloe*, she told herself; the truth was that *she* had really wanted to come. She enjoyed Logan and Chloe's company. He was so relaxed and seemed to have such a special bond with his daughter. She envied that.

She cast her mind back to her own father. She'd adored him. He was a charming, funny man who always took a few minutes to play with her when he came in from work. How she looked forward to those minutes, listening for his key in the lock, running to greet him. She could still remember his strong arms lifting her up into the air, his deep-throated chuckle. She'd thought that he really loved her. Then one morning she'd got up to find her mum sitting at the table, red-eyed. It was Hannah who told her their dad had gone away to live with another woman. She'd kept hoping he would come back home but he never did. She'd been so excited the first time he'd come to take her and Hannah out for the day, foolishly thinking that he would realise he loved them all so much he didn't want to leave them, that he'd ask to come back home again. But the happy, fun-loving father had been replaced by a polite stranger, only half-listening to her and constantly checking his watch as if he couldn't wait to get away. He took them to McDonald's, asked them how they were but didn't listen to their answers and ignored Saffy's pleas to come and live with them again. The next time he took them out, months later, Saffy didn't beg him to come home. Soon the visits fizzled out. She hadn't heard from him for years.

For Chloe it seemed it was the other way around. Her mother was the one who hadn't wanted to know. She felt sorry for the little girl; it must be hard when she heard the other children talking about their mums or saw them holding their mums' hands around the shops, but she had her dad, and Logan doted on her. She remembered what Hannah had told her when she was young and was crying for her dad. 'Don't bother about him, Saffy, it doesn't matter if he doesn't love us. We have Mum. As long as Mum loves us we're okay.'

Years later she'd read in an article in a magazine that children could survive all sorts of knockbacks and hardships, as long as they knew that they were loved. She'd been lucky, she'd had Mum and Hannah who had both loved her. Gradually it had stopped hurting that her father hadn't. Later, when she was in her teens, Mum had met Jon and remarried and he had taken her into his heart, been the dad she'd never had.

She shivered, realising that the water had gone cool, and turned on the hot tap to warm it up. Mum and Jon had both moved to France a few years ago. It had all worked out in the end. She hoped it would with Logan and Chloe too. Logan, with his sun-kissed good looks, endearing grin and easy-going disposition, didn't seem to be short of admirers. Not that he was perfect; she'd already seen his bossy side and reckoned that he liked to be the one who steered the ship. Though it seemed Jade did too so maybe that's why they'd clashed. But Chloe was adorable. She hoped that one day the little girl would have a stepmum who showed her the love Jon had shown her and Hannah.

She swatted away the thought that she hoped one day she might have a little girl like Chloe. She'd accepted years ago that she would never have a family and was absolutely fine with that.

❄

'Saffy and Oscar are coming, Daddy!' Chloe shouted. She'd been looking out of the window, eagerly waiting for Saffy to come out of Liwus Helyk opposite. It concerned Logan how fond of Saffy Chloe had become in the past few days. Had it been wise of him to invite her over again tonight? He didn't want Chloe being upset when Saffy left on Friday. Still, it was done now, and Chloe would soon get used to life without Saffy again. As would he.

He'd miss her though, he had to admit that. She was like a ray of sunshine, so cheerful and upbeat, so ready to help, yet stubborn too. He remembered that incident on the roof when he'd been sure she was going to fall and break her neck. The strength of his fear had shocked him. As had the flood of passion when they had kissed last night. The desire to continue, to suggest that they go up to his bedroom, had been almost irresistible but there was no way he was letting Chloe walk in on him with a woman in his bed.

So what was he doing inviting her over again tonight?

'I'll answer it!' Chloe shouted as the bell rang and was out in the hall before he could call her back.

He heard Oscar bark, and Chloe squeal in delight then Saffy said, 'Hello, Chloe.'

'Come in! Do you want a coffee?' Logan called from the kitchen.

'Yes please. I've brought some Christmas pudding and cream for afters. We had some left over from the party.'

Logan watched through the open doorway as Saffy took off Hannah's duffle coat and wellingtons to reveal a lemon fluffy jumper and skin-tight jeans. She looked totally gorgeous. Then she took Chloe's outstretched hand and they both walked down the hall into the kitchen. Oscar followed, tail wagging happily.

'There you are.' Saffy let go of Chloe's hand, took half a Christmas pudding and a carton half full of cream out of the carrier bag she was holding and placed them on the table. 'We might as well use them up.'

'Thanks.' Logan made the coffee and handed a mug to Saffy. 'Shall we eat in the living room by the fire?' he suggested, reaching up on the shelf for a tray. 'I've got a lasagne in the oven, it'll be ready in few minutes.'

'Sounds good to me. Shall we carry on in, Chloe?' she asked, then called over her shoulder to Logan, 'Or do you need me to carry something?'

'You go ahead. I can manage here.'

When Logan walked into the lounge a few minutes later with three bowls of lasagne on a tray, Saffy and Chloe were sitting, feet up on the sofa, watching *Marvellous Mandy* – Chloe's latest favourite programme – and Oscar was stretched out in front of the fire. 'Tuck in,' he said, placing the tray down on the table.

'Yum, thanks. That smells tasty,' Saffy said as she reached for a bowl. She dipped her fork into it and chewed a mouthful. 'It's delicious.'

After the programme had finished they played a couple of board games then Logan said it was time for Chloe to go to bed.

'Will you read me a story please, Saffy?' Chloe asked.

Saffy was about to agree but Logan butted in. 'Let Saffy rest for a bit, Chloe. I'll read you a story.'

❄

'Will I be able to go with Mummy tomorrow, Daddy?' Saffy heard Chloe ask as she stepped out of the bathroom. The bedroom door was open and she could see Logan sitting on Chloe's bed, reading her a story.

'I think so. As long as it doesn't snow again overnight,' Logan replied. 'Mummy will phone in the morning to check.'

'Will you be sad here all on your own?' Chloe asked.

'Don't you worry about me, I've got lots of work to do.' Logan kissed her on the forehead. 'You make sure you have a good time with Mummy and Nanny and Grandad. I'll be fine.'

Not wanting to intrude on their moment together, Saffy crept down the stairs, her mind going back to the very few times she and Hannah had gone out with their father. As a child she had never wondered how her mother felt about that but now she wondered if it had hurt her to let them go with him when he had ditched them all for another woman.

Would Jade's next step be to introduce Chloe to a new man, if she had one? Would she ever want Chloe back? If so, how would Logan deal with that? She pushed away the thought; it wasn't her problem. She had only just met Logan and Chloe but they were occupying far too much space in her mind.

She went into the kitchen and filled up the kettle – she didn't think Logan would mind her making a coffee – then took two cups off the draining rack. The kettle had just come to the boil when she heard Logan behind her. 'Fancy something a bit stronger than that?' he asked. 'I've got some wine – or brandy to put in the coffee, if you prefer.'

'Brandy in the coffee sounds perfect,' she replied. 'Has Chloe gone off to sleep now?'

He crossed the room, opened a cupboard and took out a bottle of brandy, unscrewing the top before replying, 'No, she's reading. I think it'll take her a while to drop off. She's excited about seeing her mum and grandparents tomorrow.'

His face gave nothing away as he poured the brandy into the two mugs of coffee.

'It's not easy, is it?' she asked softly.

He raised his eyes to hers and she saw a glimpse of pain there. 'No, but I want Chloe to feel loved by both her father and her mother, and I'm willing to work with Jade for that to happen.' He made his way to the door. 'Fancy watching a film?' he asked, glancing over his shoulder at her. 'I'm guessing you'll want to see a romcom?'

'Then you're guessing wrong, I like thrillers. In fact, there's a new drama started on Netflix… do you have Netflix?'

'I do. And are you referring to *Code Black Spider*? I've been waiting for that series to start.'

'That's the one. It's the first episode tonight.'

She followed him into the lounge, where Oscar was still sprawled out in front of the fire. Logan sat down, in the same position as the previous night and Saffy sat beside him, tucked her legs under her, cupped her hands around her mug and said, 'I'm ready to go.'

It was gripping viewing. Saffy held her breath a few times and laughed aloud as Logan nearly jumped out of his skin at one particularly scary bit.

'You needn't mock, you were hiding your face behind the cushion,' he told her, playfully tossing his cushion at her.

She grinned. 'I know. It's a bit "edge of the seat" isn't it? Have they released any more in the series or do we have to wait until next week for the next episode?'

Logan picked up the remote and flicked through the programme guide. 'Nope, we have to wait. Anything else you fancy watching?'

Just then Logan's phone, which was lying on the coffee table, rang. He leaned forward and glanced at the screen. 'God, it's Jade. I'm going to have to answer it as it's probably about tomorrow. Sorry.'

'That's fine.'

He picked up the phone and swiped the screen to answer as he stood up and walked out of the room. 'Jade.'

She heard the murmur of voices from the kitchen and tried very hard not to eavesdrop. Then she had a WhatsApp from Hannah.

I can't get a flight until Friday, so sorry. We'll be home about two. I hope you can still stop to see us.

Damn, she wouldn't have long with them. She wanted to get back for Robbie and Duncan's party on Saturday. Still, she could come down another weekend.

I can stop overnight but I'll have to go back early Saturday morning. I'll come down and see you again, soon. I promise, she messaged back.

That's okay, I know you have things to do. So sorry to have left you on your own like this. See you on Friday. Can't wait to get home.

There then followed a bit of a text conversation about the twins, and how people had been messaging her to say what a good time they'd had at the party and how wonderful Saffy was – which really pleased Saffy – and other chit-chat. Hannah signed off just as Logan came back into the room. He looked drained.

'The snow's cleared enough for flights to resume but there's a backlog so Hannah won't be back until Friday,' Saffy told him. 'I'm guessing Jade's still picking up Chloe tomorrow as the roads are clearer now.'

Logan sat down and took a long swig of his drink. 'Yes and she's hiding something from me, I know she is. She's never taken Chloe overnight before; it's come completely out of the blue and she hasn't given me much warning.' He looked at Saffy, his eyes clouded. 'I don't trust her.'

'What do you mean? Do you think Jade won't bring Chloe back?' Saffy asked. She'd heard of cases where parents had split up and one of the parents had run off with the children. But that was usually when the parents were arguing over who would have custody of the child and Logan had said that Jade had never bothered to see much of Chloe.

Logan seemed to be considering her question for a moment, then he shook his head. 'No, it's not that. I mean, she walked out and left Chloe with me so I don't think she's going to suddenly decide she wants custody of her, but I wonder why it's suddenly so important she has Chloe overnight.' He drained his mug. 'I guess I'll find out soon enough.' He got up. 'I think I need something a bit stronger now. How about you?'

'Wine would be good. A rosé, if you have it. Actually, I could go and get some from Hannah's, we've loads left,' she said, suddenly feeling guilty that she seemed to be making a habit of drinking Logan's alcohol.

'I've got a fabulous French one. He returned a few minutes later with an opened bottle and two glasses – and yes, it was a very nice wine. Saffy savoured the rich liquid as it slid down her throat. After the brandy in the coffee she was starting to feel very light-headed, but in a nice way. 'What will you do with the whole day to yourself tomorrow? I bet it's not often you get a Chloe-free day and night,' she asked, in an attempt to show the positive side of the situation.

'No it isn't. When did you say Hannah is back?' He took a sip of his wine and turned his head so that their eyes met. Saffy thought that she had never seen such mesmerising eyes. It was as if time stood still as their gazes locked. Neither of them even blinked. She was sure he was holding his breath, as she was too. Finally, she released her breath and licked her lips.

'About two on Friday afternoon.'

'In that case, what are you doing tomorrow?'

Still their eyes were locked and as if in unison they were both moving their heads closer, closer until their noses were almost touching.

'I thought I'd take Oscar for a walk along the harbour and the beach, if dogs are allowed on the beach, that is. '

'They are in the winter.' Deep blue eyes held hers. 'Fancy company?'

'That sounds good,' she replied softly.

She wasn't sure who reached for whom but suddenly they were both kissing, hugging, caressing as if they never wanted to let each other go.

Chapter Twenty-Four

'Daddy!'

Logan and Saffy sprang apart as Chloe's voice drifted down the stairs. Saffy quickly rearranged her jumper as Logan stood up, tucked in his shirt and buckled his belt. 'Coming, poppet.' He stopped at the doorway to mouth 'sorry' then shot out of the room.

What was she thinking of, making out with Logan when his daughter lay sleeping upstairs? This could have been a really embarrassing situation. It was time she went home. Saffy picked up her bag, called Oscar to her, then went out into the hall, slipped on her coat and boots and fastened Oscar's lead to his collar. She stood at the bottom of the stairs wondering what to do. She could hear Logan talking to Chloe and didn't like to interrupt but it seemed rude to just go, as if she'd bolted and run. She paused, then shouted, 'I'm off now, bye, both of you!' and was out of the door before Logan could come down and change her mind. Not that he probably would. She was sure he was just as embarrassed as she was.

She trudged through the icy mishmash of snow covering the ground, over to Liwus Helyk. Back to an empty house again. Not that it usually bothered her; she lived alone and enjoyed her own company the odd nights she was in, but it was different in someone else's house. It was hard to settle. She longed for Hannah to come home, to chat to her and Lee, to cuddle the twins, then return home to her normal life. A life without Logan and Chloe. Without complications.

She would miss Logan, though. She felt so comfortable with him, as if she had known him for ages. Too comfortable. She slotted in with him and Chloe as if she was part of the family and that wasn't the way she wanted to feel. She was pretty sure Logan didn't either. He'd emphatically told her that he had no intention of introducing another woman into Chloe's life just for them to walk away, as Jade had done. She reckoned he'd be pretty annoyed that Chloe had almost caught them making out on the sofa.

'Never mind, I've got you to keep me company, haven't I, boy?' she said as she rubbed Oscar down. He licked her face affectionately then went over to his basket and started chewing one of his new squeaky toys.

Saffy poured herself a glass of wine then reached for the phone as it rang. It was Logan. 'Sorry about that,' he said, when she answered. 'Chloe had a bad dream.'

'That's fine. I understand. It was time I went, anyway.'

'Do you still want me to come for a walk with you and Oscar tomorrow?'

No, warned her mind but she ignored it. 'Sure. I guess I'm going to need Hannah's wellies and duffle coat again?' Honestly, the last few days she hadn't exactly looked the height of glamour.

He chuckled. 'Only for the walk. Then how about we go for lunch at a dog-friendly pub? You can come home and change into your posh coat and boots for that, if you want to.'

'Deal. Shall we meet about eleven?' she suggested. 'I've got a couple of things I need to do first thing.'

'Me too. Eleven's fine. I'll call for you.'

So much for keeping away from him and Chloe. Still, Chloe wouldn't be there, and it was better than spending all day on her own.

She showered and changed into her pjs, then settled down with her laptop to write up a proposal for the two creatives she'd met at the local shops the other day – the Christmas gift maker and a craftsman who made gorgeous jewellery from silver and natural gemstones – outlining their potential and what they would bring to buycreative.com. But for once she found it hard to concentrate. It seemed empty in Liwus Helyk, as if the house itself was missing Hannah, Lee and the twins. Pictures of them were everywhere, visual records of the love they all shared, the family days out they'd had. As Saffy looked at them she felt a stirring of longing for the cosy life her sister had. She shook off the feeling. It wasn't that cosy, was it? Not with the twins ill and not being able to come home for Christmas. And never being able to go out without a babysitter – like Logan and the other single parents she'd met on Christmas Day. No, family life wasn't all it was made up to be. She was free to live her life as she pleased; she didn't need a partner or a child.

Not that she had a choice about having a child. The consultant had been very clear about the fact that her remaining ovary was so scarred she was highly unlikely to ever conceive. Saffy had felt a momentary pang of regret then shoved it firmly to the back of her mind. She'd only been twenty-four and settling down with a family was the last thing on her mind. She was so grateful to be without the regular pain she had endured over the last decade that the possibility of not being able to have a baby if she decided she wanted one in the distant future didn't concern her. She'd thrown herself into her career, working hard and playing hard and was happy with the way her life was. Still was happy. She reached out for her phone as it buzzed to announce an incoming text. It was from Robbie.

How's it going, hun? You will be back for our engagement party, won't you?

She wouldn't miss it for the world. *I'm travelling back early Saturday morning so I'll deffo be there*, she replied.

She then messaged Meg to ask her if she was going to the engagement party.

You bet! was Meg's reply. By the time they'd exchanged a few texts about what they'd been up to over Christmas, with Saffy briefly mentioning how helpful Logan had been, and Meg wanting a detailed account of every encounter, which Saffy skimmed over knowing that Meg would instantly be matchmaking, it was gone eleven o'clock. Saffy put away the laptop, made herself a hot drink and went up to bed. She couldn't wait to go home now, to get back to her friends, her work, her life. The few days she'd spent in Cornwall had unsettled her and she didn't like the feeling.

❄

Checking Chloe was settled, as he always did, Logan stood watching his little daughter's chest rise and fall as she slept. She looked so peaceful and innocent that he always felt overwhelmed with love, no matter how difficult a day he'd had with her. And there had been plenty of difficult days when she was a toddler. But tomorrow night she wouldn't be here. She'd be miles away with Jade and Jade's parents. He wouldn't see her sleeping or be jolted awake by Chloe bounding onto his bed.

Why did Jade suddenly want to play a bigger part in Chloe's life? He knew he ought to be pleased, for Chloe's sake. She needed to know that her mum loved her. It was good for him to have a break too, some time for himself to catch up with work, or go on the occasional date and be himself, Logan, for a few hours. Sometimes he longed for adult company, especially adult female company; even his work was mainly home-based and his life could be pretty solitary. He should embrace this new development with Jade. Yet he felt uneasy. He didn't trust her. What if Jade had a new man in her life, someone she was serious about, and wanted to introduce Chloe to him? How would he feel about that? He knew Jade had had a few boyfriends since their split but Chloe had never met them. And to be honest, he didn't want her to; he didn't want her to ever call anyone else 'daddy'.

'Daddy!' Chloe murmured in her sleep.

Logan bent over and kissed her forehead. 'I'm here, poppet. I'll always be here.'

He waited until she settled again before he went into his own room, walking over to the window and looking out over the road to Liwus Helyk, where Saffy was sleeping in the room opposite to him.

He saw Saffy's shadow at the window opposite and wondered if she could see him. Then she waved and he knew she could. He waved back and watched as she drew the curtains. He imagined her undressing and climbing into bed. Did she wear that onesie to bed? he wondered with a smile. He imagined waking up beside her, her face being the first thing he saw when he opened his eyes, make-up free, her hair tousled. He imagined slowly unzipping that onesie, to reveal her naked body underneath…

He shook his head. Saffy was going home on Friday. Attracted as he was to her, there was no future in it. And even if she lived closer there would still be no future in it because Saffy had made it clear that she didn't want children. So there was no way she would be interested in a relationship with a man who had a child.

Tomorrow he would have a few hours' time out with Saffy, then it was back to his normal life, just him and Chloe.

That's the way it had always been and that was the way he wanted it to stay.

Chapter Twenty-Five

Saffy let Oscar off the lead and he bounded off along the snow-speckled beach. Here and there, patches of dark brown sand peeped through the white, a tantalising glimpse of better weather. In the middle of the beach was a lone snowman, his arms already melting – built by someone when the snow had first fallen, she thought, imagining a young family going for a stroll along the beach and stopping to scoop the snow up into balls, laughing as they formed the snowman's body, then his head. Beyond the beach the icy ocean was still, as if frozen, only the occasional white wave, stiff as whisked egg white, breaking the surface. 'It looks… spectacular,' she said in awe.

'You should see it when it's really frozen over,' Logan told her. 'That really is something.'

'It was summer last time I came down but I didn't have time to go to the beach,' Saffy said. 'I expect you and Chloe go a lot in the summer.'

'Every day after school. I surf a lot and I'm teaching Chloe too. She's great at body-boarding, rides the waves really well.'

'I can just imagine you both, clad in your wetsuits, boogie boards under your arm,' Saffy said, then wished she hadn't because the image that flashed across her mind of Logan in a very tight wetsuit was a little too enticing. 'Can you surf properly? You know, upright on the board? Riding over foamy, high waves?' she asked.

'Sure. You'll have to come down in the summer and we'll take you surfing with us,' he said.

'Maybe I will. I'd like to come down more often. It's a beautiful place, even if it does look more like a ghost town right now.' The wind blew her hair across her face and she swiped it away. 'Hannah adores living by the sea. She said she takes the twins to the beach every weekend. I can see why. It's so vast and awesome. I prefer it in the summer though,' she added.

'Me too, but whatever the weather there's something about the sea that makes everything slip into perspective.' Logan looked thoughtful. 'Whenever I feel bogged down with work, or life in general, I take a walk along the beach, gaze out at the ocean, and I always feel better.'

'Nautical therapy, that's what Hannah calls it,' Saffy said. 'But I guess you already know that.' It suddenly occurred to her that Logan probably knew a lot more about her sister, and her family, than she did.

Logan nodded. 'She's a kind woman, your sister. A lot of people in this village are really fond of her. She's got a heart of gold and is always willing to help.' He bent down to pick up a shell and hurled it into the ocean, where it disappeared without trace. Oscar ran over and barked at him, as if asking him to throw another one.

Saffy scooped up a shell too, studying the intricate pattern, running her thumb over the smooth surface before tossing it into the half-frozen sea. 'Whenever something awful happened on the news, you know like a train crash, Mum used to say that we should look for the helpers – there are always helpers. That's what Hannah is, a helper.'

'Your mum's a wise woman.' Logan shoved his hands in his jeans pockets and stared out at the sea. 'Sometimes I think that people who have tough lives turn out better than those that are given everything on a plate. Chloe's mum, Jade, was completely spoilt. Sharing or considering anyone else's point of view is completely alien to her. I don't want Chloe to grow up like that.'

'What about you? Do you have brothers and sisters? Are your parents still together?'

He nodded. 'A brother, Callum, two years older than me. My parents have been married thirty-five years, childhood sweethearts, they've retired to Scotland now. They've had their arguments, but they adore each other. That's what Chloe deserves, two parents that love each other. I should have been more careful.'

She frowned. 'It takes two to make a baby, but only one to cause a break-up,' she reminded him.

'I know. I love Chloe to bits and am so glad I've got her in my life, but she was the result of me and Jade getting drunk one night and forgetting to use our usual precautions. If I'd used a condom, as I normally did, it would never have happened. I knew me and Jade weren't forever, we were just dating casually. I owed Chloe more than that.'

'Mum always felt guilty about her marriage with Dad not working out, and him not wanting to bother with us. She was always trying to make up for it. But we didn't blame her. She wasn't responsible for how Dad acted. She loved us and took care of us the best she could, that's what mattered.' She turned to Logan and saw the pain in his eyes. 'All kids need is someone to love them, they can cope with anything else. And Chloe has you.'

Logan put his arm around her shoulder and hugged her to him. 'You're sweet-natured too, like your sister, only I reckon you're a bit tougher, not so much of a homebody.'

Saffy giggled. 'Hannah's the tough one. You cross her at your peril! Me, I walk away from conflict. I can't stand falling out with anyone so avoid arguments at all costs.'

'Is that why you're still single? Because you walk away when the going gets tough?' he asked. 'It's obviously not lack of male attention because you must get plenty of that.'

He was smiling but she sensed something in his tone. Did he think she was like Jade? She considered her answer. 'No, but I don't think relationships should be hard work, although of course there needs to be give and take. And I'm not into changing anyone. People are who they are and I accept them for that or leave them alone. I expect others to do the same for me.' She took a breath to calm herself as memories of how Joe had treated her came flooding back. 'It doesn't seem right to me that you're attracted to someone and then as soon as you get with them you spend the whole time trying to change them.'

He hugged her tighter. 'Are you talking about a former boyfriend?'

She nodded. 'I've seen other people in relationships act like it too.'

'It's not a bad philosophy,' he agreed. 'Now how about we have a walk along the harbour, it's only a few minutes away, then make our way to the pub? I'm ready for a drink and a snack. Unless you want to go home and change? Not that you need to, you look perfectly lovely as you are.'

She shrugged, feeling comfortable enough with him that she didn't care if she was wearing Hannah's yellow duffle coat and wellies. 'Lead the way, my tummy's rumbling,' she agreed, calling Oscar to her and slipping on his lead.

The harbour was a few minutes around the corner. It was small and in a sheltered position, with a few fishing boats moored along the ancient brick wall, and had a snow-splattered expanse of beach leading out onto the pavement then road. Beyond that a selection of now-closed shops lined the harbour front. Saffy imagined it in the summer, bustling with tourists, the shops open, plying their wares – seaside rock, candyfloss, nautical knick-knacks and souvenirs, mussels. 'What a shame it's all closed up,' she said wistfully.

'Not all.' Logan pointed to a little beach café, nestled in the corner, its red and white striped shutters up. The words 'Hot drinks' were scrawled on a sign beside it. 'Fancy a hot chocolate?'

Saffy almost clapped her gloved hands in delight. A hot chocolate was just what she needed. As she and Logan sat on a bench overlooking the harbour a few minutes later, sipping their hot drinks and watching the boats bobbing up and down on the almost frozen Atlantic she felt ridiculously happy. She was so glad she'd answered Hannah's plea for help or she would never have met Logan. What a shame she had to go home on Saturday. She pushed the thought from her mind. She wasn't going to think about that now, she was going to enjoy being in the moment. This time she was spending with Logan was like a slice out of real life, a magical time just for the two of them. She didn't want to go back to Liwus Helyk, didn't want to go back home. But she had to.

They arrived at the pub half hour or so later. As soon as they walked in, someone shouted Logan's name, and they turned around to see Marta, Toni, Ariane and Geoff, who looked very cosy together.

'Come and join us!' Geoff called, bringing two more chairs to add to their table. The afternoon passed in a whirl of chatter and laughter (although Toni made a point of never speaking directly to Logan) while the children played in the play area and Oscar, exhausted by the walk along the beach, slept by Saffy's feet.

'Well, I'll have to be going and get these two to bed,' Ariane said. 'We're not all child-free for the night,' she said, casting a meaningful glance at Logan.

'Now now, jealousy doesn't become you,' he teased.

'When's Hannah back?' asked Geoff.

'Tomorrow afternoon and I'm back home early on Saturday morning,' Saffy replied.

'Well, I hope you come down and see us all again soon,' Ariane said as she scooped up her coat and bag. 'See you around, Logan.'

'Time for me to go too.' Geoff called his son over. He nodded at Saffy. 'Have a safe trip home.'

'Are those two an item?' Logan asked Marta as Ariane and Geoff left together.

'If they aren't, they soon will be. They got very pally Christmas Day. Seems like they weren't the only ones,' she added pointedly.

'Hannah's flight home has been delayed and seeing as Saffy gave up her Christmas to organise our party it would be rude to leave her alone,' Logan replied.

Is that the only reason he asked me out today? Saffy wondered. Judging by the look on Marta's face she wasn't convinced but she turned away to speak to Toni without saying anything further.

Gradually the parents left, one by one, until there was only Saffy and Logan. They remained there for another hour or so, chatting, sipping their drinks, enjoying each other's company. Saffy wondered what the next step would be. Logan had asked her to spend the day with him, and she had. It was almost six now. He hadn't said anything about the evening. Did he want to spend that with her too? And did she want to spend it with him? Or would they both go to their separate homes and spend it alone?

She considered it as she sipped the last of her drink. Logan too had only centimetres of liquid in his glass. They couldn't drag this out for much longer.

Logan swigged back the remains of his drink and put his empty glass down on the table. 'Fancy coming back to mine for a bite to eat?'

he asked. 'We could actually sit and watch a grown-up film too, with Chloe out the way, while Oscar snoozes by the fire. I've still got some of his food and a bowl so he can have tea at mine too.'

'I'd love that, thank you,' she replied. Back at home she never minded spending an evening alone, she was surrounded by her own things and there was always plenty to do, but she felt restless at Liwus Helyk. The family pictures on the wall, box of toys in the lounge, brightly coloured plastic cups and plates in the kitchen cupboard, the family souvenirs and mementoes all reminded her that this wasn't her home. Not only that, it was a home she would never have. A family home, filled with the love and laughter of children.

Chapter Twenty-Six

It had been a perfect day, Saffy thought as she tucked into the spaghetti carbonara Logan had rustled up whilst she fed Oscar. Logan was such easy company, she'd never felt so comfortable with someone before, she really didn't want this day to end.

They'd put their meals on trays and taken them into the lounge, listening to some music as they ate, while Oscar, exhausted by his day out, lay snoring softly by the fire. Saffy loaded the dishwasher while Logan made another hot chocolate, laced with brandy, and brought out mince pies and cream. Then they snuggled up on the sofa and watched an old movie. It was a perfect end to a perfect day.

'I'm afraid I'm going to have to go,' Saffy said, stirring at last. She really didn't want to, she wanted to stay here, cuddled up to Logan. But it was late.

'Thank you for a lovely day.' Logan wrapped his arms around her and nuzzled her nose. 'You're pretty amazing, you know.'

'You're not bad yourself,' she replied, playfully tapping his nose then trailing her finger down, stroking his stubble before tracing the outline of his lips, his sharp intake of breath sending darts of desire through her body. He reached out his hand and stilled hers, easing the finger gently into his mouth, brilliant blue eyes locking with hers as he slowly and sensually sucked it. Then she gently eased her finger out of his mouth, wrapping her arm around his neck and leaned forward to kiss him on the lips. He pulled her to him, deepening the kiss, his hand on the back on her head, strong fingers running through her hair. His tongue was sensuously probing the inside of her mouth whilst his body was pressed against hers, his arousal evident, and she was filled with an almost uncontrollable desire to tear off his clothes, feel his bare skin beneath her fingers.

'Fancy spending the night here?' he asked huskily.

'I thought you'd never ask,' she whispered in his ear.

Then they were pulling each other's clothes off and his body was just as taut and perfect as she thought it would be, and they were walking up the stairs, stopping to kiss and caress on every step. Then Logan opened his bedroom door and they crossed the room as one, and lay on the bed, kissing, caressing, lost in the pleasure of each other.

❄

Saffy stirred and lay for a while, enjoying the warmth of Logan's body spooning hers. Yesterday had been fun and last night sensational. It was as if she'd been granted a few magical days out of her normal life and she didn't want them to end; she wanted to lie like this a little longer, wrapped in Logan's arms. Any moment now Logan would wake up and normal life would take over. Today Chloe was coming home. And so was Hannah, so this was the one and only night they would spend together. Tomorrow she had to go home, back to her life, her job. Say goodbye to Logan.

She pondered over the possibility of them keeping in touch, of her coming down once a month maybe to see Hannah and catching up with Logan again. But how could that work? Logan had made it clear his priority was Chloe – as it should be – and there was no way they could have any intimacy around her. This was a one-night-only event.

'Morning, sexy.' She felt the brush of Logan's stubble as he trailed kisses down her neck. For a moment she lay still, enjoying the sensation, then she lazily turned around.

'Morning.' She snuggled into his chest, feeling the fine hairs brush against her breasts.

'How did you sleep?' he murmured against her hair.

'Zonked out. How about you?'

'Same.' He kissed her forehead. 'It was quite a session.'

'Well, if you'd been more of a once-a-night man we could have finished it earlier,' she teased.

'Finish? I've only just started.' He pulled her closer to him. 'Fancy a replay?'

Did she?

'I don't mind if I do,' she replied. 'If you've got the energy, that is.'

He had.

❄

Afterwards, they lay wrapped in each other's arms, as if they were both savouring the moment. Then Logan leaned up on one elbow and kissed her on the forehead. 'I hope I'm not making a fool of myself here,' he said softly. 'I've never met anyone like you, Saffy. I think we've got something special and… I don't want to let it go. I'd like to keep seeing you. If you'd like that too.'

What exactly did he mean by that? Was he suggesting that they be an item, that she become his girlfriend? Or did he just want to keep in touch? Saffy looked up at him. 'I'd love to. I was thinking that I'd like to come down and see Hannah more often, maybe once a month,' she said casually. 'Perhaps we could meet up then?'

'That sounds good. We could go for a meal or watch a film? Annie next door would sit with Chloe so we could have an evening out.'

And then what? She'd go back to Hannah's while he went home alone? *Take it as it comes, Saffy, don't overthink it,* she told herself. She nodded. 'That sounds good to me.'

'Great, because I don't want you to walk out of my life.' He lowered himself down on her, kissing her on the lips. She wrapped her arms around his neck and pulled him closer.

Loud barks from downstairs made them pull apart. Damn, she'd forgotten all about Oscar. He'd been downstairs sleeping by the fire all night.

'I'll let him out,' Logan said, flinging back the duvet and reaching for his jeans. 'You stay there and wait for me.'

He returned a few minutes later and they resumed where they'd left off. When they were both finally ready to get up, Logan went down to make breakfast, leaving Saffy to shower in the very masculine en suite. As she pulled on the dark blue towelling dressing-gown that was hanging on the door she heard her phone ping. She went to answer it and saw a message from Hannah to say they'd landed and would be home in about an hour and half. She glanced at the clock on Logan's beside table. Gone twelve already. This week seemed to have sped by. She made her way down the stairs, pausing halfway as she heard Logan's voice on the phone.

'Hello, poppet, have you had a nice time?'

She peered over the stairs and saw Chloe's picture on his screen. She must have video-called him, because she was pretty sure Logan wouldn't have called Chloe until she had gone.

'It's been super. Mummy wants me to stay another night,' Chloe said. Then she waved. 'Hello, Saffy! Why are you wearing Daddy's dressing-gown? Did you get your clothes wet in the snow again?'

Shit! Chloe had seen her. Best to brazen it out. 'Hi, Chloe!' She waved, then moved away from the screen and mouthed 'Sorry' to Logan.

'Saffy spilt coffee over her dress, so I'm going to pop over and get her something else to wear from Hannah's,' Logan said.

'As if!' A dark-haired, very glamorous-looking woman peered over Chloe's shoulder. 'Well, seeing as you have company, I'm sure you'll be very grateful for me having Chloe for another night.'

Saffy heard Logan's sharp intake of breath but he managed to keep his voice controlled as he said, 'Chloe, you go and play, poppet, while I speak to Mummy. I'll see you later.'

'Okay, Daddy.' Chloe blew him a kiss. 'Bye, Daddy, bye, Saffy.' And she ran off leaving a very angry-looking Jade.

'So this is the Saffy Chloe's been talking about. It didn't take you long to move her in, did it? I bet she was in the door as soon as Chloe was out.'

'What I do is nothing to do with you, Jade, we split up years ago. But for the record, Saffy is not my girlfriend and is not moving in. Now I want Chloe back today as we arranged or I'll make sure you never have her overnight again. Do you understand?'

Not my girlfriend. Well, she guessed she wasn't, even though they had just arranged to keep in touch with each other. And she didn't want to move in, although he didn't have to be so emphatic about it, Saffy thought as she went back upstairs to get dressed, wishing she'd done so before she came down, then the situation wouldn't have been so awkward.

She was dressed and made-up when Logan came up the stairs, carrying two cups of coffee. 'Sorry about that.' He put the cups down on the bedside table and sat on the edge of the bed. Although he was trying to mask it, she could see that he was very agitated.

'I'm sorry for coming down in your dressing-gown, I didn't realise Chloe had FaceTimed you. Not having kids, I'm not too up to date with what they get up to nowadays. I had no idea six-year-olds used FaceTime.'

'I put it on her iPad so she could call me and talk to me if I was out. I told you Annie babysits now and again.' Logan sighed. 'I think things with Jade are going to get messy. She suddenly seems to want to play a bigger part in Chloe's life.'

'That's a good thing, isn't it?'

'I don't know.' He got up and walked over to Saffy, putting his arm around her. 'I hope none of that made you feel awkward.'

'It's fine. It's not as if I'm your girlfriend or anything.' She hadn't meant that to come out so brittle. What the hell was the matter with her?

'I didn't mean that how it sounded, I just didn't want to complicate things with Jade, and Chloe.' He kissed her on the cheek. 'Are we okay?'

The kiss melted the lump of annoyance. 'Yes, of course. But I have to go now. Hannah texted to say she landed about half an hour ago. She'll be home soon and I want to tidy up and be there to welcome her.'

'You'll come and see me before you leave?' he asked.

'As if I would go without saying goodbye.' She kissed him. 'But I want to spend some time with Hannah tonight, and also give you some time with Chloe.'

'Okay, I'll text you later,' he promised.

As Saffy walked down the path with Oscar, away from Logan's house, she wondered whether she'd made the right decision in agreeing to keep in touch, to come down and see him. Logan and Chloe came as a pair, and it was obvious that Chloe was already fond of her – what had Jade said? 'This is the Saffy Chloe has been on about.' Plus it seemed like things were getting complicated between Logan and his ex. Did she really want to get involved in all that, as much as she was attracted to Logan, and adored Chloe?

❄

Damn, Chloe couldn't have FaceTimed him at a worse time, Logan thought. He couldn't ignore the call, not when Chloe had been away for her first overnight stay. He'd thought he could answer quickly before Saffy came down, expecting her to get dressed first, not come down in his dressing-gown. Not that it should matter; Jade had had several partners during the years they'd been apart, but he could see by the look on her face that she didn't like it and had a horrible feeling that she was going to use this against him, that this sudden interest in Chloe wasn't a one-off.

Jade always had an agenda, and always acted out of self-interest. Whatever happened, he didn't want Chloe to be hurt. She'd got used to not having Jade in her life but he knew it bothered her. Chloe often said she wished he and Jade lived together, and that she had a little brother or sister. It's what all kids wanted, to be part of a loving family, for their parents to live together. He'd been lucky enough to have that and felt eternally guilty that he couldn't offer Chloe the same. He was willing to step back a little, to forget his own feelings, and allow Jade to play a bigger part in Chloe's life but any sign of her upsetting Chloe and he'd be reining her in. One night was enough for now; Chloe wasn't used to being away from home. He would always put his little girl's interests first and intended to make sure that Jade did the same.

He walked over to the window and watched as Saffy unlocked the door of Liwus Helyk and went inside with Oscar. They'd spent a fantastic day and night together, but Chloe phoning and Jade's attitude had suddenly made things awkward. As much as he liked Saffy, a relationship, however casual, was a complication he didn't need at the moment.

Chapter Twenty-Seven

Saffy had barely had time to walk Oscar, put the heating on, change her clothes, fill the kettle and get out some cups when she heard the front door open.

'Saffy! We're home!' Hannah shouted.

Oscar pricked up his ears and went bounding out into the hall, wagging his tail and barking with joy as he ran around Hannah and Lee.

'Well, someone's pleased to see us,' Lee chuckled. 'How are you, boy?'

'He's been no trouble at all,' Saffy said, rushing to help them inside, hugging Hannah, then Lee, before bending down and talking to the twins, who looked all shy and bashful. 'They've forgotten me!' she said to Hannah, feeling guilty that she hadn't kept up more contact with her sister.

'They'll soon remember you again. Now let's have a cuppa then you must tell me everything. Everyone's been messaging, full of praise about the party. They all had a fantastic time. And Robbie and Duncan were a big hit too, so pleased they're back together. Marta said they were showing everyone their engagement rings. How romantic.' Hannah unbuttoned Miles's jacket whilst Saffy unbuttoned Lily's. 'And she said that you spent the day with Logan yesterday – never underestimate the power of WhatsApp,' she explained, seeing the surprised look on

Saffy's face. 'Marta was dead jealous. She's been after Logan for ages but he's not interested in her.'

'I'll take the cases upstairs then sort out the twins while you two have a catch-up,' Lee said, pulling two of the cases along the hall. 'Just give me a few minutes.'

'You're a superstar.' Hannah blew him a kiss.

'Don't worry, there'll be payback,' he called as he hauled the cases up the stairs.

'There will be too,' Hannah told Saffy, her eyes twinkling.

They picked up a twin each, Hannah holding Miles and Saffy holding Lily, carried them into the kitchen and made coffee, sitting the twins at the table with milk and biscuits. Oscar had settled down now and was chewing his bone.

'I'm so glad the twins are okay. It must have been so awful for you,' Saffy said.

'It was. But it's over now and I'm really grateful that you took over and organised the party for me. Thank you so much.' She reached out and touched Saffy's hand. 'And for being there for me when I was so worried about the twins, your messages and calls meant so much to me.'

'It's fine. I was worried about them and felt so sorry for you. It must have been hard to be out there, with the twins so ill.'

Hannah looked over at her little son and daughter tucking into their milk and biscuits, crumbs over their faces and a mess on the table around them. 'It was. If anything had happened to them…'

Lee came in a few minutes later and took the twins off for a nap, leaving the sisters to chat.

'Right, now tell me about Logan,' Hannah said, giving her the 'I'm not letting you go until you tell me everything' look Saffy knew so well from her childhood.

'There's nothing to tell, really. His Christmas cake was delicious – we've saved you a slice, by the way – and he and Chloe have kept me company a little. She's a cutie, isn't she?'

'She is. Do you think Logan is a cutie too?'

'Well, er…' Saffy felt her cheeks grow hot. Damn, Hannah always had the knack of worming everything out of her. 'Yes, he's very nice.'

'*Nice?* A lot of women think he's really sexy. In fact a few of them were vying for his attention last Christmas,' Hannah said, teasing. 'Are you immune to his appeal?'

'Well, he is kinda sexy and he was really helpful with all the party stuff. And he rescued me when I was locked out – even though I'm sure I could have managed by myself,' she added, explaining what had happened as she was sure that Hannah's neighbour would tell her anyway.

'Oh gosh, you mean you fell off the roof? You could have been really hurt!' Hannah said, her hand to her mouth. 'Oh, Saffy. I'm so sorry, you've had an awful Christmas, haven't you?'

'Not at all, it's been good actually. I wasn't hurt, just a couple of bruises, and I enjoyed the party.' She paused as her phone buzzed, and glanced at the screen. It was a message from Logan. *Really enjoyed last night…* flashed across the screen, then disappeared. But not before Hannah had seen it.

'And what did you do last night?' she asked, a grin spreading across her face.

Saffy decided it was best to confess and, without going into too much detail, told Hannah what had been going on.

Hannah looked delighted. 'I was so hoping you two would get on. Logan's such a lovely man.'

'He is. We've decided to carry on seeing each other. I'm hoping to come down about once a month – if you don't mind putting me up? And maybe Logan and Chloe can come up to Birmingham too.'

'Of course we can put you up. It'll be lovely to see more of you,' Hannah said with a squeal of delight. 'I can't believe you actually stayed overnight. That's a first for Logan. He must really like you.'

'Jade had Chloe overnight so we spent the day together, then the evening and it just sort of happened,' Saffy replied.

Hannah's eyes widened. 'What? Jade had Chloe overnight?' She leaned forward, elbows resting on the table. 'Wind it back and tell me from the beginning.'

So Saffy explained, and about Chloe phoning while she was wearing Logan's dressing-gown. 'Jade wasn't very pleased.'

'Well, it's none of her business. She waltzed out and left Logan to bring up Chloe by himself and has hardly seen her since. Don't let her bother you. She's no right to be upset about anything Logan does. It's about time he had someone in his life.'

'He has seen other women since they split up,' Saffy reminded her, thinking of Toni's friend Sonja, and there must have been more.

'Yes, but never at the house. He's always kept them well out of Chloe's life. He must be really smitten with you to let you in.'

That made Saffy think. She liked Logan, and Chloe, but she knew she couldn't let whatever they'd got together become anything serious.

She didn't want to say goodbye either.

Just then one of the twins started crying. 'Back in a mo,' Hannah said as she got up from the table, leaving Saffy with her thoughts.

*

The rest of the day passed quickly, playing with the twins and catching up with Hannah and Lee. Saffy felt closer to her sister than she had for a long time and was determined not to leave it so long before she came down to visit again. She wanted the twins to get to know her, to be part of their lives. She might not be able to have children of her own, but she had a nephew and niece she could spoil.

Saffy had a quick message from Logan to say that Chloe was going to be home soon and asking her if she would have time to pop over later for an hour. 'I know she'd like to say goodbye to you. We both would.'

Should she? What would Hannah think? She hadn't seen her sister for months and it seemed wrong to desert her to go over and see Logan. Even though she was dying to see him again.

'Go on, I don't mind. Me and Lee have got a million and one things to do,' Hannah suddenly said.

'What?' Saffy asked, puzzled.

'I heard your message come through and by the look on your face, it's from Logan. I'm guessing he's invited you over and you want to go but don't want me to feel upset that you're not spending the whole evening with me.'

Saffy looked up at her sister's smiling face. 'How do you do that? I swear you were a witch in your last life.'

Hannah chuckled. 'I know you so well. Honestly, you pop and see Logan for a bit while we get the kids to bed, unpack etc. We've had a catch-up, and can have a drink together later – you will be back later, I presume?'

'Of course I will,' she promised.

❄

'Daddy!' Chloe threw herself into Logan's arms. 'I've missed you.'

'I've missed you too, poppet.' Logan scooped his daughter up so her face was level with his and they rubbed noses, then he kissed her on the cheek. 'Have you had a nice time?'

'The bestest time ever. I slept in the bed Mummy slept in when she was little like me. And I met my aunties and my cousins.' She held up four fingers. 'I have that many cousins.'

It was a bit of a family gathering, then. Butterflies flittered uneasily in the pit of Logan's stomach. What was Jade up to?

'And I've got loads and loads of presents. Mummy's saved some at Nanny and Grandad's house so I have some toys to play with next time I go. Mummy's going to take me again in a couple of weeks.'

Logan looked over Chloe's head to Jade, standing behind her. Jade's green eyes met his and he saw the determination there. Okay. He needed to address this. He kissed Chloe on the forehead then gently put her down. 'Why don't you take your new toys into the lounge and you can show me them in a minute? I need to talk to Mummy first.'

'Okay.' Chloe scooped up the big bag Jade had just put down on the floor. 'Will you come and say goodbye to me, Mummy, before you go?'

'Of course I will,' Jade replied. 'Remember what I promised you. You're going to see a lot more of me from now on.'

Logan fought down the anger surging inside him. Did Jade really think she could call the shots and just waltz back into Chloe's life as if nothing had happened?

'We need to talk. Come into the kitchen,' he said firmly, walking on ahead and leaving Jade to follow him. She did.

He closed the door, then crossed his arms and leaned back against the worktop. 'What are you playing at?' he demanded.

'I'm not playing at anything. I want to see more of Chloe. I want to build a relationship with her,' Jade said, folding her arms too and meeting his stare with a determined one of her own. This was how it had always been with them, he remembered. Jade decided she was going to do something and that was it. She did it.

'You've never wanted to before,' he reminded her.

'I know.' Her voice softened. 'I was wrong to walk away from her. I realise that now. But I want to make it up to her. I want to see more of her, my family want to see more of her. She's my daughter too,' she added.

'You didn't care about her being your daughter when she was up all night teething, ill for weeks with croup, when she had to stay in hospital overnight with concussion after falling off her bike.' He could have cited a long list of incidents that Jade had been absent for. 'Where were you then?'

She looked a bit shamefaced. 'That was then, this is now. I want to be here for her from now on. I *intend* to be here for her from now on. And if you fight me over this I'll go to the courts.'

'Chloe lives with me. I decide when you see her, and if you take her away overnight. I'm her legal guardian,' Logan reminded her.

'Legal? So that was decided by the court, was it? When did this happen, as I wasn't informed?'

Logan felt a wave of nausea. That was one thing his mother had advised him to do when Jade left but he hadn't seen the need. Jade had made it quite clear she didn't want custody of Chloe.

'She's been living with me for her whole life. I've been her sole guardian since she was less than one year old,' he retorted.

'Yes but I have legal rights too, as her mother. I have the right to see her when I want to and if you don't let me I'll go for custody of her.'

Go for custody. The words were like a knife slicing his heart. Was Jade really going to try to take Chloe off him?

'You gave up any rights to Chloe when you walked out on her. I'm happy for you to see her. I've never stopped you. But she's in my care and I'll decide what's best for her, so you run everything by me first before making promises to Chloe. Do you understand?'

He tried to keep his voice low, although he was shaking with anger. How dare Jade threaten to take Chloe away?

'You're always the perfect one, aren't you? So confident in how right you are, that you're the better person, that you know everything.' She put her hands on her hips and tilted her chin. 'I know I messed up, Logan, but that doesn't change the fact that Chloe is my daughter. I love her too. And I intend to keep seeing her. If you think I'm going to let your girlfriend take my place and become Chloe's mum then you're very much mistaken.'

'Saffy is not my girlfriend.'

'Really? Just a one-night stand then? Charming.'

He wasn't going to let her turn this into an argument, not with Chloe here. Logan clenched his fists as Jade turned and walked out of the kitchen.

'I'm going now, Chloe. I'll see you soon, darling. Do you have a goodbye kiss for me?'

'Bye, Mummy.'

Logan stood in the doorway of the kitchen, watching as Jade and Chloe hugged, panic stabbing his heart as he saw the delight on his daughter's face as her mother hugged her.

Jade couldn't take Chloe from him, could she?

Chapter Twenty-Eight

As soon as Logan opened the door, Saffy could see by his dark eyes and the frown etched across his forehead that he was troubled over something.

'Is Chloe back?' she asked, remembering the conversation that morning when Jade had demanded to keep Chloe for another night.

A patter of feet along the hall as Chloe rushed to greet her answered the question before Logan could.

'Saffy! Come and see all the presents my mummy and nanny and grandad and aunties bought me!' she said, grabbing Saffy's hand and pulling her along the hall. 'I've got lots more at their house too. And Mummy said she's going to buy a house by Nanny and Grandad, so I can see them more often.'

'Hey, watch you don't pull my arm off,' Saffy teased, seeing the shock on Logan's face at Chloe's last remark. She shot him a 'speak to you in a minute' look as she followed Chloe.

Judging by the pile of toys Chloe showed her, Jade and her family had certainly gone out of their way to make the little girl happy. Is that why Logan looked so tense? She spent a little time ooohing and aaahing over the gifts Chloe showed her, then excused herself saying she needed a drink.

Logan was in the kitchen drinking what looked like Scotch.

'That bad, eh?' she asked sympathetically.

'I'm only having the one, don't worry. I'd never be drunk in front of Chloe. But yeah, it was pretty bad.' He picked up the bottle. 'Want one?'

'A small one, with a dash of orange juice if you have it.'

She waited until he'd fixed her drink and handed it to her before asking, 'What happened?'

'Jade's decided that she wants to play a bigger part in Chloe's life and says if I don't let her she's going for custody.'

He looked so wretched that Saffy's heart went out to him and she instinctively wrapped her arms around him in a hug, then stepped away in case Chloe came in. 'Look, Chloe hardly knows Jade, does she? The courts aren't going to take custody away from you and give it to her.'

'That's just it. I never went for legal custody, I didn't see the need.' His eyes were clouded. 'Jade made it clear that she didn't want to take care of Chloe and I couldn't see her changing her mind over that.'

'Even so, Jade walked out and you've been Chloe's sole carer for almost all of her life,' Saffy pointed out. 'I'm sure there's no way the courts will uproot her and send her to live with her mother, who is practically a stranger to her. That is if Jade is serious about going for custody. Do you think she is?'

He took a slow sip of the amber liquid then shrugged. 'I've no idea, to be honest. Jade can be pretty stubborn and she seems determined to see more of Chloe.' His gaze met hers. 'She said there's no way she's going to let "my girlfriend" replace her and become Chloe's new mum.'

Ouch. So this was her fault for walking in when Chloe video-called him and letting them both see her in his dressing-gown. Damn.

'Sorry,' she said. She hesitated. 'But what if Jade has actually realised what she's missed and genuinely wants to be a mother to Chloe? Is that such a bad thing?'

'She walks away from Chloe, hardly sees her for years then decides to waltz back in her life and take her off for nights away whenever she feels like it.' Logan sounded bitter. 'She doesn't deserve a second chance to be a mother to her.'

Saffy thought back to how her father had walked away from them, the infrequent visits then nothing at all for years. Would her mother have let him back into their lives if he'd wanted to? And would she have wanted her mother to allow him? She knew she would. It wasn't so much the divorce that damaged children, it was the absent parent, the one who walked away and stopped caring. The wounds of feeling like one of your parents didn't love you enough to be part of your life never really healed. You papered over the hole, but it was always there.

'Maybe not,' she said quietly. 'But Chloe deserves a second chance to get to know her mother, doesn't she?'

A muscle twitched in Logan's jaw and he walked over to the window, staring silently out. She knew he was battling with himself, wanting to do what was right for Chloe but – naturally – struggling with this new development. It must be difficult for him. For years it had just been him and Chloe and now her mother was back and there was a whole new family –grandparents, aunts, cousins – wanting to spoil his little girl.

She put down her glass and crossed the kitchen to him, touching him lightly on the arm. 'You said yourself that Jade is very career-orientated. She probably just wants to see more of Chloe and said she is going for custody just to show you she meant it.'

He ran his hand agitatedly through his hair. 'I never expected this. Not in a million years. I don't know how to deal with it. Of course I want, have always wanted, Jade to be part of Chloe's life. She needs her mother. But I don't trust Jade not to let her down again. Chloe's older now, she'll be heartbroken if her mum decides she can't be bothered to keep up regular contact again.'

'I don't know what to tell you except to remind you that Chloe's the important one in this. It's about her. Not you or Jade.' She kissed him on the cheek. 'Look, I'm sure it will all work out.'

He reached out and pulled her to him. 'I hope so.'

Then they were both kissing, gentle, soothing kisses at first, then more urgent.

'Are you two getting married?'

They sprang apart at the sound of Chloe's voice.

'I hope you are,' she said, her face shining with delight. 'Then I might have a sister. My cousins Maisy and Lena are sisters. I'd like to have a sister.'

Shit. This was exactly what she didn't need.

'Of course not. We were just saying goodbye because I have to go home tomorrow,' Saffy told her.

Chloe's eyes filled with tears. 'I don't want you to go home.'

This was getting too complicated. Saffy felt like she was being suffocated. One minute she was having a light-hearted romance and the next minute she was the cause of a custody battle and a little girl wanted her to provide a baby sister for her.

'I have to go home. I'm back at work soon and need to get back to my flat. But when I come down again to see Hannah and the twins I'll come and see you and Daddy too,' she replied.

'When? Next week?' Chloe asked.

'It might be a while…'

Logan butted in. 'Saffy lives a long way away, poppet.'

'I need to go now. I have to pack ready to go home early in the morning, and me and Hannah have lots to discuss.' Saffy bent down and kissed Chloe on the cheek. 'Bye, Chloe.'

Chloe wrapped her arms around Saffy's neck. 'Bye. I'll miss you.'

'Go and play with your toys while I see Saffy out, then it'll be time for bed,' Logan told her. As soon as Chloe went out of the room he turned to Saffy. 'You're leaving very quickly, I thought you were spending a couple of hours with us. It's like you can't wait to get away.'

'Sorry… I… er…' She struggled to find the words to explain how trapped she suddenly felt.

'Have you changed your mind about us keeping in touch?' he asked, his eyes on her face.

She bit her lip and lowered her gaze. Best to just say the truth. 'No, but I think I should step back a bit and let you sort out this custody thing with Jade. You've got enough on your plate without me adding to it.'

She saw the disappointment in his eyes. 'Look, I'm not after a substitute mother for Chloe so that I can win a custody battle with Jade, or someone to provide a sister for her if that's what you're thinking. She's just a little child, she doesn't understand what she's saying.'

'I know that.' She swallowed. 'But we've only known each other a few days, spent one night together. Things are moving a bit fast…'

'And you like your life uncomplicated. That's fine. I should have known that,' Logan said sadly. 'I'll let you out.' He walked past her, into the hall and opened the front door. 'Goodbye, Saffy, it's been nice knowing you.'

That goodbye sounded pretty final. She wasn't sure that was what she wanted. 'Look, I'll be down to see Hannah again and…'

'Oh, don't worry about that promise you made to Chloe about coming to see her. We won't hold you to it.'

❄

'You're back quick! I thought you'd be over there for a couple of hours yet,' Hannah said as Saffy walked in.

'Change of plan,' Saffy replied stiffly. It was ridiculous but she felt like she was about to burst into tears. *For God's sake, you've only known Logan a few days,* she told herself.

But what a few days it had been.

Lee cast a look at Saffy's face then got up out of the armchair he was sitting in. 'I've got things to do so I'll leave you two to talk.'

'Thanks, hun.' Hannah blew him a kiss. She reached out and touched Saffy's arm. 'Let's go into the kitchen.'

Right, spill,' she said when she'd made them each a cup of coffee.

Saffy filled her in with the latest events. 'I should never have got involved with Logan,' she said. 'I didn't mean to. He's good company, and Chloe's a nice kid. We hung out together a bit, had a good time. That was all I wanted. Then I was going back to my life and work.' She sighed. 'Now look what's happened.'

'Do you like Logan? I mean really like him?' Hannah screwed her eyes into tiny slits as she scrutinised Saffy's face, just like she used to do when Saffy was a rebellious teenager.

'Yes, I do…'

'If he hadn't got Jade being awkward and Chloe wanting you to get married and supply her with a baby sister, would you like him even more?'

'I guess so,' Saffy admitted. 'But he does have those two things, so I reckon we should finish it now. I don't want to be getting any fonder of him or Chloe, because no matter how we feel about each other I'll never marry him and I'll never be able to give Chloe a baby sister – or brother.' Tears pricked her eyes and she instinctively lowered her head so that Hannah wouldn't see them.

Too late. She felt Hannah's hand on top of hers, gently squeezing it. 'Saffy, you know that it isn't one hundred per cent certain that you can't have children.'

'The consultant made it clear that it would be nothing short of a miracle if I did.' Saffy fought back the tears and lifted her head to look at her sister. 'What's the point of me getting close to anyone? There's no future in it.'

'I wondered when this would surface. You buried it down so deep, refused to even talk about it, that I knew one day it would come to a head.' She leaned closer. 'Is this why you've buried yourself in your work? Never had a long relationship since Joe?' She paused. 'Joe was controlling and selfish, Saffy. Not every man is like him, most aren't. And even though he's opinionated, I know Logan isn't like that. He's kind and thoughtful. And a future doesn't always need to include children.'

Saffy bit her lip. 'I know. And to be honest, I wouldn't have wanted a baby with Joe. Actually, I don't even know if I want children. I've never met anyone I wanted to get serious with, and I'm happy with my career so it's not really bothered me.'

'Until now?' Hannah asked gently.

'It's this Christmas. Seeing the bond between all the parents and their kids on Christmas Day, it reminded me of how much Mum loved us and struggled for us. And meeting Logan – he adores Chloe and she adores him. Then worrying about the twins while you were away. It all brought up feelings I didn't know I had. Made me think about having a family of my own, but I can't and never will. And that's fine. I'm okay with that.' She brushed the stupid tears from her eyes with the back of her hand. 'But I'm not going to ruin someone else's life because of it.'

'Not everyone wants children, Saffy. And if someone really loves you then they won't mind, you will be enough for them.'

'What if you and Lee couldn't have had children? Would you both be happy?'

Hannah sat back in her chair. 'I don't know. Once you have children it's hard to imagine not having them – but there are other options, sis.'

Saffy pulled herself together. What was the matter with her, getting all upset like this? She'd only known Logan a few days. She'd been quite happy with her life before and probably once she got back home she'd be happy with it again.

'Take no notice of me. I think I've got caught up in all the Christmas "mush". Besides, Logan's made it quite clear he doesn't want us to see each other again so let's leave it at that.' She forced a bright smile on her face. 'Never mind me. Tell me about your holiday. Are the twins okay now? No side effects at all?'

They chatted for a while, then Hannah yawned. 'Sorry, I'm so tired. The journey was exhausting. I think I'm going to turn in, if you don't mind?'

'Good idea. I'm whacked myself. And I'm afraid I have to leave early in the morning.'

'I know. It's a shame we haven't had more time together but it's been lovely to see you and catch up.' Hannah pushed her chair back and stood up. 'You won't let all this with Logan stop you from coming down and seeing us, will you?' she asked. 'I'd love to see more of you and for the twins to get to know you. You're their only aunt.'

She'd forgotten that Lee was an only child. 'I'll definitely come down more often,' she promised.

But how would she feel if she bumped into Logan while she was visiting Hannah?

She'd be fine, she told herself. Once she got back home, back to her flat, friends and work, she would forget all about him. Like she told Hannah, she'd got carried away with all Christmas 'mush'. A sort of winter holiday romance.

Chapter Twenty-Nine

'It's a brill party, isn't it? And you look fantastic, by the way,' Meg said, joining Saffy at the drinks table Robbie and Duncan had set up.

'Thanks.' After the last few days of wearing mainly jumpers, jeans, Hannah's duffle coat and wellies, Saffy was glad of an opportunity to dress up – especially in the gorgeous black Hollywood evening gown that she'd chosen from the costumes Duncan had hired. Robbie and Duncan's engagement party was the perfect antidote to her post-Cornwall blues. She was feeling better already.

'I'm glad Robbie and Duncan made it up, they're so good together.' Meg poured herself a glass of orange juice. 'I bet they had a ball at your Christmas party too.'

'They were in their element. You know how they love a party. They announced their engagement as well, which helped break the ice. Between us, we totally nailed the party, thank goodness.' She stared as Meg took a sip of the juice. 'Aren't you drinking?'

Meg's hand flew instinctively towards her tummy. Then she leaned forward and said in a whisper, 'I wasn't going to say anything, but I have to tell someone. I'm pregnant. I did the test this morning. But please, please keep it to yourself? We're not telling anyone yet, not until we're sure everything is okay.'

Saffy was momentarily stunned. 'You're having a baby?'

'Yes,' Meg said, with a tiny smile. 'Isn't it wonderful? It means we'll be bringing the wedding forward because I don't want to be showing, and it'll be more of a low-key affair but we're both so happy. You should have seen Stefan's face when I told him, he actually had tears in his eyes.'

Meg looked happy too; her cheeks were glowing, her eyes sparkling. Saffy smiled. 'Congratulations. I'm really pleased for you both.'

'What are you two gossiping about?' Stefan asked, walking over to join them, a half pint of beer in his hand. He took one look at Meg's face and grinned. 'You've told her, haven't you?'

Meg nodded. 'I had to tell someone. You don't mind, do you?'

'Nah, I'm busting to tell everyone myself. I want to announce it to the world.' Stefan put his arm tenderly around Meg's shoulder and kissed her on the cheek. 'I can't believe I'm going to be a dad.'

'You're going to be a dad?' Robbie repeated from behind them. 'Oh my goodness, that's fantastic.' He raised his glass. 'Hey, everyone, Meg and Stefan are having a baby.'

Within seconds Meg and Stefan were surrounded by a crowd congratulating them, shaking their hands, slapping them on the back. Saffy smiled as she watched Meg and Stefan brimming with happiness amongst all the congratulations. She was so happy for them and refused to dwell on the fact that she would never feel that happiness herself.

'How did things go with sexy single dad once we left?' Robbie asked, when they finally found time to catch up.

'Disastrous.' Saffy filled him in.

'Shame. He's quite a hunk and I could see you were both well into each other,' Robbie sympathised. 'Is it definitely dead in the water?'

'Dead and buried,' she told him. 'Now fill me in on what's been happening. Have you made any wedding plans yet?'

'Not had a chance, hun, with all the party preparations, but it's next on the agenda and will definitely be this year. It will be spectacular, naturally, and we want you to be chief bridesmaid. Please say you will.' He put his hands together in mock-prayer and adopted a beseeching look on his face.

Saffy grinned. 'You bet I will!' She couldn't wait. She knew that Duncan would make sure he and Robbie had the wedding of the year. It was one event she definitely didn't want to miss.

'I knew we could count on you!' Clowning around, Robbie kissed her hand. 'We'll provide the gorgeous dress and all the finery so you'll get to be a glamourous princess for the day.'

'Sounds good to me.' Duncan would probably take charge of the wedding décor, and Robbie the wedding outfits; he had impeccable taste so the dress was bound to be amazing.

It was a fantastic evening. Just what she needed. How stupid was she, pining over someone she hardly knew? Not to mention getting so upset that she couldn't have children when she had such fabulous friends, a job she enjoyed and a fantastic life, Saffy thought as she rode home, very merry, in a taxi later that night. And Ajay had messaged her earlier to say he was very impressed with the spreadsheet she'd done for the product meeting, and he'd liked the profiles she'd submitted for the two creatives she'd met down in Cornwall. She really felt like she had good chance of getting that promotion. She didn't need Logan in her life; it was perfect as it was.

❄

Just as he'd done every night since Thursday, when Saffy had burst into his life, Logan stared out of his bedroom window at the one opposite, the room Saffy had slept in when she was there. Only now she'd gone home to her single life. A life without him.

He pulled the curtains closed and turned away from the window. He had to stop thinking about Saffy – they'd had a holiday romance, that was all. They'd enjoyed each other's company for a few days, spent an unforgettable night together and now it was over. He had other, more important, things to deal with.

He sat back down on the bed and swiped the screen to his text messages so he could read Jade's latest message again. He read it slowly, assessing every word.

I'm sorry we argued last night, Logan. I really don't want to argue with you, or – believe it or not – hurt you. This isn't personal. I know I did wrong to leave you to bring up Chloe alone, I should have seen her more and I want to put that right now. All I'm asking is to see her regularly, to take her out, for my family to get to know her. I won't back down on this, Logan. Chloe is my daughter. I want to be a mother to her. I'd like it if we could meet up and talk about how we can arrange this. If you feel you can't do that then the legal route is my only option.

It was all very formal and very Jade.

For half an hour after receiving the text Logan had stood by Chloe's bed, watching her sleep, as he often did, trying to imagine not having her in his life every day, sharing her with Jade. There were times, he had to admit, when he'd have been glad of a night off, for the chance to do things you couldn't do with a young child around, and if Jade had wanted to have an arrangement like that when she'd first walked out he would have readily agreed. But she hadn't. She had hardly seen Chloe over the last five years. She had no bloody right to walk back into their lives, expecting to play mummy again and dictating the terms.

Then he remembered Saffy's words. That he might not think Jade had a right to a second chance at being a mother but Chloe had a right to a second chance to have her mother in her life and to get to know her other family – a whole new family of aunts, uncles and cousins that she had never met. And she'd been so happy to go and stay with her nanny and grandad and other family at Christmas.

Saffy was right. He knew she was. He had to forget about his own feelings and do what was best for Chloe. And whilst that definitely wasn't giving her up or giving in to Jade's every demand, it did mean he had to be prepared to meet her halfway. He had to be prepared to share his little daughter. Their little daughter.

He hit the reply button and started typing:

I'm prepared to give you a chance to play a bigger part in Chloe's life, but please don't let her down. She's old enough to know now and be hurt if you walk away again. I'll meet up with you once she's back at school and we'll discuss it. But remember, Chloe's home is with me and that's the way it's going to stay.

He read the text over again then pressed 'send'.

Chapter Thirty

One month later

'Can I see you in my office for a few minutes, please, Saffy?' Ajay asked as he walked past her desk with a pile of folders.

Saffy crossed her fingers behind her back as she followed her boss into his office. This was the day he was appointing the new business development manager, and she was feeling pretty hopeful that Ajay would choose her. She'd been working really hard, staying late at the office to finish work, and had developed marketing plans that had increased sales for three of their partners.

'Sit down please, Saffy.' He nodded at the chair on the other side of the desk. She pulled it out and perched on the edge of it.

Ajay picked up his pen and twiddled it around in his hands. 'Now, Saffy, I know you really wanted the position of business development manager, and I have considered it very carefully.' He paused. 'But…'

He was giving it to someone else! Saffy immediately forgot all about her resolve not to show her disappointment and blurted out, 'But I've worked so hard, increased sales and written proposals for new creatives to join us!'

Ajay nodded. 'I know you have, which is why I think you're better suited to another position that has just come up.'

Another position? What did he mean?

Ajay tapped his left hand with his pen. 'The thing is, we're planning on expanding. At the moment we're centred in the Midlands, and yes, you and the other reps travel around the country for meetings, but we need another office, a permanent base.'

Expanding? Where was he thinking of sending her?

'We finally decided on Exeter,' Ajay continued. 'We do a lot of business in the West Country and Exeter is in a good position to reach most of Cornwall and Devon but also to travel up country too.' He leaned back in his chair. 'So we need a product development manager to build up a team of creative partners in that area, and seeing as you've already suggested two, and have connections down there, I think you'll be ideal for the position. What do you say?'

That took her by surprise. She wasn't sure what to say. It was a brilliant career opportunity – but it would mean relocating, a lot more responsibility, more work. The hard work and responsibility didn't bother her but relocating did. She had a great group of friends and loved her flat.

'Let me tell you a bit more about it. I realise it's a big step but I can only give you until the end of the week to make your decision. I need to fill this position quickly, the new office opens next month.'

Next month! Talk about moving fast. She listened as Ajay told her what the new post would entail, the salary – enticingly more than she was getting now – the relocation allowance, and that although she would be office-based, she would spend a lot of time finding and meeting with creatives, and could do some of the work from home. It sounded tempting. Very tempting.

'It's a challenging position and I think you're the right person for it. You've got a lot of initiative, are proactive and get on well with the clients. The marketing plans you've developed for our existing creatives are excellent, as are the proposals for the new ones. But I understand if you decide it's not for you.' He leaned forward. 'I'd appreciate it if you keep this to yourself, Saffy, it's not common knowledge yet. And let me know your decision by Friday morning. If you have any further questions, feel free to pop in and ask them.'

She was being dismissed. 'Okay. And thank you for offering the post to me,' she said, standing up. Thank goodness she was meeting Meg at lunchtime and could talk to her about it; she thought she was going to burst.

❄

Meg looked thoughtful when Saffy told her about the job offer. 'It sounds a great opportunity.'

'I know. And I'm the first one Ajay's offered the position to.'

'It means moving away from your lovely flat and your friends, though. We won't be able to meet for lunch and you won't see Bump grow up.' Meg placed her hand over her still-flat stomach.

'I know but…'

'I know, it's a big move for your career, so you need to think about it carefully. And you'll be nearer to your sister, of course.' She stirred the straw around in her orange juice. 'What about Logan? It means you'll probably bump into him too if you see more of Hannah.'

Saffy had told her all about her 'fling' with Logan and how it had ended.

'I'm sure we can both manage to be polite if we see each other,' she said.

'Do you still have feelings for him?' Meg asked.

'Of course not, I told you it was a silly Christmas holiday fling.'

Pre-pregnant Meg would have questioned her further but thankfully mum-to-be Meg was too busy with plans for the baby, and her wedding to Stefan to probe. Because if she was forced to be honest, Saffy had to admit that she wasn't over Logan. He had left an impression on her that the numerous other men she had dated hadn't. She often relived their night together in her mind and, yes, wondered how he and Chloe were, but she was sure she had made the right decision to step back and let Logan sort out the mess with Jade. Even though she had to admit that she missed both Logan and Chloe terribly.

❄

Logan read the letter from Jade's solicitor, informing him that Jade was seeking custody of Chloe, for the third time. He could hardly believe this was happening. Up until Christmas Jade had barely bothered with Chloe and now she wanted to uproot her from him, her home, her school and everything that was familiar to her. She had announced she was planning on moving back to Bristol, near her parents, and then demanded to have Chloe stay every other weekend. He'd agreed to once a month, reminding himself of Saffy's words that Chloe had the right to get to know her mother. He thought of Saffy a lot. The few days he'd spent with her were stamped indelibly on his heart but he knew he'd made the right decision to finish it with her. He had to concentrate on Chloe, to sort out this custody battle with Jade; he couldn't afford any more complications in his life, or any more upset for Chloe.

Logan had then set the wheels in motion to formally get full custody of Chloe – something he could kick himself for not doing when Jade first walked out, knowing she'd have signed the papers back then with no hesitation. But the threat to the control over her access to Chloe was presumably what had prompted this letter back from Jade, suddenly demanding full custody. Ruth, his solicitor, had assured him that there was no way the court would uproot Chloe and give Jade custody, and not even joint custody, seeing as Jade lived in a completely different area, which would disrupt Chloe's schooling. She thought however that the court would find Jade's request to have Chloe stay with her every other weekend a reasonable one. 'I know Jade walked out and left Chloe with you, and hasn't bothered much with her until now, but she is still her mother, Logan. I think the court would want to encourage Chloe to have a relationship with Jade.'

So that was it; he had to let his precious little girl go and spend every other weekend with Jade.

'I'm not trying to stop Jade from seeing her. I just don't want Chloe to get hurt. I'm scared that Jade will get fed up of playing mummy again, and Chloe will be devastated,' he told Hannah when he went to pick Chloe up. Hannah had collected her from school and she was now playing upstairs with the twins.

'You can't stop her getting hurt, love. All you can do is be there for her if she does,' Hannah told him. 'I know it's hard for you but Chloe having a relationship with her mum is a good thing, isn't it?'

'I realise that and I want her to have her mum in her life. God, it's hard being a parent, isn't it?'

'The hardest job in the world. Luckily I had a bit of practice with Saffy. I was practically her surrogate mother as poor Mum was working so much.' She switched on the kettle and took two mugs off the rack. 'Fancy a cuppa while the kids are playing?'

Saffy. The mention of her name still had the power to hurt him.

Hannah narrowed her eyes. 'You and Saffy, it was only a fling, right?'

'Sure. Your sister's got her city life, her career and her friends. She's not really the kind of girl who'd want to get involved with a single dad going through a messy custody battle, is she?'

Hannah gave him a quizzical look. 'She's interested in her career, of course, why shouldn't she be? She's young and single but she's got a good heart and we've grown very close again since Christmas. She was really supportive of me then, and always asks after the twins now.'

An image of Saffy playing Twister with the kids flashed across his mind. She'd joined in with gusto. And that laugh!

'Yeah, she was brilliant at the party on Christmas Day,' he said. 'And the two guys – it was a lot of fun.'

'Robbie and Duncan? I've never met them, what are they like?' Hannah asked as she handed him a mug of coffee.

'They're great.' As they sat chatting away Logan thought how much his life had changed since Christmas. Nothing was certain any more.

Chapter Thirty-One

'Listen, babe, we'll miss you but Exeter isn't that far away. You could easily drive up on a Friday evening straight from work and spend the weekend with us. Our spare room is yours whenever you want it. It's not that far to drive down and visit your sister either, it's the best of both worlds.' Robbie shoved another handful of peanuts in his mouth and chewed them thoughtfully. 'This is a fantastic opportunity, you'll be doing the job you've always wanted to do. What's with the hesitation?'

Saffy spread the butter on the warm baguette slowly. How could she explain to Robbie when she didn't really understand herself? 'It's a big decision to up sticks and move,' she said slowly. 'I love this flat and being able to meet up with you and Meg at lunchtime.'

'Enough to turn down a promotion?' Robbie narrowed his eyes suspiciously. 'This is about Logan, isn't it? You're worried that you'll bump into him when you visit Hannah?'

'No, I'm not!' Saffy said indignantly. Honestly, when Robbie had asked if he could pop over from work on Thursday evening to discuss wedding preparations with her, she hadn't expected him to give her the third degree about her new job offer.

'You've never been a very convincing liar,' Robbie told her. He nodded towards the oven. 'I think the pizza's done.'

'Oh shit!' Saffy glanced at the oven door where she could see the now dark-brown pizza bubbling, grabbed the tea towel and opened the oven, standing back from the hiss of hot smoke. 'It's a bit well done, sorry,' she said, as she took out the almost unrecognisable ham and pineapple pizza and placed it on top of the oven to cool.

'What's new?' Robbie grinned. He picked up the bowl of salad Saffy had just prepared. 'At least you do a mean salad.' He nodded toward the open door leading into the lounge. 'Shall I take it through?'

'Thanks.' Saffy transferred the pizza onto a plate, cut it up, picked up the plate of buttered baguette and followed him through. Two plates and cutlery were already placed on the coffee table and Robbie was now sitting on the sofa, dishing himself out some salad. She put the pizza and bread in the middle of the table and sat down beside him. 'It's been ages since we did this.'

'That's because we live too far away from each other to just pop in.' He picked up a slice of pizza and bit into it. 'Which is why it doesn't make sense that you're hesitating over this new job. I mean, I'll miss Friday night meet-ups after work and the odd weekend lunch but everything's changing for all of us. Meg's having a baby and getting married. I'm getting married.' He looked at her, puzzled. 'This is the job of your dreams and as much as you love us all, I don't believe you're thinking of turning it down just because we all won't be able to meet up as often.'

'I didn't say I was thinking of turning it down. I'm just considering all things carefully. It's a big decision.'

'It's Logan, isn't it? Admit it. I could see the connection between you two at Christmas and you haven't been the same since. You've lost your spark.'

How could she explain to Robbie when she wasn't sure what she was feeling herself?

'It's not that I've still got feelings for him. It's just that I don't want things to be awkward. And I don't want to break my promise to Chloe.'

Robbie looked surprised. 'What promise?'

'That when I came down to visit Hannah I'd pop in and see her.'

'And you can't do that because…?'

'Because Logan made it clear he didn't want me to. We're over.'

'In that case, don't worry. He's the parent, it's his responsibility to deal with Chloe and you're released from your promise.' Robbie picked up another slice of pizza. 'So, remind me, what exactly is stopping you from taking this fantastic promotion?'

She'd been asking herself the same question all week. She kept thinking of how Chloe had hugged her, begged her to visit. How would the little girl feel if she found out that Saffy had been to visit Hannah and the twins but not popped in to say hello to her? *Kids are like that, she'll have forgotten me by now,* she reminded herself, *especially now that she's got her mum back in her life.* 'I guess I feel like I've let her down. But you're right, it's up to Logan to explain to her that we've fallen out.'

'Maybe you'll *unfall* out.'

She shook her head. 'No chance of that. I'm not getting involved with a man with a child desperate to have a little sister. It'll only end in heartbreak.'

'Not everyone's like Joe.' Robbie took another bite of pizza and chewed it thoughtfully. 'Joe was a selfish moron and definitely not right for you. If a guy really loves you he won't dump you because you can't have a baby.' She'd confided in both Robbie and Meg after the consultant had told her the results of her operation.

'If a guy wants children – or more children in Logan's case – it's not fair to deprive them of that. It's my problem. I don't want to make it anyone else's.'

'Not being able to have kids of your own is hard, but it isn't the end of the world, hun. There are other ways to have a family. Me and Duncan have been talking about it. We'd like a family in a couple of years.'

'Maybe… but it's not just that.'

'Well, the Saffy I know and love wouldn't turn down the job of a lifetime just because it didn't work out with a guy.' Robbie stood up. 'I'll make us a coffee, shall I?'

'Yes, please. Black for me.' As Robbie disappeared into the kitchen, Saffy thought over his words. He was right. The truth was that the only reason she was hesitating over this job was because she didn't want to bump into Logan again. It had been a long time since she'd fallen for someone in such a big way and she was struggling to cope with it. Well, she needed to get over it. This was too big an opportunity to miss.

❄

'I'm really pleased you're accepting the position, Saffy,' Ajay said when she told him her decision the next day. 'You're the ideal person for the job and I know you'll do it well.' He shook her hand, his face all smiles. 'We'll help with relocation expenses but we need you down there this time next month.' He looked at her questioningly. 'What about your flat? Do you have to sell it? Give notice to your landlord?'

'I own it. I'll put it in the hands of an agency and rent it out for a while, until I decide whether to sell,' she told him. She'd decided this in the early hours of the morning when she'd still been tossing and turning about her decision. That way, if the job didn't work out, she still had her home to come back to.

'Great, that's all sorted then. Now take a seat while we discuss all the finer details.'

Saffy left Ajay's office feeling sure she had made the right decision. She was excited about finding new craftspeople and artists to add to buycreative.com's database. And she loved Exeter, it was a picturesque and bustling city. This was a brand new chapter in her life and she was going to seize it with both hands.

She phoned Hannah to tell her the news later that evening. 'Oh, Saffy, that's brilliant. Congratulations.' Saffy could hear the TV in the background and the twins playing. She could imagine the scene in her head and was suddenly filled with a longing to see her sister and the twins again. 'And, of course, it means that we'll be able to see more of you too. That'll be wonderful.'

'It will. I've missed you all. How are the twins?'

They chatted for a while, exchanging news, ending with Saffy promising to come down for a weekend soon. When she ended the call, Saffy was even more sure that she was making the right decision. She missed her sister and would love to be part of the twins' lives. As for Logan, she was sure they were both adult enough to be polite if they bumped into each other. She'd been getting herself into a stew over nothing. Tomorrow she'd call a letting agent to find someone to rent her flat for six months and start packing. A new life was waiting for her.

❄

'I don't want to go to Mummy's this weekend. I want to stay at home,' Chloe said, on the verge of tears. 'Please don't make me go.'

Logan had wondered if the novelty of seeing her mother would wear off and Chloe would want it to be just him and her again. Now what did he do? He'd agreed with Jade's solicitor that she could have Chloe every other weekend. He couldn't force the little girl to go though, not when she was so upset, and he couldn't help feeling pleased that she preferred to stay home with him instead. But although he wanted to tell her that she didn't have to go, he knew that he should try to persuade her.

He crouched down in front of her. 'Mummy's expecting you, poppet, and she'll be really disappointed if you don't go.'

'I don't want to.' Chloe sniffed and huddled into the corner of the sofa.

Logan frowned. This wasn't like Chloe. He sat down beside her and wrapped his arm around her. 'Tell me why not,' he coaxed.

'I don't like Grant.' Chloe sniffed again.

Logan froze. 'Who's Grant?'

'Mummy's boyfriend. He's really grumpy.'

'Did he shout at you?' Logan asked, fighting down the urge to phone Jade right now and ask her what the hell was going on.

'Yes.' Chloe sniffed. 'I want to stay here with you and play with my toys.' She looked up at him beseechingly. 'Can I, please?'

He remembered thinking that Chloe had been quiet when she came home from staying with Jade last time but had thought she'd just been tired. He hated it that she'd been so upset and hadn't confided in him. And he was angry with Jade that she'd let one of her man friends shout at his – their – daughter. He'd a good mind to tell her she wasn't having Chloe overnight again. He was sure that if he told his solicitor that Chloe had begged not to go, she would say he didn't have to make her.

Then he remembered Saffy's words. 'You might not think that Jade has a right to a second chance but Chloe has a right to a mother.'

He had to sort this, for Chloe's sake. Then at least he could say, hand on heart, that he'd tried to keep her mother in her life. He kissed Chloe on the forehead. 'I'll speak to Mummy and tell her you don't want to go and see what she says. Maybe Grant won't be there.'

He left Chloe watching the TV and went into the kitchen to dial Jade.

'I hope you haven't phoned up to make up an excuse, Logan.' As usual, Jade was on the attack. 'We've agreed that I pick Chloe up today and have her overnight.'

'I know.' Logan hesitated. *Keep calm,* he told himself. *Try not to be accusing.* 'The thing is, she's crying that she doesn't want to come.'

'You've put her up to that!' Jade shot back.

'I absolutely have not. In fact, I've got a date for tonight.' He hadn't, but he wanted Jade to know that she wasn't the only one who had someone in their life. Except he didn't, did he? He'd lost the only person he wanted in his life. *Stop thinking about Saffy, you've got an important issue to deal with here.* 'Chloe is crying that she doesn't like Grant. She said he shouted at her.'

He heard Jade's sharp hiss. 'Grant has never shouted at her. Yes, he told her off – she spilled her food on the floor and wouldn't clear it up. But he certainly didn't raise his voice.'

Logan bristled with anger. How dare some guy he didn't even know tell his daughter off? 'Chloe has only stayed over with you a few times and you think it's okay for your latest man to tell her off? No wonder she doesn't want to come and stay again.'

There was a pause and… was that a quiver he heard in Jade's voice? 'She really doesn't want to come?'

'No.'

'Please can I speak to her? Can I FaceTime her?'

Jade had added herself to FaceTime on Chloe's iPad when Chloe had stayed over last time, which really annoyed Logan so he had immediately blocked her, insisting that all contact came through him first. He didn't want Jade calling Chloe whenever she felt like it.

'I'll pass her the phone, you can talk to her,' he agreed.

He went back into the lounge and held out his mobile. 'Mummy wants to talk to you.'

Chloe shook her head. 'I don't want to talk to her. She'll try to make me go and stay with her.'

'Please put her on, Logan,' Jade begged.

She actually sounded upset. Logan held out the phone again. 'Mummy really wants to talk to you. Please talk to her, poppet.'

Chloe shook her head and crossed her arms.

'I'm sorry, Jade, she won't. I can't make her,' he said.

'Then I'm coming over.'

'No you're not,' he said firmly. 'You're going to have to be patient, you can't just waltz into Chloe's life and expect it all to go smoothly. I'll talk to her over the weekend, see if I can persuade her to go out with you for the day next weekend. And no Grant.'

'You've turned her against me, haven't you?' Jade accused. 'I'm going to speak to my solicitor and make sure I get full custody. You can't stop me from seeing Chloe.'

Chapter Thirty-Two

Three weeks later

'Hello, Saffy, have you come to visit Hannah and Lee?'

'Ariane! I didn't know you worked here!' Saffy said, surprised to see her standing behind the shop counter. 'How are you? And yes, I'm down for the weekend.'

'I started here a few weeks ago. I do a few shifts during school hours and the kids go to their dad's every other Saturday so I work weekends then.' She smiled. 'It's lovely to see you again. We all had such a good time at the Christmas party, thanks to you.'

'It was a pleasure, I enjoyed it too.' Saffy took her purse out of her bag. 'You might be seeing more of me in future. I've been promoted and moving to Exeter soon and am hoping to pop down and see Hannah, Lee and the twins most weekends.'

'That's fantastic. I know Hannah would love that,' Ariane said.

'Daddy! There's Saffy!'

Saffy spun around as she heard the familiar voice, a smile spontaneously leaping to her face as she saw Chloe running towards her.

'Saffy! You're back!' Chloe hurled herself at her and Saffy instinctively bent down and gave the little girl a hug.

'Hello, darling. Yes, I'm back for the weekend. How lovely to see you.' As Chloe wrapped her arms around her neck, Saffy looked over the little girl's shoulder to Logan, her heart doing a somersault as those familiar blue eyes met hers. The sandy hair was a bit longer now, the stubble she'd run her fingers over a little more unkempt than she remembered. He looked tired and strained, she thought, wondering if that was anything to do with Jade. Hannah had told her that she was fighting Logan for custody of Chloe. 'Hello,' she said, feeling a bit awkward.

'Hello, Saffy. How are you?'

'I'm good, thanks. I've come to stay with Hannah and Lee for the weekend,' she explained needlessly. 'How are things with you?'

'Okay.' He nodded. 'Good to see you again. Enjoy your weekend.'

'Thanks.'

'Are you coming to visit us?' Chloe asked, tugging at Saffy's sleeve. She turned to Logan. 'She can, can't she, Daddy? I want to show her the doll's house Mummy bought me.'

Saffy's eyes flitted to Logan's face again. 'Er…'

Chloe was tugging her hand. 'Please, Saffy?'

'I'm sure Saffy's too busy. She's come to visit her sister and the twins, not us, Chloe,' Logan butted in. He stepped forward and took hold of his daughter's hand. 'Come on, poppet, we've still got a lot of shopping to get.'

'Me too, I've got lots to do,' Saffy said quickly.

'See you around, then.' He turned and walked out of the shop with Chloe, leaving behind the basket of goods he'd been about to pay for.

'Daddy, you forgot the shopping,' Saffy heard Chloe say as Logan left the shop but Logan carried on walking. He obviously couldn't wait to get away from her. She couldn't believe how much it had shaken her to see him again. She thought she'd got over him but no, the attraction was still there. Not for him though, obviously – which was a good thing. She had a new job, new life; she didn't have time right now for complications and with Logan it would definitely be complicated.

Shame, though. She liked him. A lot.

Too much.

She turned back to Ariane, feeling a bit embarrassed. Had she noticed how eager Logan had been to get away from her?

'He's not been himself lately, it's all this business with Jade,' Ariane said.

'I'm sure it will all work out okay,' she said vaguely, not wanting to discuss Logan's private business. 'Can I have some milk and a loaf, please? We're right out.'

'Of course. They're just over there.' Ariane pointed to the shelves on the right wall of the shop.

'Thanks.' Saffy picked them up, paid for them and left the shop, her mind still on Logan. He'd looked so strained. She wondered what Jade was up to now.

As she turned the corner to walk back to Liwus Helyk she saw a silver Mercedes convertible pull up outside. She stopped and watched as a tall, very well-dressed woman with short dark hair got out. There was something familiar about her. Then she realised it was the same woman she'd seen on Logan's phone when Chloe FaceTimed him while Saffy was wearing his dressing-gown. Jade. The woman walked up the path and knocked on the door. Had she come for Chloe?

She ought to go, not stand and watch, but she couldn't seem to move.

The door opened and Logan stood on the doorstep, Chloe beside him. 'Mummy!' Chloe shouted, running out to hug Jade.

'What are you doing here?' Saffy heard Logan demand. He didn't seem pleased to see her.

*

What the hell was Jade doing, turning up out of the blue? They had an agreement that she messaged and they both arranged a suitable date first. Had she come to take Chloe? Well, there was no way he'd let her, but he had to tread carefully; he didn't want to argue with her in front of Chloe. Ever since that weekend three weeks ago when Chloe had refused to go with her mother or even speak to her, Jade had pulled out all the stops to win the little girl over, sending presents of new clothes and expensive toys. Chloe was delighted, although she still refused to go out with Jade, insisting that she wanted her mother to come and visit her instead. So Jade had come – without arranging it beforehand, as usual.

'I wanted to see Chloe,' she said. 'I had a meeting in Bude and it was too good an opportunity to miss. It's not a problem, is it? She is my daughter.' She looked down at Chloe. 'You want to see Mummy, don't you?'

'Yes!' Chloe gave her a hug, then suddenly peered around her and started waving. 'Saffy!'

Logan glanced up and saw Saffy about to cross the road towards Liwus Helyk. She turned as Chloe called and waved back, looking awkward. She had obviously seen Jade and was trying to avoid them. Chloe ran over and started talking to her.

'I see your girlfriend is back again,' said Jade.

'She's not my girlfriend,' Logan told her. He ran his hand through his hair. 'Look, I don't want to argue in front of Chloe so you can come in and see her for a bit, no more than half an hour though. I've got things to do.'

Jade pouted. 'I want to discuss access with you. The solicitor's bills are costing me a fortune so I was hoping we could discuss it calmly and work something out.'

Logan considered this. He couldn't afford the legal bills either. 'Okay, but I don't want to discuss it now, not in front of Chloe. We'll meet up one of the days when she's at school.'

'I'm out the country soon. I want to sort it before I go.' Jade pointed to Saffy, who was still talking to Chloe and said loudly, 'Can't your girlfriend look after Chloe for a while, so we can talk?'

'Oh yes! Can she, Dad?' Chloe asked. 'Can I go with Saffy and see the twins?'

How embarrassing. That was typical Jade. She never stopped to think how anyone else felt about a situation. 'I've told you that Saffy—'

'I could take Chloe to see the twins for half an hour,' Saffy told him.

Logan went to protest but Jade butted in. 'That's settled then. I'll see you later, darling,' she said to Chloe. 'You run off with that lady while I talk to Daddy.'

There she was again, taking charge as if everything was down to her. Logan could feel his anger rising but he kept it in check. He wasn't going to cause a scene in front of his little daughter, but he'd be telling Jade a few home truths once they were alone.

'I'm sorry to put this on you, Saffy, but if you don't mind it would really help,' he said.

'No problem.' Saffy took Chloe's hand. 'Come on, Chloe. I bet the twins have lots of games they want you to play with them.' She shot Logan a sympathetic look. 'I hope you sort things out.'

'That was bloody embarrassing. Me and Saffy are finished. We haven't seen each other since Christmas,' Logan snapped, glaring at Jade. 'You'd better come inside because I don't intend to have an argument on the doorstep for the whole street to hear.'

'I haven't come for an argument. I want to sort things out between us, without the lawyers,' Jade said as she followed him inside. 'All I want is to see my daughter on a regular basis. Surely, that isn't too much to ask.'

'I'm going for full custody, Jade, and my solicitor is confident I'll get it,' he warned her.

'I know,' she admitted. 'And so is my solicitor. Look, Logan, I don't want to fight any more. I know I'm in the wrong. I walked out on Chloe and have hardly had anything to do with her the last few years. I regret that.' She followed him into the kitchen and pulled out a chair, suddenly looking rather forlorn. 'I hate myself for walking out on my daughter. Especially now…' She swallowed and tears brimmed in her eyes. Logan was taken aback as he saw how distressed she was.

'What is it?' he asked gently. Then a horrible thought struck him. 'You aren't ill, are you?'

She shook her head. 'No, not ill, but I am pregnant again.'

That shocked him. 'What?'

'I know. Who'd have thought it?' She opened her handbag and took out a photo, passing it over to him. He stared at the middle-aged man in the picture.

'This is Grant, I take it.'

She nodded. 'We've been seeing each other for almost a year now. He wants me to marry him.'

Well this certainly was a day for surprises. 'And are you going to?'

'Yes. I'm ready to settle down now. I want to make a home and have this baby.' She patted her tummy. 'I guess loving this baby so much made me feel guilty about leaving Chloe. I wanted her back, to make it up to her. But I can't turn back the clock. I did what I did and I have to live with it.' Tears welled up in her eyes again.

Logan sat down beside her, not sure what to say.

'What I can do is be a better mum to her from now on.' Her eyes met his and he could see that she was serious. 'Will you let me do that? I promise I won't go for custody and I won't cause any problems. All I want is to have Chloe to stay at least one weekend a month, preferably two, and some of the school holidays. I want her to be part of our family, mine and Grant's. I know he was a bit stern with her at first, but that's just his way. He loves her and I promise he would never hurt her. What do you say?'

Chapter Thirty-Three

'Hi, come in. Saffy told me Jade had turned up out of the blue, how did it go?' Hannah said warmly.

Saffy looked up from the Hungry Hippos game she was playing with Chloe and the twins, watched closely by Oscar, who barked excitedly every time one of the hippos snapped at the balls. She'd guessed it was Logan when the door knocked but deliberately left Hannah to answer to give her time to compose herself. She didn't want Logan to have any idea how much it had shaken her to see him again.

'Thank you so much, Saffy.' He came in with Hannah, looking a lot happier than he had half an hour ago. 'I can't tell you how grateful I am. You too, Hannah.' Then he spotted the game they were playing. 'Who's winning?'

'I am but Saffy's quite good too,' Chloe said.

'I bet she is. And the twins are a lot younger than you, remember, so give them a chance.' He bent down and swooped Miles up into his arms. 'How are you doing, little fella?' Then he bent down to stroke Oscar, who had come up for some fuss too.

'Has Mummy gone?' Chloe asked.

'Yes, she just stopped by on her way from work. But she's going to see you next weekend. Is that okay?'

'Will Grant be there?'

'Yes. He and Mummy have a new house they want to show you. It's near Nanny and Grandad's house.'

Chloe looked unsure. 'Do I have to go?'

'No you don't, but it might be nice to see your mum's new house, don't you think? And Mummy has promised Grant won't shout at you again. Will you give him another chance?'

Chloe considered this. 'I s'pose.'

'Do you have time for a cuppa?' Hannah asked. 'I was about to make one for me and Saffy.'

'Love one.' Logan put Miles down and knelt down to Chloe. 'Are you okay playing with the twins while we all go and have a cuppa in the kitchen?'

'Okay, we'll play with the fire station – but if they start to moan I'm bringing them in to you,' Chloe agreed.

'Deal.' Logan held up his hand and Chloe high-fived it. Then he smiled at Saffy. 'That means we have about five minutes.'

Guessing he wanted to talk to her and Hannah about Jade, Saffy followed him into the kitchen. Hannah had already put a plate of biscuits on the table and was spooning coffee into the mugs. 'I take it that things went well with Jade?'

Logan leaned over and took a biscuit off the plate. 'After the initial few minutes, yes.' He filled them in on the details.

'She's pregnant again? Wow!' Hannah placed the mugs of coffee on the table and sat down. 'Let's hope she doesn't walk out on this one.'

'It does sound as if she regrets her action, though, and is trying to make up for it,' Saffy said. 'Which is more than our dad ever did.'

'True,' Hannah agreed.

'I think she's genuine. I've never seen her so upset.' Logan gazed out of the window as if his mind was somewhere in the past. 'She always seemed so cold and unemotional to me. It was all about how having a child affected *her*. But now, this baby seems to have brought out her maternal side. Something she never showed with Chloe.'

'She's older now, maybe she's realised that a career isn't everything,' Hannah told him. 'Best to make sure you still get full custody of Chloe though, in case Jade changes her mind again.'

'I will, don't worry. And we've agreed regular access and maintenance payments.' Logan turned back and gave Saffy a devastating smile that made her heart skip a beat. 'Good to see you again, Saffy, and thank you for coming to my rescue.'

'No problem. I'm pleased you've got it sorted.'

'Me too. I know I resented Jade turning up again at first but I do want Chloe to have her mother in her life. And I must admit, the odd night or weekend off would be useful. I could catch up on work and then have more time to spend with Chloe when she is home.'

Logan seemed happier now, more pleasant towards her, Saffy thought in surprise. Then she remembered how close they'd been and the gulf between them still seemed so wide.

Changing the subject, and with a twinkle in her eye, Hannah announced, 'We should be seeing a lot more of Saffy now she's been promoted and moving to Exeter.'

Was that a spark of interest she saw in Logan's eyes?

'Really? Well congratulations, Saffy. Is it the same line of work?'

'It's for the same company. A promotion, actually. We're opening a new branch in Exeter so we can expand more into the West Country and I've been given the post of sourcing new creatives down here.'

'My main office is in Exeter too. When are you moving down?' Logan asked.

'Next Saturday. I start the job on the Monday,' Saffy told him.

'Oh, Logan, didn't you say you were popping in to your Exeter office on Saturday morning? I'm guessing you don't want me to look after Chloe now as she'll be with Jade, but maybe you could drop in on Saffy, give her a hand getting straight in her new flat?'

Saffy shot her a look. Trust Hannah to interfere and try to matchmake.

Logan paused. 'Yes, I could. If you want me to that is, Saffy?' He turned to her as he asked the question.

Well, that was a change of heart from 'couldn't wait to get away from her' in the corner shop. Mind you, Hannah had almost twisted his arm. Still, she would like to get back on a friendlier footing with him, especially as she was hoping to pop down and see Hannah regularly. Besides, Robbie and Duncan would be there too, so it wouldn't be just the two of them.

'Thanks. Robbie and Duncan are helping me move in and I'm sure would love to see you again. I'll WhatsApp you my address. I'll be there all day.'

'I'll see you sometime in the afternoon then.' Logan stood up. 'I'd better be off now.'

'Don't forget Sunday lunch tomorrow. I'll be dishing up at one-thirty,' Hannah reminded him.

Logan hesitated. 'Are you sure? Don't you want to spend the time with Saffy? You must have a lot of catching up to do and I don't mind.'

'Don't be daft, Saffy and I have got plenty of time to catch up. She's here until Sunday evening – and it's nothing to dish up a meal for two more people,' Hannah told him.

'Then, yes, we'll be there. Thank you.' He looked at Saffy. 'I'll leave you two to chat then. See you both tomorrow.'

'See you,' Saffy replied.

As soon as Logan and Chloe had left, she turned to Hannah. 'Are you trying to matchmake?'

Hannah turned on her innocent 'what, me?' look. 'Logan's a friend, he's a single dad, he gets on well with Lee and we often invite him to lunch. You don't want me to cancel on him, do you?'

'And what about inviting him to drop in on me in Exeter?'

'I thought it would be nice for you to see a familiar face. Besides' – Hannah shot her a knowing look – 'anyone can see you both fancy the pants off each other.'

'I do not!' Saffy said emphatically.

'You do. And he fancies you too, but you both think it won't work.'

'It won't. Logan wants a stay-at-home mum to look after Chloe, and probably another child. That's not, and never will be, me.'

'I doubt he wants that at all,' Hannah replied. 'And what is it you want?

Saffy considered this. 'What I don't want is to be tied down to someone. I've just got this fantastic promotion and I don't want to be held back.'

'Being with someone doesn't mean you can't have a career too,' Hannah reminded her gently.

'It makes it more difficult. It's different for you, Hannah, you're motherly. All you've ever wanted is a family. You enjoy looking after people, you always have. You were like my substitute mother…'

'Because I had to be!' Hannah retorted. 'Do you really think I wanted to be? That I wouldn't have preferred to go out with my friends, have a bit of fun sometimes instead of always having to look after my kid sister?'

Her angry words stunned Saffy. She had never stopped to think what it must have been like for Hannah having to look after her all the time. Hannah had been young too; of course she would want to be out with her friends. All the time Saffy had been resenting her older sister bossing her around, Hannah had been resenting it too. She bit back the angry retort that it wasn't her fault when she noticed the tears in Hannah's eyes. She was really upset. 'I'm sorry.' She reached over and touched Hannah's hand. 'I've never stopped to think what it was like for you. It must have been hard. And I was an awkward brat sometimes,' she admitted.

'You were a normal teenager, and I loved you. But I wanted to be your big sister, Saffy, not your mother. I wanted to be the one you confided in, not resented. I wanted us to be close, like we have been since Christmas. I really appreciated how you helped me out then, and how you messaged me every day to see how the twins were. It was like I finally had a sister.'

Saffy's heart went out to her. She got up and hugged Hannah tight. 'I'm sorry, sis. All I wanted was for Mum to have time for me, to look after me instead of you doing it. It was hard for both of us. And for Mum.'

'I know.' Hannah sniffed. 'Take no notice of me. I shouldn't have said all that.'

'Yes you should. I've been selfish, wrapped up in my own life, and you gave up a lot for me to have that life.' She squeezed her sister's shoulders. 'I promise to be there for you from now on. How about I start by taking the twins to the playground? Give you and Lee some time together?'

Hannah's face lit up. 'Really? Thanks, that would be great.'

'I'll go and get our coats,' Saffy said.

As she went into the hall to get the coats Saffy cast her mind back to Hannah's words about Logan. 'You two both fancy the pants off each other.' Well, it was true, she did fancy Logan like mad. Who wouldn't?

He was drop-dead sexy and really caring too. Did he fancy her? What if he did? It made no difference. As she had told Hannah, they would never make it work so it was best for them both to save each other some heartache and not even attempt to have a relationship. Friends; that was all they'd be from now on.

It was a pity she hadn't thought of that before she went to bed with him, though. It was hard to get the images of him kissing her, caressing her, out of her mind.

Chapter Thirty-Four

'Push me higher, Auntie Saffy,' Lily squealed. 'Right up to the trees!'

'Hold tight then!' Saffy said, giving the safety swing another push. Lily clung onto the rails and screamed in delight. She loved going high, whereas Miles was more cautious. He liked to gently swing to and fro, moving his head from side to side to study his surroundings, pointing to the birds, or a passing dog or cat. Nothing much slipped past Miles's eager eye but Lily lived her life at a faster pace and was always too busy having fun to take much notice of what was happening around her.

Saffy was enjoying spending time with the twins. She had never been one for babies; yes, they were sweet and nice to cuddle, but she preferred toddlers and older children who had developed their own personality. She loved watching them learn to walk, to talk, do different things.

'Saffy!'

She spun around at the familiar voice. Chloe was running toward her, closely followed by Logan.

'Great minds think alike,' he jested. 'Are you on auntie duty?'

'Yes, I thought I'd give Hannah and Lee a bit of time alone.' She turned back as Miles shouted, 'Push, Auntie Saf. Push!'

Chloe ran over to the slide and swiftly climbed the steps.

'Be careful!' Logan warned her. 'One step at a time.'

'Push please, Yuncle Loggy,' Lily called.

They stood side by side for a few minutes, pushing the twins on the swings, while Chloe ran up and down the slide.

'You must be pleased about your new job. And I know Hannah will be chuffed to see more of you,' Logan said.

'I am. And yes, I'll be pleased to see more of Hannah and the twins.' She paused as Miles held up his arms and demanded 'Out!' She bent down to lift the little boy out of the swing and cradled him in her arms – accidentally brushing against Logan's thigh. Tingles coursed through her body and memories of her fingers running over that naked thigh at Christmas flashed across her mind. Two months ago, yet it seemed a lifetime. 'I didn't realise that the company you worked for was based in Exeter.'

'Higher!' Lily demanded, obviously not tired of swinging yet.

Logan gave Lily a gentle push. 'Yes, and I'm thinking of working from the office a bit more now that Chloe is settled at school, especially on days where she has after-school clubs.'

Miles started to struggle in her arms. 'Down!' he demanded in a very firm voice.

'Out!' Lily demanded, lifting her arms.

'I think these two want to run around now,' Logan said, lifting her out of the swing.

'I'll let them for a few minutes then I'll take them back home.' She put Miles down and they both watched as the twins ran off. Chloe immediately followed them, stood between them and held both of their hands. 'She'll make a great big sister,' Logan said.

'Let's hope Jade has the sister she wants,' Saffy replied.

'She won't mind, she'll love the baby whether it's a boy or girl. She's been begging me for ages for a little brother or sister. Slower, Chloe,' he called as Chloe ran across the grass, still holding the twins' hands.

She was a lovely little girl, Saffy thought. Logan was right, she'd make a great big sister. She wondered if he minded his ex-partner having a baby with another man. He didn't seem to. She guessed his feelings for Jade were long gone. What about his feelings for her? Was Hannah right? Did he still fancy her as much as she still fancied him? But even if he did, did he want another child? And if he did, did he want it more than he wanted her?

❄

Sunday lunch was a lovely, relaxing affair. Saffy enjoyed herself immensely. Lee and Hannah's fondness for each other was evident to see, and the twins were a delight. Miles emptied his dinner over his head – much to the consternation of his parents – and Lily spent most of the time blowing raspberries. Chloe had persuaded Logan to buy her a joke book she'd seen in the supermarket when they went shopping yesterday afternoon and insisted on telling joke after joke. The rest of the adults took this in good humour but Logan clasped his hand to his forehead and groaned. 'Why did I let her talk me into buying that perishing book? She's going to drive me mad for the next week or so until she tires of it.'

'I remember you being like that, Saffy. Someone bought you a joke book for your birthday when you were about eight and we had to listen to the same jokes for weeks. Drove us insane!'

Saffy grinned. 'I bet you were the same but luckily you have no older siblings to tell tales on you.' She turned to Logan. 'I warn you now that she likes to come out with some very embarrassing stuff that she says I did when I was little and I'm not even sure half of it is true.'

'I'm the oldest too,' Chloe said. 'So my little sister or brother won't be able to tell tales on me but I will about them. I think being the oldest is really good.' She opened her book again. 'Can anyone get this joke?'

Logan groaned. 'Put it away for a while please, poppet, and go and play with the twins. They're getting bored.'

Chloe pulled a face but Miles chose that moment to call her so she got down from the table and ran over to play with him. She adored the twins.

The rest of the afternoon passed pleasantly; they went into the lounge, where Lee opened a bottle of wine and they shared anecdotes and memories of their childhood. Saffy was fascinated to discover that Logan's parents used to run a newspaper shop. Logan and his brother helped out on Saturdays and had a paper round each. 'Mum and Dad used to love going around stately homes at the weekend,' he said. 'That's what made me so interested in architecture. I used to study the designs of the houses, it fascinated me.'

'It sounds a very interesting job, and handy that you could work from home when Chloe was little. You must miss going into the office and mixing with people though. Is that why you're thinking about working from the office more now Chloe's older?' She would hate to work from home; she'd miss the hustle and bustle of the office, the interaction with the others.

'Yes, that's why I have a meeting on Saturday, to sort out the finer details. I won't go in every day, and I need to make sure I can have time off if Chloe is ill. She comes first and I'm all she's got. Well, I was,' he corrected himself. 'Now it seems that she has her mother, a soon-to-be stepdad and a new baby too.'

'How do you feel about that?' Saffy asked him softly.

'I don't mind. Jade and I were over years ago. I just hope that she doesn't get so busy with the new baby that she drops Chloe again. She's older now and it will hurt her badly if she's got close to her mum and then doesn't see her any more.' He shrugged. 'I guess it's a chance I'll have to take.'

'You can't protect her from everything, you can only be there for her if things go wrong,' Saffy told him. 'I know that's easy to say when I don't have any kids...'

Logan grinned. 'And you might think you don't want any right now, but you wait, the bug will bite you when you don't expect it. I can hardly believe Jade's about-turn. She actually seems excited about this child.'

'I'm glad. And yes, that does happen to some people but not to me.' She rose to her feet. 'Anyone want a top-up?'

'Just bring another bottle in, there's one in the fridge,' Lee said.

She kept her face away from them all so that they wouldn't see the tears that had sprung to her eyes because suddenly she wasn't sure she was fine with it any more. Right now she didn't want children, but maybe in a few years she might. She'd enjoyed spending this weekend with the twins and Chloe, and the knowledge that she might never have children of her own was unexpectedly painful.

Saffy made her way to the kitchen, feeling slightly wobbly. She must have had too much to drink, that was why she was feeling tearful, she thought as she opened the fridge. She tensed as she heard footsteps behind her. *Please don't let it be Logan,* she prayed. *I don't want him to see me like this.*

'Saffy.'

Thank goodness, it was Hannah.

'Are you okay, hun?' Hannah held out her arms and hugged her. 'Are you feeling upset about the children thing?'

Saffy nodded. 'I don't know why it's suddenly hitting me. It's silly, I dealt with it years ago and was fine with it. It must be spending all this time with you and the twins.'

'And Logan and Chloe.' Hannah's eyes searched her face. 'You love him, don't you? I can see it in your eyes. I think he loves you too.'

'Well, there's no future in it. Logan loves kids. Anyone can see that. Sooner or later he'll want a brother or sister for Chloe too and start to resent that I can't have any children.'

'I'm sure he won't. You need to broach the subject with him, see how he feels.'

Saffy wiped the tears away with her sleeve. 'It's not something I tell everyone, Hannah, and we aren't even an item.' She sniffed. 'And I'll make sure we never are.'

'You could be robbing yourself – both of you – of a really great relationship.'

'I don't want Logan's sympathy,' she said determinedly. 'Promise me you won't tell him.'

'I promise. But I think you're making a big mistake,' Hannah told her.

Why did she have to break down like that? She'd accepted it years ago. She didn't want or need sympathy from anyone. Least of all Logan.

❄

He'd longed to reach out and touch her, to draw her to him and kiss her, to make love to her but he hadn't. He'd kept a respectable distance, chatted lightly about the twins, Chloe, Saffy's job when all the time he was longing to ask her if they could give it another try, see if they could make a relationship work.

Why hadn't he?

Was it really because of Chloe? Chloe had her mother back in her life now, a baby brother or sister on the way, and she really liked Saffy. He wasn't talking anything serious, just a few dates. What harm would it do? There was definitely strong chemistry between them. Maybe he could ask Saffy if she felt the same when he popped in to check out her new flat next week.

Chapter Thirty-Five

A week later

'Where do you want this, Saf?' Robbie asked, pushing in the white-wheeled ottoman with the light beech lid. 'I'm presuming the bedroom?'

'Yes please, under the window,' Saffy replied, putting yet another box down on the floor. She had no idea she'd collected so much stuff! Thank goodness Duncan and Robbie were helping her move in.

'It's a nice place, plenty of character,' Duncan said, carrying in the big Tiffany lamp Saffy had fallen in love with at an antique shop a couple of years ago.

'It's not as nice as my old flat, but it'll do for now,' Saffy said. 'Once the position is confirmed as permanent, and I'm sure I want it to be, I'll sell my flat and buy one down here.'

'Yes, make sure you like it before you uproot yourself.' Robbie nodded. 'Now, that's the last of the boxes so how about I put the kettle on?'

'Good idea, I'll just take this through into the bedroom.' Saffy picked up the black plastic bag she'd chucked all her duvet covers and sheets into.

'I've got something to go with the coffee.' Duncan popped out to the van and returned five minutes later with a plastic container containing a large cake, and Logan by his side. 'Look who I found downstairs,' he said with a grin.

Saffy looked up from the box she was unpacking and her pulse danced as her eyes rested on Logan, looking devastatingly handsome in a dark grey suit, white shirt and blue tie. Whoa!

'Sorry I'm a bit early. The meeting didn't last as long as I thought,' he told Saffy.

'No worries,' she said. 'You look smart. I didn't realise your meeting was such a formal one.'

'Not really formal but I thought I'd best make a good impression. I don't want everyone thinking I've let myself go and spend all my day in pjs or trackies just because I work from home.'

'Don't you?' Duncan asked him. 'I often do when I'm working from home.'

'Designer ones, naturally. So if anyone pops in he still looks totally gorgeous,' Robbie added, popping his head around the kitchen door.

Duncan grinned. 'I wouldn't wear anything else.'

'I might do if I didn't have to get dressed to do the school runs. Mind you, I admit I spend most of my time dressed in jeans and a T-shirt or jumper.' He glanced around at the pile of boxes and bags in the room. 'I'd offer to help you sort all this out, but I can see you've already got plenty of help.'

'We're just the delivery men, we're off after we've had a cuppa and a slice of cake, so you can take over from us,' Duncan told him. 'I'll go and slice this up.' He went to join Robbie in the kitchen, conveniently leaving Logan and Saffy alone.

'So this is it, D-day,' Logan said, gazing around. 'How do you feel about the big move?'

Saffy thought about it. 'Truthfully? Excited and a bit nervous at the same time. I'm made up about the job, it's a big step forward for my career and I'm so looking forward to building up a group of creatives and helping them sell their goods. But I'm going to miss my work colleagues. It'll be whole new team at Exeter.'

'You'll be fine. You're outgoing, mix well and are obviously great at your job or you'd never have been given the position.'

She hadn't expected him to lavish such praise on her. 'Thank you.'

'Break time!' Robbie kicked open the door with his foot and walked in carrying a tray with four mugs of coffee and some saucers. Duncan followed, holding a plate with the now sliced chocolate fudge cake on it.

They placed the tray and cake down on the table. 'Okay, tuck in,' Robbie said.

'That cake looks scrumptious but I think I'd better take this jacket off first, I've only just had this suit dry-cleaned.'

Saffy watched as Logan eased off the jacket, memories of the hot, toned body beneath that shirt flitting across her mind. *Stop staring at him!* She tore her eyes away and reached for a mug of coffee. When Logan sat down beside her, his jacket placed on the back of the sofa, she'd composed herself again.

They all chatted for a while, light, easy conversation about amusing moving house anecdotes.

'Honestly, when we moved into our place we couldn't get our huge cream sofa through the front door. We had to take the door off the hinges. And, of course, we had to move in on a Sunday, didn't we, because of work, so all the neighbours were out watching,' Robbie said.

'Yep, so Robbie waved at them all and invited them in for a cup of coffee,' Duncan continued. 'Only we all ended up having wine. That was our first party, amid a pile of boxes, bags and other clutter.'

'It was brilliant. It broke the ice and all the neighbours helped us get straight.'

'When I moved down to Cornwall Chloe wasn't even two,' Logan said. 'I'd hired a van, and my brother and his wife had come to help. We put Chloe in the dining room with a load of toys, and her favourite film on the TV and kept popping in and checking on her. But she crept out without any of us spotting her and decided to visit the woman next door. She walked in on her when Annie – Mrs Mackintosh – was in the bathroom and helped herself to one of her freshly made cakes. Thanks goodness Annie saw the funny side but I shudder to think what might have happened if Chloe had wandered into the road. Mind you, Annie fell in love with her and became my regular babysitter so it all worked out,' he added.

'What about you, Saf, any house-moving stories to share?' Robbie asked, as he bit into a slice of cake.

'There's one I still feel guilty about,' Saffy said. 'We moved around a bit when I was a kid, lots of rented places, and we always took our family cat, Mr Tibbs, in a cat carrier and kept him indoors until he got used to where he lived. But once, when I was about five, I was so excited about us having a big garden – we'd only had a small yard before – that I couldn't wait to show it to Mr Tibbs. I let him out of his case and he was off like a shot. I cried for days but luckily he turned up at our old house a week later. The neighbours phoned to let us know and Mum went to collect him. Every time we moved after that Mum and Hannah banned me from touching Mr Tibbs' case.'

They all chuckled.

❄

She was beautiful, Logan thought as he watched Saffy talk, and so expressive, her hands waving as she talked, her expression changing from guilt to worry and laughter as she told the story. She was so warm and genuine as well as sexy and gorgeous. The whole package. He'd never known anyone like her. And he didn't want to lose her.

After the coffee and cake, it was time for Robbie and Duncan to go.

'We're going to miss you,' Robbie said, putting his arm around Saffy's shoulder and giving her an affectionate squeeze.

'We sure are. Don't be a stranger. Come and spend the weekend with us now and again,' Duncan told her.

'I will,' Saffy promised. 'Anyway you guys will be too busy planning your wedding to miss me.'

'We definitely won't. You're our chief bridesmaid, remember?'

'I'm looking forward to it!' Saffy told them. 'Have you settled on a date yet?'

'Not yet, but it'll be around August/September while it's still summery.' Robbie answered this time. He turned to Logan. 'You must come too, bring Chloe. Children are definitely allowed.'

Logan was too surprised to answer at first; his mind was racing. If he accepted, would that make things awkward between him and Saffy? On the other hand, it would give him chance to see more of Saffy, and looking beautiful all dressed up as a bridesmaid too. He could accept and back out if things were too awkward with him and Saffy. 'Thanks, I'd love to.'

'That's settled then. We'll send you an invite as soon as we've fixed a firm date.' Robbie air-kissed Saffy on both cheeks and shook Logan's hand. Duncan did the same and then they were both gone, leaving the flat feeling very empty and Saffy looking awkward. Just like he felt.

'How about I help you get straight then we could go out for a meal?' he offered.

Saffy thrust her hand through her tousled hair and surveyed the pile of boxes. 'That would be great but…' She paused.

'Go ahead,' he encouraged her.

'Well, I don't want you to ruin that smart suit.'

'That's not a problem.' He took off his tie and put it on the back of the sofa with his jacket, unfastened the top two buttons of his shirt and rolled up his sleeves. 'There. I'm ready to go. Anything else?'

'And – can we have a takeaway instead? I really don't feel like getting all dolled up to go out tonight. I need to settle in and get my things straight before work on Monday.'

'No problem. And when you've had enough of me, tell me to go. Right?'

'Right. But that won't be until all this is sorted out,' she said with a grin.

He grinned back and picked up a big box. 'Now where do you want this?'

❄

With Logan's help it only took a couple of hours to get straight. Yes, lots of her things were still in boxes, but they were in the correct rooms so she could unpack at a later date. The important stuff – the microwave, toaster, coffee machine, her full-length mirror-cum-jewellery-box, work files, bed linen and towels – was all out and ready to be used. Now all she had to do was hang the curtains and make up the bed.

Logan handed her a cold can of Coke. He'd popped out to the shop to get supplies, leaving her to carry on with the unpacking.

'Nearly there,' he said. 'You'll soon have it looking like home.'

'I need to hang the curtains, it's getting dark now, and then I might leave the rest until tomorrow,' she said, popping the ring pull open and taking a big gulp of the refreshing drink. 'I'm knackered.'

'Will your curtains fit these windows?' he asked.

'Yep, I checked. The only thing I don't have is a blind for the bathroom. I'll hang a towel over the pole for now.'

'You're three storeys up and the glass is frosted. No one will be able to see in,' he reminded her.

'I know, but I get spooked if I don't have curtains or a blind at the windows and it's dark outside,' she confessed.

'Really?' He checked his watch. 'There's a big furnishings store only ten minutes' drive away, and it sells blinds. Want me to measure the window and we'll go and get one? Or I could go and get it while you carry on here?'

Did she? She could have hugged him. 'Oh, would you? A cream one will do fine. Thanks so much.'

'I'll be half an hour max,' he told her, grabbing his jacket and taking his wallet out of the inside pocket.

'No, I'll give you the money.'

She reached for her bag, tripped over a box on the floor and fell against him.

'Whoa!' He placed his hands on her shoulders to steady her.

'Thanks,' she mumbled, trying to ignore the effect his hands touching her skin was having on her.

'You're welcome.' Tender blue eyes smiled down at hers. Then he lowered his head and kissed her lightly on the lips and she couldn't ignore her feelings any longer.

Chapter Thirty-Six

Logan caught his breath as Saffy wound one arm around his neck and one around his waist and leaned into him, returning his kiss with passion. It was as if he'd ignited a fire she'd been trying to quench. His hands slid to her waist as they kissed deeper, then one slid under the bottom of her T-shirt, onto soft bare skin. He felt a shudder run through her body as he caressed her back, moving his hand upwards, underneath the back of her bra. Their kisses were more intense now, and her hands were pulling the bottom of his shirt, tugging it out of his trousers so she could run them over his bare back too. God, she was hot – make that sizzling.

It was as if they couldn't get enough of each other. They were kicking off shoes, tugging at each other's clothes, kissing, caressing, then they were lying naked on the rug on the floor and he was thinking it was a good job he'd put a packet of condoms in his jacket pocket just in case and he needed to get one right now… but wow, what was she doing?

❄

Later, as they lay curled up in each other's arms on the sofa, and she couldn't even remember how they'd got there, Saffy closed her eyes, savouring the feeling of contentment. She wanted to lie here forever, to shut out the world, to enjoy this feeling of just her and Logan; the smell of him, the closeness, the way he was looking at her now, gazing into her eyes. It was almost as if he loved her. Did he?

Because she loved him.

There. She'd admitted it to herself, the truth she'd been refusing to face since she met Logan. She loved him. Although where they went from here, she had no idea. Chloe was away this weekend so Logan was free to spend time with her, but what about other weekends? Would he expect her to stay at Hannah's and pop over to visit? Or maybe he didn't expect anything at all, maybe this was a one-off again?

'You're looking thoughtful.' Logan tapped her nose playfully. 'Are you having regrets? Or have I tired you out?'

'Neither.' She leaned forward and wrapped her arms around her shoulders, suddenly cold. 'I think I might turn the heating on.'

As she went to get up, Logan pulled her back. 'Wait. I want to talk to you. Please.'

He reached down and pulled a throw up from the floor, tenderly wrapping it over her to keep her warm.

Okay, so where exactly was this going?

Logan wrapped his arm around her shoulders, hugging her to him. 'Can we put our cards on the table? I think it's important that we're honest with each other.'

So this is where she got the 'can we keep this casual and away from Chloe' speech, which was fine by her; she had a new job, a new home, she didn't need complications in her life. Even if she did love him.

'Sure,' she agreed.

He kissed her on the forehead. 'Bottom line is that I love you.'

She shot upright and turned to face him, hardly able to believe her ears. 'You do?'

'Yes.' He pulled the throw that had fallen from her shoulders back around her. 'I won't be able to concentrate if you don't cover up,' he said, leaning forward and kissing her on the forehead.

This was beginning to sound serious. She met his gaze and steeled herself for what he had to say.

'The question is, do you love me?'

She could see the love in his deep blue eyes as he held her gaze and hoped he could see the love reflected back in her own eyes. She nodded emphatically. 'Yes.' She leaned forward and kissed him on the lips. 'Definitely.'

And then they were kissing again. When they finally came up for air Logan pulled away a little, his eyes searching her face. 'So how about we take the next step and make this a relationship?'

A relationship? What did he mean by that?

'As in, see each other regularly?' she asked.

'As often as we can. Maybe we can meet up in the week, or at weekends. One of the plusses of Jade wanting to be in Chloe's life is that I get child-free weekends.'

He only wanted to see her when Chloe wasn't there? Did that mean he saw this as a temporary relationship? A fling? Yet he said he loved her…

He must have seen the confusion in her eyes because he suddenly stiffened. 'It looks like you aren't ready for that. You want to keep things light?' He reached down for his boxers. 'Maybe I ought to go.'

She steadied his hand. 'Not ready for what?' she asked gently.

'To be my girlfriend. To tell people we're an item.'

'And what about Chloe? You both come as a package.' It was important that she knew exactly what he was asking of her.

'I'm not asking you to be a substitute mum to Chloe, Saffy. I thought we'd got a connection here, we've just said we love each other. But yes,

I want you to be in Chloe's life too. To be part of our family.' His eyes were searching her face. 'Is that what you want too?'

'Of course.' There was nothing she wanted more, but what if he wanted to extend that family? For them to have a child together? She had to tell him that wasn't possible before they got too involved. She had to give him the chance to walk away now. It would hurt but not as much as if she'd become part of their family and then had to tell him. She couldn't cope with going through that again, and this time she knew the rejection would be far more painful than it had been with Joe. She tried to find the words to voice the fears that were whirling around in her head. 'But, I have to tell you something. A family isn't for me…' she stammered. 'It never will be.'

Suddenly he was up and starting to get dressed, his face all closed and tight. 'Normally I'm okay with casual, normally that's what I do. But I stupidly thought we were more than that. I thought you liked Chloe, that you accepted us as a unit.'

He was dressed now, reaching for his jacket. He was going to walk out if she didn't say something to stop him but she felt like she was frozen, she couldn't move, couldn't speak. She made one last attempt.

'I do. Chloe's a lovely little girl. I'm just trying to say…'

He turned to her, his eyes full of sadness. 'Goodbye, Saffy. Good luck with your new job and new life.' Then he was out of the door. Out of her life.

Chapter Thirty-Seven

How had they gone from professing their love for each other to Logan walking out? Saffy thought dismally as she stood at the window, watching him walk to the car, his jacket slung over his shoulder, his movements slow, dejected. She'd hurt him; she hadn't meant to, she hadn't been able to find the words to explain what she'd wanted to say: that he could never have a family with her, that if he was with her he would have to settle for Chloe being his only child.

Tears gushed to her eyes. She wiped them away with the back of her hand and turned away from the window. Half-blinded by the tears that wouldn't stop coming, she made her way over to the sofa and slumped down on it, drawing up her knees and hugging them tight, as she looked around at her clothes scattered on the floor. How had it changed from that passion to this emptiness? Surely if Logan loved her, he would have tried to understand?

She sat up as the words she'd said repeated in her mind. 'A family isn't for me and never will be.' God, that sounded awful. No wonder he was so hurt. He thought that she meant Chloe. That she didn't want to take on Chloe.

She had to phone him, to explain. But what if he reacted like Joe? What if he said that he couldn't be with someone who could never have children? Well, at least she could give him the choice. She couldn't bear for them to break up because he thought she didn't want Chloe. She adored that little girl. She had to phone him. Where had she put her phone? It had been on the table with Logan's car keys before they started tearing each other's clothes off.

Logan's car keys. Her eyes rested on the bundle of keys on the floor under the table at exactly the same time as the door knocked.

Logan. He'd come back for his keys.

She wrapped the throw around her, picked up the keys and shuffled over to the door.

'Sorry to disturb you but I've left my keys,' he said stiffly as she opened it.

'I can't have children,' she blurted out. 'That's what I was saying. Not that I didn't want Chloe.'

He stared at her, stunned. 'What?'

'I can't have kids. That's why I said a family wasn't for me. I wasn't talking about Chloe. I love Chloe. But if you stay with me, she'll have to be your only child.' She bit her lip, blinked back the tears and watched his expression. The icy coldness was replaced by bewilderment, surprise – was that relief? Then compassion.

'Saffy.' His tone was suddenly tender and he stepped inside, closed the door behind him with his foot and took her in his arms. 'Why didn't you tell me this before?'

'When?' she asked. 'We haven't exactly been in a relationship, have we? We just…'

'Made love a couple of times,' he finished for her.

She nodded, enjoying the comfort of his arms around her. 'It's not something you say to everyone you meet or hook up with, is it? I can't have kids.'

'But we said we loved each other…' He had his arm around her and was easing her –almost tripping over the throw – towards the sofa as they talked.

'I know. And I tried to tell you but it came out wrong. It came out like I wanted to keep things casual because I didn't want to take on Chloe.'

They sat down, facing each other, and she pulled the throw close around her shoulders. 'The problem isn't Chloe, Logan, it's me. I won't ever be able to have children. If you and I stay together, you'll never have another child. That's a really big deal. I want you to think about it, make sure you're okay with it before this goes any further.'

He gently placed his hands both sides of her face. 'I love you, Saffy. You're enough for me. It doesn't matter whether we have a child together or not, that doesn't change how I feel about you.'

She could see the love in his eyes and knew he meant it, for now. She had to be sure that he realised what he was committing himself to.

'And what about in a couple of years' time? You might feel like you want a child then.'

'I'm not hankering for another child. I only want you. You'll always be enough for me,' he promised. 'What about you? Would you like to have a child?' His tone was tender and he'd moved so close she could feel his warm breath on her neck.

'I don't know. But I would like to have the choice.' She tried to catch the sob but it was out before she could stop it. Then she felt his arms around her, and he spun her around, pressed her head in his shoulder, and held her as she cried.

'I'm so sorry,' he whispered into her ear. 'I realise this must be really tough for you.'

It felt so good in his arms that she wanted to stay there forever. 'Sorry, I don't normally get upset over it,' she mumbled, taking the hankie he offered her and wiping her eyes. 'I came to terms with it years ago.'

'It's a big thing, Saffy, massive. You have every right to be upset about it but please don't think that it matters to me. Having you in my life is enough for me.'

She looked up at him. 'Are you sure?'

'Positive. And if at some time in the future we both feel like we want a child together there are other options we can explore, but whatever happens, you are enough for me.'

'And you – and Chloe – you'll always be enough for me,' she told him.

'Good.' His lips found hers and they kissed, their bodies melting against each other. Then Logan raised his head, still holding her tight, his eyes meeting hers. 'Look, I'm not expecting you to move in or be a mother to Chloe but we come as a package. There are times when she'll be with me and I need to know that you're okay with that.'

How could he even ask that question? She loved spending time with Chloe, surely he knew that? But she understood it was because Chloe's own mother had walked out and left her and he didn't want his little girl to be hurt again or to feel pushed out.

'You must know that I adore Chloe. We even share a love of polar bears,' she reminded him.

He kissed her on the forehead. 'You're brilliant with her. But there are times I might have to cancel things we've arranged at the last minute because she's ill, or I can't get a sitter.'

'That's not a problem,' she assured him.

'Can I take it that we're in a proper relationship then?' he asked, his eyes brimming with love.

She nodded. 'You can.'

Then they were in each other's arms, kissing and caressing again and this time when they made love it was like a commitment to each other, a promise of a loving future together.

When they were both finally sated and she lay snuggled up to Logan's bare chest, feeling his arms cradling her, Saffy thought that she had never felt happier.

'How do you feel about me staying over tonight?' Logan asked softly, as he traced her lips with his thumb. 'Would you prefer to be on your own, to settle in?

She couldn't think of anything she'd like more than to have him stay with her. She wrapped her arms around his neck. 'I'd love you to stop over.'

'Then how about I order us that takeaway? I don't know about you, but I'm starving.'

She rolled over on top of him and tapped his nose teasingly with her finger. 'I can't think how you've worked up such an appetite.'

He smiled up at her. 'Takeaway, then finish tidying up and bed?'

'You really do have only one thing on your mind, don't you?' she said. Then he pulled her down and started kissing her again and it was another hour before they finally had the takeaway.

Chapter Thirty-Eight

It was gone ten when they woke, opening their eyes at the same time and smiling at each other as they lay face to face. They'd fallen asleep that way, and although they must have moved several times in the night, had somehow woken in the same position.

'This is how I'd like to wake every day, with you being the first thing that I see when I open my eyes,' Logan said, wrapping his arms around her, his eyes ablaze with love.

'Me too,' she whispered back. 'But I think we're going to have to settle for the occasional weekend for a while.' Logan had Chloe and Saffy had a six-month lease on this flat; there was no way they were going to live together in a hurry. Neither of them wanted that yet, though. Saffy wanted to concentrate on her career for a while and she knew that Logan wanted to give Chloe time to get used to them being together before they took things any further.

'I know. We'll get there gradually,' he said. 'As long as we love each other we can work anything out.' His eyes held hers. 'You do love me, don't you?'

'Absolutely.' She moved in for a cuddle and they embraced for a while. She loved it, this feeling of happiness, that all was well with the world, which enveloped her whenever Logan held her in his arms. She didn't want to move and disturb such a precious moment but she needed the loo, and a drink, in that order.

'Fancy a cuppa?' Logan asked, as if he'd read her thoughts.

'Please.' She eased herself out of his arms. 'And the bathroom.'

'Tea or coffee?' He pulled himself up, watching admiringly as she threw back the covers and looked around for her dressing-gown. Damn, she hadn't unpacked it – hadn't unpacked anything except the pillows, duvet and bedding so they could make the bed.

'Tea please, one sugar,' she said as she headed for the bathroom. 'And don't keep staring at me!' Then she turned as she heard him chuckle. 'What's so funny?'

'When you headed off to the bathroom like that, all self-conscious. It reminded me of when I called to bring the vegetables and you were wearing your polar bear onesie. You looked so awkward at being caught dressed in it.' His eyes were dancing with laughter.

'I was,' she said, returning his grin. 'But hey, it got me top marks with Chloe. We bonded over polar bears.'

'So you did.' Suddenly he stopped laughing and his eyes deepened as they lowered.

'Now what are you staring at?'

'Fancy coming back to bed for a bit?'

'You're insatiable. Go put the kettle on,' she ordered, but her face lit up with a smile as she walked into the bathroom and shut the door.

❄

When they'd showered, and Logan had fetched breakfast supplies while Saffy unpacked, they went for a walk by the river, strolling hand in hand as if it was the most natural thing in the world. As she sat on the bench, watching the ducks, Saffy felt that she would burst with happiness.

They had lunch out then went back to the flat, where they sat talking, sharing stories about their childhoods, and their pasts, their likes and dislikes. It was as if they were trying to pile it all in that afternoon because they didn't know when they'd get the chance again.

The afternoon flew by and Saffy felt a sense of loss when Logan glanced at his watch. 'I'm sorry but I have to go. Jade's bringing Chloe back at six.'

'That's fine. Give Chloe my love,' Saffy said. 'I'll phone you later.' *When will we see each other again*? she wondered. Perhaps she could visit Hannah on Saturday and spend some time with Logan – and Chloe – then.

'I'm in the office on Wednesday, maybe we could meet for lunch,' Logan suggested.

'That sounds good… and I could pop down to see Hannah at the weekend. Or is that too soon?'

'Of course not. I wish I could see you every day.' He paused, an anxious look coming over his face. 'I wish you could stop over with me but…'

'But you want me to stay over at Hannah's until Chloe gets used to the idea of us being together?' she finished for him. She'd already guessed that. Knowing how protective Logan was of his little daughter, she was quite sure that he wouldn't want her to sleep over.

'For a little while, if you don't mind? I don't want Chloe to think it's normal for grown-ups to sleep together as soon as they get together.' He looked a bit awkward. 'I'm sorry, I know it sounds a bit prudish and as if I'm pushing you away.'

'It's not a problem. I don't think I'm comfortable with Chloe finding us in bed together just yet either. We can save that for the weekends she's at her mum's.'

'Deal. It's only for a month or two.' He caressed her cheek with his fingertips. 'You're really special, Saffy, you know that?' His lips were mere centimetres away from hers now.

'You're not too bad yourself,' she said.

Then their lips met and there was no more talking.

Chapter Thirty-Nine

August – Five months later

'Saffy!' Chloe came running in and threw her arms around Saffy. 'I was hoping you hadn't gone home yet.'

'I thought I'd stop and see you.' Saffy pulled the little girl down to sit beside her on the sofa. 'What's your little brother like?' Jade had given birth to a little boy last week so Grant had fetched Chloe to take her to show him.

'He's so cute. I wish we had a baby,' Chloe said. 'Do you think you and Daddy might have a baby?'

Saffy swallowed and looked over at Logan. What did she say to that? *Tell her the truth,* she thought, *otherwise she'll keep asking.* 'No, because I can't have any children, I'm afraid,' she said slowly. 'Not everyone can have babies.'

Chloe's eyes widened. 'Oh, poor you.' She gave her a big hug. 'Never mind, you can share me with Daddy.'

Tears pricked Saffy's eyes as she smiled down at the little girl. 'Thank you. I'd like that.'

'It doesn't matter, Saffy and I are very happy how we are,' Logan added, then quickly changed the subject. 'What's your little brother called?'

'Sam. He's so tiny. I held him on my lap for a bit but then he did a poo and Mummy had to change his nappy.' She pulled a face. 'He cries a lot in the night though.' She scrambled off the sofa. 'Can I have some crisps?'

'Sure, there's some in the kitchen cupboard,' Logan told her. As soon as Chloe disappeared into the kitchen he went over to Saffy, sat down beside her and put his arm around her shoulder. 'I'm sorry about Chloe. Did she upset you?'

Saffy shook her head. 'She's bound to talk about it, especially now that she has a new baby brother, so I thought it was best to be honest, then she won't keep asking.' She fixed her eyes on Logan's face, searching. 'Are you sure it doesn't bother you? I'll understand if you think you can't deal with it. It's perfectly understandable that you might want another child.'

'I've told you, all I want is you.' He leaned forward and kissed her. She wrapped her arms around him and hugged him tight. This man and Chloe, that's all she needed. They hugged in a comfortable silence for a while then Logan relaxed his hold and looked down at her. 'I've been thinking, your contract on your flat is up soon, isn't it?'

She'd been thinking about that herself only last night. 'Yes, next month.'

'So how do you fancy moving in here? You spend most of your time here anyway and I can't think of anything I'd like better than to wake up with you every morning.' He placed his hand under her chin and gently lifted her face so he could read her expression. 'Is it too soon for you? Do you prefer your own space? I understand if you do.'

She couldn't think of anything she'd like more than to wake up with Logan either. And to share her life with him and Chloe. 'I'd love to move in with you,' she assured him. 'Should we make sure Chloe is okay with it first, though?'

Logan kissed her again, for a very long time. When they came up for air, he called Chloe downstairs.

'What's up?' she asked, looking from one to the other. 'You both look very pleased.'

'I've asked Saffy to move in with us and she's agreed,' Logan told her. 'Is that okay with you?'

'YESSS!' Chloe screamed, running and putting her arms around Saffy. 'When are you moving in? Today?'

'We haven't actually discussed when yet but in a couple of weeks,' Saffy replied, pleased at the little girl's response. She'd formed quite a bond with her over the last few months and had been pretty sure that Chloe would be happy to have her around on a more permanent basis, but you never could tell.

Chloe gave Logan a hug next then went back upstairs to play.

'How about I ask Annie to babysit and we go out for a meal to celebrate?' Logan suggested.

'I've got a better idea. Let's go for a pizza and take Chloe with us,' Saffy replied.

'Are you sure?' Logan asked.

She reached out and squeezed his hand. 'We're going to be a family so let's start out how we mean to go on. You and I can have a night out alone another time, but today I want us to celebrate with Chloe.'

❄

Later that night as they lay in each other's arms in bed, after a celebratory pizza with Chloe, Logan thought he'd never felt happier. He could still barely believe that Saffy had agreed to move in with him.

He had been plucking up the courage to ask her for weeks but knew that he was asking a lot of her, to take on a ready-made family, and even though the issues with Jade were sorted for now he was pretty sure more would come up in the future. He had to make sure Saffy knew what she was letting herself in for. He so desperately wanted this to work out and was prepared to back off and let Saffy move at her own pace, if necessary. He didn't want her to feel trapped in any way. He didn't want to risk losing her.

He squeezed her shoulder gently and asked softly, 'You are really sure about moving in, aren't you, Saffy? Chloe can be a handful at times. Obviously, I'll look after her as much as I can but there will be times I'm at work and you'll be left in charge. Are you okay with that?'

She raised her head and smiled at him. 'No problem. I love Chloe, you know I do. And yes, I know it won't be all plain sailing but together we'll sort it.'

And he was sure they would. When Jade had left him he'd known that Chloe was solely his responsibility, that her happiness and welfare were all that mattered. He'd resigned himself to living alone for the foreseeable future because he would never trust another woman enough to let them into Chloe's life again. Then Saffy had come along and wrapped herself around his heart. And he felt certain that she would never let him down, that she would love Chloe almost as much as he did. He couldn't be any happier than he was right now. This was what he wanted forever.

'What about your flat in Birmingham? Are you still going to rent that out?' he asked.

'I was thinking of selling it because I feel really settled down here. It's lovely to be near Hannah and the twins and now we're together I definitely won't be going back to Birmingham to live. I could carry on renting, of course, but the rent just about covers the mortgage so I don't make any profit from it. And I feel like that's my old life, I want to draw a line under it.' She turned onto her back and gazed up at him. 'If I sell I'll probably be left with a couple of grand when it's all settled. I guess it could get me a new car.'

'Or pay for a honeymoon.' He watched the expression on her face change from surprise to… was that delight? The words surprised him too; he hadn't planned them. They'd just popped out but now he thought about it, yes, he would like to marry Saffy.

'Are you proposing to me?' she asked.

'Hang on.' He got out of bed and went into the bathroom. Finding what he wanted he returned to the bedroom then got down on one knee and held out his closed hand. Saffy sat up and hugged her knees.

'Saffron Baxter, will you please marry me?' he asked, opening his hand to reveal a tiny purple sparkly hairband

Saffy giggled. 'Yes please.'

Logan grinned and slid the purple band onto the ring finger of her left hand. 'I now pronounce us engaged,' he said. 'We'll go shopping in the week and get you a proper ring.'

'I think I like the purple band.' She smiled. 'So what do we do now?'

'Now we consummate our engagement,' he said, pulling back the bedclothes and getting into bed.

❄

'Engaged!' Hannah squealed in delight as Saffy showed her the diamond engagement ring she and Logan had chosen whilst Chloe was at school. They were telling Chloe when she came home from school later but couldn't resist sharing their news with Hannah and Lee. 'That's marvellous. You two are perfect for each other!' She threw her arms around Saffy and gave her a big hug, then did the same to Logan. 'This is the best news I've had for ages.'

Lee kissed Saffy on the cheek and shook Logan's hand. 'Brilliant news. This calls for a celebration.'

Hannah clapped her hands. 'Yes, we must celebrate. There's a bottle of cava in the fridge.' Saffy watched her sister in amusement. She was positively brimming with happiness. 'When's the wedding?' she asked.

'We haven't decided, we only got engaged last night,' Saffy told her.

Lee returned with the bottle of cava and four glasses on a tray. 'Sorry it isn't the real stuff but at least it's bubbly.'

He popped the bottle and carefully poured the fizzy drink into the glasses, giving them all one each.

'To Saffy and Logan!' he said.

'Saffy and Logan!' Hannah echoed.

Saffy felt Logan's hand clasp hers. She turned to him, smiling. 'To us,' he said, clinking his glass with hers.

'To us,' Saffy echoed.

As Logan's eyes met hers she wished she could freeze this moment forever, put it in a frame marked 'the happiest I've ever been' and treasure it.

Chapter Forty

September

Robbie and Duncan's wedding was a spectacular affair, as Saffy knew it would be. Both the grooms looked incredibly handsome in snow-white suits and waistcoats, with a black shirt and white tie for Duncan and a white shirt and black tie for Robbie. Saffy's dress was a gorgeous pale blue, exquisitely cut with a diamanté bodice. Robbie's nephew was a pageboy and Duncan's niece was a flower girl. The best man – a mutual friend of the grooms – was dressed in a black suit, pale blue shirt and white tie.

'Don't they look fantastic?' Meg asked, cuddling her baby daughter. As soon as she and Stefan had found out they were having a little girl they'd postponed their wedding for eighteen months so their daughter could be a flower girl. Meg had asked Saffy to be her chief bridesmaid too.

'They certainly do,' Saffy agreed. 'And so happy together.'

Robbie and Duncan hadn't been able to keep their eyes off each other, and both wore broad grins for the entire ceremony.

'Talking about happy, have you and Logan set a wedding date yet?'

'There's no rush, we've only been living together a couple of weeks,' Saffy told her. Moving in with Logan had made her happier than she'd ever imagined but neither of them had discussed the wedding since they had got engaged.

'I was wondering if you wanted to have a double wedding with us next summer?' Meg asked mischievously.

'I'm not sure. We haven't had time to discuss it yet but I want something a bit low-key,' Saffy replied. To be honest, good friend as Meg was, she wanted her and Logan's wedding day to be a special day just for the two of them – well, three, Chloe would be bridesmaid, of course. They hadn't really discussed wedding plans though. Things had been so hectic. She'd tell him about Meg's suggestion tomorrow and see what he thought of the idea.

Just then Robbie and Duncan took the floor for their first dance and everyone turned to watch them as 'Perfect Day' by Lou Reed started playing.

'This is such a lovely song,' Saffy said. And apt, she thought. It had been a perfect day.

'Just look at them, they look so happy,' Meg sighed as Robbie and Duncan glided across the floor in a smoochy waltz. 'I can't wait for our wedding next year.' She kissed her baby on the forehead. 'Ella May will make a beautiful flower girl.' She turned to look at Chloe dancing with a couple of other little girls. 'Chloe will make a gorgeous bridesmaid too,' she added.

'Yes she will.' Robbie and Duncan's wedding had been lovely but Saffy felt that she wanted something different. Everyone had summer weddings. She quite fancied a winter one. Scarlet bridesmaids' dresses with white sashes, white fur capes over their dresses. Chloe would look so cute like that.

'Fancy a dance?' Logan suddenly appeared at Saffy's side and held out his hand. She took it and followed him onto the dance floor. As he held her waist she rested her head on his shoulder. She wanted this man in her life forever.

The music changed to 'You are the Best Thing' and Logan pulled her even closer. 'How do you fancy a Christmas wedding?' he whispered. 'We could book it for the weekend before Christmas and then we can celebrate our first Christmas together as a married couple.'

A Christmas wedding? He'd been thinking along the same lines as her. They might even have snow.

'That sounds perfect,' Saffy said happily. 'That would make it the best Christmas ever.'

'I can't believe that we only met last Christmas,' Logan whispered in her ear. 'I guess this means that I'll no longer be eligible to join the Lonely Hearts Christmas dinner, seeing as I'll be a married man.'

'You won't get out of making the Christmas cake that easily, you'll be family and we'll definitely be spending Christmas at Liwus Helyk,' Saffy said. 'That is if you want to?'

'I very much want to. It's part of Christmas for me and Chloe, and it's your sister's party that brought us together.'

'It brought me and Hannah together too. We're closer than we've ever been.'

'We could have the twins as bridesmaid and pageboy,' Logan said. 'Then it will be a real family affair.'

'That would be perfect.' Saffy smiled. 'Hannah always hoped her Christmas get-together would end in a wedding for someone. I bet she never guessed in her wildest dreams I would end up being the bride.'

Logan wrapped both arms around her as the music slowed down. 'Happy?'

'Ecstatic.'

'Me too.'

Then, as the closing lyrics to 'You are the Best Thing' played out they both joined in, gazing into each other's eyes as they moved to the music.

A Letter from Karen

I want to say a huge thank you for choosing to read *Snowy Nights at the Lonely Hearts Hotel.* I really hope it gave you a happy glow and made you feel all warm and cosy inside. If you did enjoy it and want to keep up-to-date with all my latest releases, just sign up at the following link. Your email address will never be shared and you can unsubscribe at any time.

www.bookouture.com/karen-king

I hope you loved *Snowy Nights at the Lonely Hearts Hotel* as much as I enjoyed writing it. Cornwall will always have a special place in my heart – it's so beautiful whatever the season. It was a pleasure to recall snowy winters, mulled wine, log fires, carols and twinkling fairy lights and to write about love, family and friendships.

If you enjoyed reading my book I wonder if you could spare the time to write a review for me. I'd love to hear what you think. It doesn't have to be a long one, and I'd be very grateful as reviews make such a difference helping new readers to discover my books for the first time.

I love hearing from my readers too so do get in touch on my Facebook page, through Twitter, Goodreads or my website.

Thank you again for choosing my book to read.

Love Karen xx

KarenKingRomanceAuthor

karen_king

www.karenking.net

Acknowledgments

This story is set in Cornwall, a place I will always hold close to my heart. I'm delighted to visit it again, this time in winter, and remember all the good times and friends I had when living there. Thank you for the memories.

Many thanks to Isobel Akenhead for approaching me and inviting me to write for Bookouture and for being a fabulous editor; her expertise and guidance has made this a stronger story. Also to Jennie Ayres for her excellent copy-editing and to Alexandra Holmes and all the Bookouture team.

Also to all my fantastic Facebook friends for the support, advice and laughs. You are all stars.

To my family. My wonderful husband Dave, who is always 'the wind beneath my wings' and my four amazing grown-up daughters who are a constant source of inspiration and 'chick lit' knowledge. I love you all.

Finally, a big thank you to my readers for buying my books, taking the time to message me, write reviews and spur me on to write more stories. And to the many reviewers and bloggers who are kind enough to give me space on their blog, take part in my blog tours and help promote my books. You are all wonderful.

CPSIA information can be obtained
at www.ICGtesting.com
Printed in the USA
LVHW040105301118
598739LV00007B/244/P

9 781786 815538